ICE & IRON

MERRY RAVENELL

9 Swords

Ice & Iron

Copyright © 2019 by Merry Ravenell

Cover by Seventh Star Graphics

For my peeps.

COMPLICATIONS

I hadn't wanted to be the IronMoon Luna, and I definitely did not want to be the SableFur Luna.

I was the Luna of SableFur by right of conquest, but it didn't make me the *rightful* SableFur Luna. There was one other soul with a blood claim:

Gabel.

I ran my bandaged hand over my arm. No Mark had re-appeared.

A sea of dazed faces stared blankly at the hideous, yellow-tinged puddle of fang and bone melted into the floor.

Blood and gore began to dry on all of us.

Will you make him King?

Lucas stood by Adrianna's chair, waiting for me to take my place.

Dazed and feverish, I managed the three steps. Lucas caught my hand and steadied me. I faced all the SableFur again, mouth dry, half-healed neck aching, my hands worthless half-stitched bloody masses, and pain crawling through every organ in my body.

How is that hole in your soul?

Generations of SableFur Lunas had sat on that very chair. Hard, unforgiving, unpleasant.

Exhaustion started to wrap itself around my brain. The pain in my arm grew worse. I focused my blurring eyesight on Bernhard, the Second Beta. "Where is Adrianna?"

Bernhard hesitated before he answered. How much of this had he been a party to? Had he known how far Lucas was willing to go? He looked to Lucas, and made a move towards where I sat, hand outstretched, a faint hitch in his gait.

Lucas' snarl rattled against the old walls. His prestige smothered the air. "She is Luna by right of conquest. You will answer her."

Bernhard struggled against invisible chains. His throat moved like words were caught in it. Lucas seized Bernhard by his shoulder and smashed him to one knee. "*Kneel.*"

Bernhard's shoulders visibly clenched, muscles tight and straining against his skin. "I do not know… Luna." He choked on my title, then continued to speak. "I only know she told Alph—"

Lucas snarled.

"—Magnes she wouldn't be attending."

I struggled through the haze. I just needed a few more minutes. "So she'd have waited in the house."

Bernhard shifted uneasily. "I don't know. I didn't ask."

"You are not saying she was *concerned* about the outcome of these events and went to high ground." I dug the words into him like claws going into his gut.

Lucas' cruel grip on Bernhard's shoulder didn't relent. Bernhard's thighs strained to stand.

"Check the house, now," I ordered Lucas. "Adrianna couldn't have survived Magnes' destruction. Find her, and her pups. Make sure the pups are safe. I don't want anyone running away with them, or for them to be alone right now."

Gabel had two half-brothers, and there was a very good chance they were watching their mother die in front of them.

"She may have survived," Bernhard growled, breathing hard around his effort to stand against Lucas' grip.

The death of one mate, almost without exception, killed the other. *If* Adrianna had survived, she'd have been in unspeakable agony and incapacitated. We needed to find her and her sons.

"She may be alive!" Bernhard directed this at Lucas, struggling to rise against Lucas' restraint. "And you are just naming Gianna Luna!"

"She is Luna by right of conquest," Lucas snarled. "She defeated Magnes, you will obey her!"

Bernhard pushed upward. Lucas shoved him down. The Second Beta's knees hit the ground with a crack.

Lucas grabbed Bernhard by the hair, twisting up into his war-form as he did so: a dark gray wolf with a short, plush pelt marked with deep scars and shaped with muscle. He smashed Bernhard's face into the yellow blot on the floor. *"Did youuu notttt jussssst ssseee wooolvvvvessss offf ssstarlighttt rennnnd a corruptttt Aaalphhha sssso thissss isss alllll that remainssss of him? Did you not jusssst sssee thossse ssssstarlight wooolvvvess attackkk at Luuuna Gianna'ssss commaaand?"*

Bernhard's cheek ground into the blot.

"You will obey yourrr newwww Lunaaaa!" Lucas bellowed. *"Ssssshe was cccchosssen by the Moon Herssssself!"*

Lucas flung Bernhard down and his guttural snarl rattled the floorboards, claws curled. *"Orrrr yoouuu will die byyy myyy claawssss anddd join your dammned massster."*

Bernhard rolled to one knee and weighed the cost of disobedience and revolt.

My heart raced, and it was getting hard to stay upright. I was *so* tired, and my brain was still a mess from having been

Beyond the Tides. I grabbed the arms of the chair to steady
myself. Pain ripped through my hands as stitches tore.

"*Go!*" Lucas howled.

Bernhard rose to his feet and bowed his head. "Yes, First
Beta. As you say."

He gestured for several warriors to follow him. He did not
excuse himself from my presence.

Blood dripped off my hands. I swayed on my feet as I
stood. "I am Luna now." I raised my voice as much as I could
manage without throwing up from exhaustion. "Obedience
and loyalty are all I ask."

It's all I'd asked for as IronMoon Luna, it would hopefully
save my pelt as SableFur Luna, at least for a start. Best to keep
the standards attainable and the expectations clear.

Lucas, still in war-form, knelt before me on one knee. "*And
it wwwillll be yoursssss, Luuuunnna.*"

The rest of SableFur stayed silent. Hardly the howls of
greeting and esteem IronMoon would have given. My arm
started to crawl with painful, burning prickles.

Kiery approached. "Come, Luna. There are matters that
require your attention. She will be in the main house, Lucas."

Lucas rippled his lips across his fangs. "*I wwwillll atteenddd to
thingggssss heeere.*"

Kiery pulled me down the hall's length towards the door.

She didn't say anything as she hurried me back into the
main house and up into my room. My little, empty, small room
with its ugly blue tile bathroom still stained with Aaron's
blood.

I stared at the smears of blood, dumbly, my whole body
suffused in pain and fever.

I was death-pale, except my eyes were sunken, the eyelids
rimmed red and huge ghoulish bags under them, my cheeks
drawn into concave hollows, my lips paste-pale, and the necklace of half-healed ulcer scars around my neck flushed red with

lingering festering. My dark hair was wild and ungroomed and devoid of luster.

"This had to leave a bad first impression," I rasped. I'd gone from half-crazy not-Oracle to the SableFur Luna in ninety seconds. At this rate I was going to go from SableFur Luna to casualty in record time.

"You're sick, Gianna." Kiery steadied me as I bent over the sink.

"Is that what I am?" I asked. Kiery splashed some frigid water over the back of my neck. The feverish burning got worse. I dry-heaved.

"Your hands better not be going septic. They didn't look like they were going to turn a few hours ago, but that can sneak up quick." Kiery swore as I heaved again. I hadn't eaten. Nothing came up.

"Guess it's good I didn't go with Aaron," I joked weakly.

"If a man isn't going to hold your hair back while you puke, pass him by," Kiery said as I dry-heaved again.

My knees gave out. She caught me and lowered me to the bathroom floor before I split my skull open. Pain burned in my left arm. I clasped my arm and keened.

"Don't do that!" She tried to slap my hand away. "You're going to ruin your hands!"

"It hurts," I whispered as something inside me twisted and *burned*, and the pain was so intense it blotted out everything else. My vision became nothing but starlight and fire.

Something dilated. Pure agony incinerated my nerves and mind.

The Bond thrashed like a fish kicking free of a net.

Kiery shoved her hand over my mouth to muffle my scream. She crushed my head back into the tile. "Don't scream, Gianna, by the Moon, don't let them hear you screaming!"

This pain obliterated any previous concept I'd had of pain.

The Bond thrashed and kicked, and I saw red membranes and the blood coursing over that bone crown, and Gabel walking away, away, away, leaving me in the snow, away, away, away. Something cut into me, no, it cut *out* of me.

"Don't scream!" Kiery begged, pinning me with one knee in the gut while leaning both hands over my mouth. "Don't scream!"

Something ripped open, and the pain reached a blinding crescendo, then eased, like tides moving from shore.

Kiery, breathing hard, slowly retreated and knelt beside me, knees splayed. We both panted and held very, very still.

I smelled blood. Lots of blood. One of us was bleeding, and it wasn't Kiery.

What now?

Kiery's voice shook. "Sit up. Come on. I'll help. Move slowly, just like coming out of a vision."

I whimpered as she pushed me against the edge of the tub. Tingling pain zapped my brain, but something warm and smoldering pooled in my core. My brain was such a bloated tick it couldn't move.

"Gianna." Kiery pulled at me in a whisper.

"Mmmph?" I mumbled.

"Gianna!"

The Moon sailed overhead in my awareness, steady and cool, a coal within me soothed aches and pains. I sighed again, content for the first time in a month. I was safe, and nothing hurt. Nothing at all. A corner of my brain shouted at me I wasn't safe at all, I was the Luna of SableFur and that made me decidedly *not* safe.

No, I was safe. Safe here, safe in this sea of—

Kiery slapped me. Hard.

The world came into focus.

"Hi," Kiery said, now suddenly ashen and urgent. "Wake the fuck up, will you?"

"What?" I asked, dazed. "How long was I—"

"About ten minutes," she said. She nodded towards my arm, eyes huge. "Take a deep breath before you look."

"What, I don't have an arm anymore?" I asked, taking in how I was soaked with blood, and there was, in fact, a puddle of blood under me. It extended outward across the ugly blue tiles. My arm (or my stump) hurt like hell, so if the Moon had burned it off, not a big jump.

"No… you have an arm. Just. Take a deep breath."

"Then what am I bleeding from?" The sheer amount of blood finally dawned on me. I scrambled, but the blood was slippery and my hands were useless and I dry-heaved from exhaustion.

The blood shone blue-gloss in the light.

"Oh Moon, Moon, Moon," I whispered as the surface of the blood shone blue-gloss. I'd never seen such a pool of blood. Not in light, not so smooth and clear and fresh and—

Blue-gloss tattoos.

"Oh my…" I whispered with sudden, horrible understanding of what made the blue-gloss ink. Why it always seemed alive.

Because it was.

Kiery's hands shook as she used scissors from the cabinet to cut off my blood-soaked shirt.

I took a deep breath and looked down at my arm.

My Mark had reappeared.

My arm had been carved with the three ragged bars Gabel had torn into me, but now they were integrated with a raw dance of fine lines and swirls twisting around cruel geometric edges and shapes. The open wound extended from the softness of my elbow to my shoulder cap. It wept blood from deep in the crevices of the flesh.

Is that the pattern you would have given me?

I think it is, buttercup. It would have been beautiful.

It was like something out of Hell's Own Art Gallery.

"It's—" she started to say. Then she stopped, because there wasn't a single word for the cruel, horrible beauty of the thing.

It was gorgeous in the same way Flint ripping war-forms in two was, Gabel so neatly killing Marcus, or the cruel torment of the donkey, or the void-perfection of the basement, or Adrianna kicking me in the ribs. It was beautiful in the way exquisite pain was beautiful, the roughness of Gabel's grip on my body, or raking my nails into his skin.

I'd *felt* this Mark before.

"What am I?" I whispered.

A month in a tourniquet had caused the Bond to rush back to life, overwhelming me, and now, it sat, warm and alive, but damaged and aching, within me.

Within *us*.

Sealed by a Mark that announced to everyone exactly what I was.

"You're the Balance-Keeper." Kiery pushed my face around so I had to look at her, not the Mark. "The point on which light and dark turns. And now you have the Mark Gabel would always have given you."

"If I have it, he has it, and he will come," I rasped. "We have to find Adrianna and his brothers."

"Shush," she muttered under her breath. I'd torn stitches *again*, and they were red and flushed and swollen and lined with yellow pus and crust.

"We can't just sit here with you in a puddle of blood and leave your hands looking like this," Kiery said in a low voice. "And Gabel *cannot* just show up to reclaim you. You're the SableFur Luna now, and all hell will break loose!"

"I think all hell *did* break loose?" I said, then the effort proved too much, and I dry-heaved again. Gabel showing up would be appropriate, and what else did Kiery expect to happen?

"No, that's what we're trying to prevent, remember? Stay here. Don't move."

Kiery, splashed with blood, got up and headed out of my little room. I leaned my head back against the tub and closed my eyes. "It was supposed to be you."

She paused in the doorway. Some of my blood dripped off her fingertips. "I don't think it was supposed to be either of us."

CALLING HOME

The pain of the renewed Bond was a throbbing misfortune. It was sort of like the agony of frozen hands when all the blood flowed back into them and all the nerves came alive again.

And somehow I was the SableFur Luna. Sitting in a puddle of my own blood on an ugly bathroom floor, and so weak even trying to talk to myself resulted in a dry-heave.

Kiery returned with a phone.

I caught Hix's scent. My heart spasmed.

"Who do we call?" Kiery asked, fingers over the screen. "Who do we call to say do *not* come here? Not yet, anyway."

Did Flint have a phone? I couldn't remember. I was pretty sure he didn't. Flint wasn't much for talking. "Does Flint have a number in there?"

Kiery scrolled through all of Hix's contacts. "I don't see a Flint."

Hix was dead. Tears pooled in my eyes. Eroth, maybe? But Eroth wasn't with IronMoon. Gabel had sent him to RedWater, hadn't he? I couldn't remember. It was hard to think. "Gabel," I said, gorge trying to rise again.

Kiery dialed the number and held the phone to my ear. I tried to take it. She smacked my hand away. "I'll hold it. You just tell him *not* to come here. Keep it short."

"I don't understand. He is *going* to come." And I wanted him to, didn't I?

"I'll explain when you're coherent. Do what you're told and tell him he needs to be patient."

"If he thinks I'm sick he's not going to listen," I tried to tell her.

"Convince him, Gianna. It's important. Trust me." Kiery pressed her cheek to my forehead and muttered something about how I was burning up.

The phone rang. And rang.

Then.

"Gabel is convinced you are dead, Hix."

Not Gabel. Flint's voice instead. Brittle, terse, undercut with relief. I sobbed and babbled the bad news, "Hix is dead."

"Luna?" Flint's voice rose half a note in shock. Fabric rustled. I imagined his kilt swishing around his knees as he moved through the hallways of the IronMoon heart.

"He's dead. They killed him and stabbed him in the back —" I sobbed uncontrollably.

"Are you coming back?"

"Gabel." Kiery prodded me in her best teacher-voice that could have probably summoned me from death itself. "Come on, focus. There's a lot of blood, but you can get this out."

I tried to paw at my tears. Kiery hissed *hold it together another sixty seconds*. I gathered up my fragmented mind and rasped, "Where's Gabel?"

"He is not here," Flint said. "He is in the field. I am in IronMoon's heart. Where are you?"

I took a deep breath. "SableFur. Flint, you have to find him. You have to stop him from coming here."

"Why?"

"Magnes is dead. My Mark has re-appeared. The Bond is open again." I tried to grab a handful of my hair to steady myself. Kiery smacked my hands away.

When he spoke, his voice was warm. "You succeeded. This is excellent news."

"Is it? I don't see how. I'm the SableFur Luna now. Adrianna's dead—"

"Yes, I imagine she is. How did you become Luna?"

"It would take too long to explain."

"I see. I'll go to Gabel," Flint said as if that course of action made perfect sense to him.

Kiery took the phone away from me and put it to her own ear. "Master of Arms."

"Oracle Kiery," I heard him say. How had Flint known it was Kiery?

Kiery grabbed both of the towels from the rack. She dropped one towel on the ground and started to kick it around with her foot mopping up the blood puddle. "Fuck, this is a mess. There's too much blood. Gianna's in bad shape and needs medical care. SableFur doesn't know she's still mated to Gabel, and I can't trust any of the doctors here to keep their mouths shut about the Mark on her arm. Is there anyone in IronMoon you can send, or do I have to call Aaron? Because I'd rather not involve IceMaw. The situation is explosive enough."

She knelt down on the bloody mess of towel and looped the other towel around my arm. She mouthed *don't scream* and then lashed the towel closed over my bleeding arm. I managed to not scream, but I blacked out for a few seconds. She wrestled the ends of the towel tighter.

A surprisingly dark chuckle. "As it happens, we have a human. She's in the field with Gabel now. She isn't an Iron-Moon. She's for sale to the highest bidder."

"Can she get here quickly? We'll pay double what you're

paying her." She lashed the towel into a thick knot while I tried to stay conscious.

"I will call her after this. Expect her in approximately eight to twelve hours. I suggest you have her money upon arrival."

Kiery hung up on Flint.

I dropped my head and surrendered to everything.

KIERY : DIFFERENT DREAM, SAME NIGHTMARE

Kiery ran to grab more towels and start mopping up the bloody mess on Gianna's bathroom floor.

"Crap, crap, crap," she muttered as the blood smeared everywhere. Blood was such a damn sticky liquid. She'd had to clean up Lucas' bathroom more than once because he'd come in torn up, but he'd never bled puddles. At least not in his bathroom. He'd had the good taste to take that to the professionals at the clinic.

She threw the soaked towels into the bathtub, rinsed them, then tried to mop up the blood some more. There was a second blood here too. Aaron had already bled and stained the grout.

This bathroom had seen some things.

She rummaged around in the cabinet—nothing. Not even peroxide. She piled the blood towels into the tub, then jumped in to rinse off, and threw her bloody clothes in with it. She'd just run back to her room wearing Gianna's robe.

She glanced at the newly minted SableFur Luna passed out on her miserable little bed, her arm wrapped in hand towels. The bleeding seemed to have eased up.

"Just hold on until this Ana gets her," she muttered, knowing Gianna couldn't hear her.

She ran back to her room, grabbed fresh clothes, and peroxide and ran into the kitchen. Cook was there with his stunned kitchen crew, trying to figure out what to cook for dinner.

"Cook," she said.

"Is it true?" Cook asked. "Magnes is dead?"

"Magnes is worse than dead. The Moon destroyed him," Kiery said.

"With starlight wolves?" one of the line cooks asked.

"Yes," Kiery said, trying to sound like the composed Elder Oracle and First Beta's mate she was, and not the trying-to-cover-up-a-bloodbath she-wolf she actually was in that moment. "I'm sure the wolves are still going to be hungry, but I'm also sure there's not going to be dinner. They're looking for Adrianna and her sons now. Or what's left of her."

Cook nodded soberly, and a couple of the kitchen wolves made small sounds of concern. Cook said, "She left the house hours ago."

"Adrianna did?" Kiery asked. "She left *before* all this happened?"

Cook nodded again. "Took the pups and left. Nobody else went with them."

"Tell Lucas. Gianna's really worried that the pups are alone with a dead or dying mother. If they're far from here, they need to get found," Kiery said, then, "Cook, I need some bleach. Alpha Aaron bled all over her bathroom and she didn't get around to giving it a proper cleaning."

"I'll send for—"

"I'll do it," Kiery interrupted.

"But you're an Oracle, Kiery."

Cook said that as if she was too good to mop a bathroom. Oh, the stories she could tell from her own time training. "I was Gianna's last teacher. She knows me, not the others. I can handle cleaning a mess, Cook. I've been with Lucas for years, remember?"

Cook gestured to one of the wolves, who darted into a side closet and brought her a bottle of bleach, a bucket, and a mop. Even better than the bleach she'd been hoping for.

Kiery picked up her prizes. "And in about six hours or so, a human's going to show up. Her name is Ana. She's a vet, and Luna Gianna's private physician. She's not an IronMoon, just a mercenary human who follows money. If I'm not around, let her in and make sure nobody kills her."

Cook nodded.

The bleach stank to the Moon, but it cut through the blood, and made quick work of everything. She poured it over the towels in the tub and rinsed them out, sneezing on the overwhelming stench and the burn on her hands, but she had to keep the Mark secret from SableFur, and that meant getting rid of the evidence.

Gianna hadn't moved. She risked pulling at the towel-bandages and dousing the wound with peroxide. It foamed and hissed, and Gianna twitched, but she was so exhausted and wretched that she didn't do much else.

"Well, at least it's sort of stopped bleeding," Kiery whispered to herself. It looked pretty bad: like meat that had been tenderized. She put a clean towel under it just in case and sat down on the edge of the bed to wait for the arrival of the human.

~*~ Kiery's Dream ~*~

She was at the mouth of a large cavern. A huge cavern where every-thing seemed to be bathed in fire, and ghoulish skeletal heads stared down at her from the ceiling. All around her were the press of shadowy bodies, their attention focused at the stage at the other end of the cavern.

She'd been here before.

But Magnes was dead.

The shadowy wolves were silent this time, but expectant. She couldn't see faces. Everything was shrouded in the glow of flickering flames, but the flickering brushed along the shadowy skin to reveal the bones underneath, like the reverse of clouds passing in front of the sun.

She stepped through the crowd towards the stage. The shades shuffled, jostling a bit.

They shouldn't be aware of her.

The Tides roared in the distance, and her mind wobbled.

A moment in the dream to center herself in the center of the current, then pushed forward again.

The fire and ash made it difficult to breathe. It wasn't ash, it was some kind of fetid, dry dust. She coughed and tasted something musty on the back of her throat. What was burning? She didn't smell anything burning except wax and oil, like lanterns.

On the stage—which was made of thigh bones lashed together by strips of sinew—was an altar of stone. She went up the steps, aware of the way the bones creaked under her weight, and walked to the altar.

There was a scepter made of a war-form's humerus, and the ball end dotted with fangs to make a small, spiked globe. There was a war-form skull. The lower mandible removed, and the fangs turned upside down and arranged along the top of the skull to make a crown, and the skull rested on a cloak made from a silvery-blue pelt.

Kiery touched the pelt. It had been Aaron's pelt before.

It was an Oracle's now. Gianna's.

The crowd shifted.

Adrianna, wearing nothing, strode up onto the stage. Trailing behind her were her two sons in pup-form.

Kiery had to catch herself from screaming. Her balance rocked on the Tides. She dropped to her knees onto the bones and grabbed the altar as Adrianna, unaware she was there at all, donned the crown.

The pups—her two sons—had been skinned of every shred of hair, from ears to tip of their tails, and were soaked in scabs and blood.

"No, no, no," she whispered, brain rocking dangerously.

Adrianna swept the cloak around her shoulders, and seized the scepter, and faced the shades. She raised the scepter and howled the Luna's song of victory. The shades answered. The flames trembled. The pups threw their heads back and howled.

~*~

The doorbell rang at three in the morning.

Kiery yanked out of her dream with a yelp, fell out of her chair, grabbed the floor with the flats of her palms.

The skinned, bloody pups burned in the front of her brain.

"The dream changed," she rasped to herself. The Moon had refused to let her onto the Tides for weeks, but still haunted her with dreams. The original dream had been Magnes, and the pelt had been Aaron's. Now the dream had changed: Adrianna, wearing Gianna's pelt. And the crown had changed. In the other two, the fangs hadn't been desecrated. Gabel's skull had still had its fangs.

It changed… for the worse. Somehow that was possible. Somehow doing everything the Moon had wanted had made things worse.

The doorbell rang again.

"Crap!" she breathed. She lunged up to her feet and bolted out of the room.

By the time she got there three warriors were growling at the human woman on the other side.

"Oh hey, guys," she was saying as the three wolves snarled at her and demanded she explain what she wanted. "Wow, you guys have big teeth."

"I'm expecting her," Kiery said, shoving the warriors out of the way. The woman on the other side was surprisingly tall, slender in a strong way, and while not exactly beautiful, strangely attractive, with a mane of dark hair coiled off to one side, and bright, dancing green eyes full of mischief. Her scent said she wasn't the least bit intimidated by the three warriors.

This was a human?

"Ana," she said simply, hefting the big square-sided bag on her shoulder. "I don't usually make housecalls, but I've been told you pay well."

"Who is this?" One warrior, Evan, demanded of Kiery.

"My name's Ana," the human said. "Doctor Ana. I'm Luna Gianna's private doctor."

"You're IronMoon?" Evan demanded.

Ana grinned. "I'm whatever you pay me to be, big guy."

"We have doctors," Evan said.

"I called her," Kiery said, shouldering Evan out of the way. "I'm Elder Oracle Kiery. I sent for you."

"Kiery, Kiery… oh, I know that name. Wow, Gabel wants you dead. Like not just dead, but like plaything dead."

Kiery sighed. "Yeah, I'm sure he does. Whatever. Can you come inside, please?"

"Sure, sure, where's the blood and gore?"

"Eh, that's already been cleaned up," Kiery half-lied. "It's her hands I want you to look at. She's this way."

The human turned around, stuck her tongue out, and wiggled her fingers at the males, then sauntered after Kiery.

"So why'd you call me?" Ana asked once they were in Gianna's room. "This pack has doctors."

"Because I don't trust any of them, and you shouldn't either." Kiery grabbed her and shoved her nose into Ana's hair. It was a dumb thing to do, but this weird human showing up on the heels of the most horrifying dream she could remember seemed strange.

"I was just kidding about the doing anything for cash," Ana said. "Okay, well, maybe not…"

"You *are* human," Kiery said, stepping back.

"Awww, I'm *flattered*," Ana said cheerfully. She pulled on

some gloves with a snap. "You okay? You look pasty even for an Oracle, and you're shaking. Pupils dilated to hell. Or do you just have some stuff you'd like to share?"

"I'm an Elder Oracle," Kiery said, trying to scrounge up some dignity. "I just had a dream straight from Hell."

"Damn, and then you wake up to *me*? The Moon must hate you." She turned her attention to Gianna. Took one look under the towel. "Yup. The Big Boss's got a matching one. He enjoyed the process of getting it more, though. What the hell happened to her? She's been gone like a month."

"The Bond, silver, and using her Gift too much," Kiery said. Gianna shifted in her sleep, but didn't protest. Maybe it was a good sign she was at least a little coherent if disturbed.

Ana picked up Gianna's hands and turned them over. "Well, this is a half-baked stitch job. These look like they've been run over a few times. Okay. I'll get to work."

"Is she going to survive?" Kiery asked.

"I'm a vet, not a human doctor, but my highly attuned instincts say she probably just needs some sleep and food and time. So let me get to work. You go sleep."

"Don't trust anyone here," Kiery said.

"Not even you?"

"Maybe not even me. Don't tell anyone about her arm. Not even Lucas, my mate and the First Beta. Play dumb about it."

"Why?"

"Because if this pack finds out she's still mated or re-mated to Gabel of IronMoon they will chew through all of us," Kiery said.

"Right. Got it. Bloody warlord and all that." Ana snapped fingerguns at her.

Kiery sighed and shook her head. "Where the hell did they find you?"

"Stripmall working for hams."

"I'm sorry I asked…"

WILL YOU MAKE HIM KING?

I woke to pain, and the sounds of someone moving.

I opened my eyes; they refused to focus, and I almost decided it wasn't worth the effort.

SableFur. My room in SableFur.

Gabel.

The person in my room came over to the bed and set down a metallic tray. A few objects rattled. They pulled down the blankets and sheets. Cold air ripped across my naked skin.

I managed to open my eyes again.

"Ana," I wheezed.

She pulled on a pair of surgical gloves. "So you recognize me this time, eh?"

"What?"

"You've been out of it. Seeing *all* the pretty colors. You lost some blood, and I've been giving you nice drugs. Wonderful drugs." She picked up a small vial of something, shook it in my face, and put it down. "Been learning a lot about you wolves. Had to make a little phone call to that wolf who's hot for you in the south so I could talk to his doctors, because I'm not on speaking terms with the doctors here in this fancy pack."

"Aaron," I wheezed. "You called Aaron?"

"That's his name. Aaron. I'd just been calling him Dirty Pitchfork. Haha! I told him I needed to talk to one of his doctors so you wouldn't die, and him, being the asshole gentleman that he is, said he'd come get you, to which I said not unless you wanna start a war, and of course he said *obviously* he wanted to start a war over you, and I said she won't live long enough for it to matter, so he said he'd have to schedule the war for later and gave me the referral."

That sounded like something Aaron would say. "That wolf won't take *no* for an answer."

"Nice eye, by the way. New tattoo?"

"I don't know what it is." Anita had called it a keyhole, or the hole in my soul. Lucas and Kiery had said the Moon was in my eye.

"This Moon Goddess of yours does not fuck around. She's straight up Old Testament."

"Where's Gabel? Did he come with you?"

"Not a clue. I ghosted him when Ink-Daddy called me and told me to get my pesky ass to SableFur."

"Ink—Ana, are you still creeping on him?"

She stuck out the tip of her tongue. "I admire him from an inoffensively safe distance."

"How long have I been asleep?" I tried to prop myself up. Anna swatted me and arranged my pillows. My hands had been re-bandaged once again, this time into absurdly massive mittens more like boxing gloves. I waved them around and smacked her with one. "Joke's over. Take these off."

"You *have* to let those heal," she told me sternly. "Whoever stitched and re-stitched them did a half-ass job but you're not helping. There was just enough skin left to stitch them *again* and they're sort of infected and gross. So now you get mittens of shame. Don't make me get a cone."

I scowled. I did not want mittens. I wanted to brush my hair and not look like an infant in bunting.

Ana drew up something in the syringe and then picked up my wrist. "Let's see. I got here about three in the morning you owned Magnes—Kiery told me that story, holy *shit* would I have paid to see it!—and now it's ten in the morning or so the next day. So I guess you've been out for thirty-six hours. Technically you've been awake but you've been pretty delirious."

"Two days! I—"

"Lucas has got it held down for now. He's kind of a vanilla stick in the mud, but in that capable reliable sort of way." Ana pushed me down into the pillows again. "You don't have sepsis —Kiery was certain you were going to aggressively try to die on her—but there's nothing too wrong with you I can find except for the hands and bruises, but Kiery told me you've also been Beyond the Tides a bunch. Time to catch up on all that sleep and start repairs."

I watched as she slid a needle under my skin. I licked my lips and whispered, "Flint said you've been with Gabel."

"With him? Like *that*? I'm not a skank." Ana almost dropped the syringe.

"No, I mean, with him in the field."

Ana chortled. "I was about to say yeah, I'm not his type. He's got one type and her name is Gianna. Gabel dragged me along. Don't know why. I like to think it's because I'm better at doctoring than Doctor Cuts-A-Lot but I think it's because he doesn't trust me without you around. He liked to remind me all the time he humored my presence for your sake."

I managed a watery smile. "How is he? Last you saw."

Ana clicked her teeth together. "Honestly? Sorta bonkers. He says he's seen you in a grove. I sort of believe him, because there were times we couldn't wake him up, and it scared the bejesus out of Eroth. Holding the blue tourmaline spear."

"It's true. I have the other one," I said.

"Yeah, well. Day to day your man be unravelling like a ball of yarn in a box of bored kittens. Heard all about how you two hooked up." She gave me a sideways look. "So let me make sure I've got this right. He abducts you, treats you like shit for a while, then you two reconcile. A month after you get married, you get accused of some bullshit, he divorces you because you lied to him or something." Ana snipped off some gauze with curved scissors. "Then all shit broke loose. He lost his mind, howling about the Moon betraying him and I'm sitting here like, dude, from what I heard you are Grade A asshole, and you ain't got no one to blame for all this going to fuck, but I like living, so I didn't say anything. Didn't seem to be the time to open my big fat mouth and state the obvious."

"Wise."

"Nope, I just let the God of All Holy Ink—holy shit, he's still so hot, I try not to creep on him, but holy shit—throw him around and beat some sanity back into him, and there was a lot of fur and snarling and blood and howling and stitches and more snarling and I was *almost* like check, please."

"But you stayed," I said.

"Just gotta put up with some crazy ass shit straight out of my fire'n'brimstone Sunday school, but the priest always warned us it wasn't made up." She wagged her finger at me and winked. "Anyway, so you reclaim your good name—stop me if I miss something—and in the process fuck up some pack, defeat their Alpha in some fucked up deus ex machina and dude is also Gabel's father. You become their Luna, and now you've got this thing back on your arm that ain't like it was before, and Gabel has a matching one."

I tried to grab her out of instinct, but just swatted her with the stupid bandage-mittens. "You've seen his?"

"Hell, yes, I saw it. If he was a cat, I'd tell you it cost him a few of his nine lives because I have *never* heard a scream like that, but I charge in there expecting who the hell knows what, but of course he's standing there tracing the gash with his finger like scooping buttercream icing off a cake and looking as bright-eyed full-balls-out nutso as you'd expect. Says it's just like he felt it would be, and it's amazing. Right. You do you, guy." She made a corkscrew motion at her temple. "About half an hour later Flint calls me to tell me get thee to SableFur, you guys pay triple overtime, and I am like *bye*."

I could easily picture Gabel fascinated with the bloody carving on his arm. "Gabel won't be far behind you, and I don't know what I'm going to do about it. Everyone here thinks he repudiated me and we're over."

"Um, yeah. How are you going to break the news to them that daddy's home?"

"I have no idea."

Will you make him King?

My brain was getting foggy again. "Where's Adrianna? Gabel's brothers?"

"Damn, that Kiery chick was right about you being stubborn. She said she was your last teacher."

"She was. Adrianna."

Ana paused in wrapping up some gauze. "Gone."

"Gone?" I asked blankly. "Magnes is worse than dead. Adrianna should be dead. That's how it works."

"She might be dead wherever she is," Ana said. "But she was long gone. Bags packed gone. She didn't stick around for whatever was going to happen between Magnes and Lucas, took the kids, and went to her mom's place. Or wherever. They haven't found her. They're pretty sure she's alive."

"She survived?" I asked blankly. She should be dead. She should have been *very* dead. "The Moon didn't take her? The Bond didn't?"

"No. Nobody else is missing. Wherever she went, she went by herself."

"Then there are probably two pups out there who are

alone when she dropped dead on the road," I said. "Gabel's brothers are *kids*, Ana. They're like eleven and six. Tell me they've been trying to find her. Do you know?"

"Hey, try to stay calm, okay? Yeah, they've been trying to find her. This stuff takes time. She'll turn up, or the kids will."

I struggled to sit up.

"Nope, nope, you need to stay in bed," Ana said.

"I have a war to stop and pups to find," I said.

"You look like a re-animated corpse. The only thing you're stopping is traffic. Open wide. Gotta take your temperature. Unless you want it in the butt."

"… No. And don't tell me if that's what you've been doing."

Ana smirked and poked the thermometer under my tongue while I planned my next move.

BUILT FROM BONES

My next move was to show up to breakfast. I couldn't hold a fork or feed myself with my mittens, but I could still sit in a chair and glower at people. There was an exactly zero chance I was going to let anyone feed me by hand.

Ana and Lucas could protest all they wanted that I needed to rest, but the more I rested, the closer all this got to turning into a calamity, no Dark Comet required.

There was some housekeeping I—and only I—could do. And I may as well do it considering I couldn't otherwise eat.

I sat in Magnes' chair at the head of the high table. The chair to my left—Adrianna's chair—was empty. The other wolves I had seen previously at this table when I'd come in from the First Test took their customary spots, but sober glances went all around. Other wolves, as they filed in or ate, glanced over at the high table, expressions ranging from sad to confused to undisguised anger.

The anger was no surprise. I wasn't SableFur by birth, and SableFur were never going to be pleased about an outsider storming into their prestigious, ancient pack and telling them how to run their lives. The Moon Herself could have sat my butt down in that chair and had a celestial chorus sing my praises and SableFur *still* would have resented it.

They were going to uncork the rage when they found out about Gabel. Hell, how was I going to break that news to them? Very gently?

I started with something easy and benign. "Kiery."

"Hmm?" she asked over coffee.

"Do you know when my bowls will be done?"

Kiery looked startled. "Your bowls? What bowls?"

Crap. "I came here with obsidian chunks. They were sent to the stonecutters. Or so I believed."

"Oh." She visibly relaxed. "No, I didn't hear anything about that."

"Is that a bad sign? Did Magnes just throw the stones into a pit?"

"Depends. When did you send them out?"

"About two weeks ago? Maybe closer to three. Long before they suspected I was up to no good. Do you think Magnes didn't send them at all?" I inquired, sipping my own coffee, and ignoring the pained glances I got as I invoked the name of the recently worse-than-dead Alpha.

Kiery shook her head. "If you sent them early like you say, I'm sure they're around. I'll make a few calls and find them."

Good. With luck my new bowl would be in my hands right when my bandages came off. I couldn't scry for myself, but I could still meditate, and that was better than using a rusty mirror or the blue tourmaline.

I turned my attention to Lucas as the kitchen staff set out a plate of hot biscuits. Before I could speak, the wolf that had carried in the biscuits set a small folded piece of paper just under my plate, and then retreated. I unfolded it:

Cook needs to speak to you.

Nothing scandalous there, and it could wait. I told Lucas, "After breakfast, show me what you did with Hix's body."

Angry looks from the other tables that overheard my request.

"Luna," Lucas said, giving me a once-over that revealed how terrible and sick I still looked. "A warrior wouldn't—"

"Show me," I repeated, adding bite to my tone. "He gave his life to save me and help me pass the Second Test. You will show me what you did with his body. Or are you too ashamed to? Did you just throw him in some pit to rot?"

Breakfast got very, very quiet.

"Gianna—" Kiery said softly, then stopped.

"Hix was a stud," Ana said, then she took a big bite of biscuit. She nudged Bernhard. "Hey, jam please."

"Show me. Where. You. Put. His. Body." I growled at Lucas, surprised at the low depth of the tone.

Lucas said, "There are other things for you to worry about Luna."

"And he placed his loyalty to his Luna before anything else," I shot back.

"An honor not all of us can claim," Bernhard said.

"Not yet," I bit out at him. "But give it time. You'll probably get your chance."

"I hope I do," Bernhard murmured, eyes on Lucas. "There will be no greater honor."

"This is a waste of time," Lucas said as he led me down a surprisingly well-groomed and marked forest path.

"He died my First Beta. I will do him the honor of knowing where his bones rest," I said tartly, trying to keep up with his big strides and not huff and puff too much while doing it.

"You don't understand what's happening in SableFur right now," Lucas growled. "You aren't paying attention."

"I've been drugged out of my mind trying not to die the past few days."

"That's why you should listen to me when I tell you what needs your attention and what doesn't. You don't know this pack."

"And you put me on the damn throne. You can spell out for me all the ways I'm *not* doing a good job, and how SableFur will not like me purely because I'm not a SableFur, when we have that meeting this afternoon. Right now, show me where you put Hix's body."

"Hix would understand if you can't pay your respects just now." Lucas stopped walking.

"Because SableFur would rather forget he ever existed?" I shot back. Oh no, I had every intention of making sure SableFur never forgot who Hix was. I wanted them to remember how he'd found that disgraceful little SableFur spy, how he'd exposed Anita's lies, how he'd been tortured and interrogated until Adrianna had strung him up to a pole and killed him like a common animal while my back was turned.

My marked eye throbbed, and my arm pounded.

Lucas ushered me to an ancient stone chapel in a very quiet part of the forest. Despite its age, the chapel was in beautiful repair, with its mortar reinforced over the ages and while it had no glass panes in the windows, the wood shutters were well-tended and didn't sag, and the path leading up to it shoveled free of snow and carefully tended, and the clearing free of new trees and the old ones healthy and massive, but groomed in such a way that there was a clear portal to the sky over the small stone structure.

Lucas pushed the iron door open. It did not creak.

The interior was painted with beautiful murals from our fables, the paint having been retouched many times because of the exposure to the elements. The interior was free of dust and debris, and the floors, while stone, were adorned with simple carpets woven in bright red wool.

At the far end was a stone altar. Beyond it, a wall of lit candles.

"Who maintains this?" I asked.

"Wolves tasked with it," Lucas replied.

The back wall was lined by two iron lattices of candles, and another ornate iron door with four impressive locks. Lucas had an ancient iron key ring with him. He unlocked all the locks, then pushed open the heavy wooden door on the other side.

He reached inside, and pulled a torch from a place along the wall, held it to the candles until it took a flame, and led me down a dark stone stairway.

It smelled of bones.

The stairway twisted around into a cold subterranean darkness, probably two stories down. I kept my shoulder pressed against the damp wall until warm light started to pool at the bottom of the stairs, and eventually we emerged onto a long hallway illuminated by lanterns. It was nothing but shelves made of stone, and on the shelves were various boxes made of wood, leather, stone, metal, all labeled with... *names.*

They were ossuaries. Hundreds of ossuaries.

"He isn't here, yet," Lucas said quietly as he led me down the hallway. "His body is being prepared."

Werewolves weren't particular about bodies. We burned our dead as a general rule. We rarely interred our dead, and funerals where a body lay in state were very rare, even for an Alpha or Luna. I'd never heard any different from SableFur, but apparently they had a booming mortuary business.

Just what had the Moon (and Lucas) gotten me into with this pack?

Up ahead was more light.

"This is where SableFur has been interring our dead for

hundreds of years," Lucas explained, voice hushed, and his hands folded in front of himself like a priest. "Not all our dead, just those worthy of being included. The ossuaries store the bones until they're needed."

The extremely long hallway became carved stone, more ornate as we approached an immense, underground cavern that glowed with yellow-orange light. The ancient underground chapel was large enough to host several hundred people.

Except it was made of bones. The entire thing was an ossuary.

The only thing that was not bone was the stone floor and the raw, rocky ceiling, although some efforts were being made to construct arches and buttresses of stone. Everything else was bones, even the chandeliers and lanterns. Those were made from the delicate bones of the feet and fingers woven together with wire.

"Moon," I breathed. Skulls with fangs still attached stared down at me. Femurs, tibias, scapula, vertebrae, each carefully arranged like art, depicting scenes and creating decorative mosaics. None of it was painted. Just bones in varying shades of ivory, the dark stone of exposed wall, and the orange-yellow of the lanterns and candles.

The basement in IronMoon was far worse than this, a hellish hole the Moon did not see. But a chapel built out of bones was a worthy second place. The SableFur had some… interesting… notions about honoring the dead.

"Only those most revered in SableFur's history are here," Lucas explained, tone soft. "Not every SableFur is placed down here. Not every bone is used for this place. But Hix will be here, as will you, one day, Luna."

Being part of a mosaic or turned into a chandelier didn't sound much better than being turned into a rug or blanket. "So this is where Hix's bones will rest?"

Lucas nodded. "Some of them. The rest will be placed in an ossuary until they're needed. His fangs will not be separated from his skull, as you can see. His loyalty served you until the very end, across Alpha and pack. I've left orders his spine be used first."

"So *you* administer this?" Lucas had never really struck me as the artistic type.

He shook his head. "No, but I have a say. Only a few non-SableFur have ever been interred here. It is a great honor."

Holy Moon, was that wistfulness on his face? Was getting interred here a goal SableFur warriors had? Like going to a special SableFur heaven?

Hix would not have approved nor cared about getting into SableFur heaven.

I blinked on tears and emotion. *Too bad, you stupid First Beta. You got into SableFur heaven. I hope the Moon sent you to your reward.*

"I didn't save you," I whispered. Not couldn't, or failed to, I *hadn't*.

"Luna?" Lucas asked.

"I didn't save him. I could have. I could have set him free and escaped with him," I said, tears clogging my throat. "Instead I left him in that cage knowing what was going to happen to him."

"Of course you did."

I whispered, "I could have let him out. I could have tried. I put my mission over his life."

Lucas gave me a disgusted look. "He was a warrior, he believed you were his rightful Luna and his Alpha was a fool, and he gave his life to help you."

Now I looked at him, eyes swimming with tears that didn't fall. "I know."

Lucas' expression tempered. "Adrianna had him stuck like a pig, but you gave him a better death than Gabel ever could have."

That wolf will die for you, buttercup.

"I need to stay a moment," I told Lucas as we emerged into the top chapel. "He is owed the song."

"You can't shift to wolf form to sing," Lucas said as he locked the gate. "The caretakers of this place will sing for him. They sing for all the bones."

"I don't care," I said angrily, waving my mittens about. "He was my First Beta. He died for me."

"Hix would not want you to rip your hands apart again."

"I—"

Lucas walked out of the chapel. "He's the first wolf you sacrificed, but he's not the first you've killed and not even close to being the first you sent to their death. He won't be the last. Come on, we have a meeting in an hour."

There was so much blood on my ruff, and before this was over, I feared I'd be soaked in it.

ADRIANNA :
NOTHING/EVERYTHING LEFT

The agony was almost beyond bearing.

Adrianna clutched between her breasts. Her heart still beat, but it didn't seem to be there. All that was left was a gaping, tattered hole that opened up onto an abyss.

"Mom," her oldest said, touching her shoulder carefully, timidly. He was trying to sound brave. His voice trembled. The younger one looked from behind him, eyes huge and terrified.

"I'm alright," she said, breathless and holding in screams.

"Are you dying?" he asked.

"Not a chance," she growled. The Moon had destroyed her mate, and the cruel sliver of crescent laughed at her, snarled at her, shoved her like a challenger she couldn't shove back. All she could do was endure and refuse to fall into the pit.

"They're waiting."

"Who is?" she asked.

"Everyone," the oldest said, confused. "You sent for them, remember?"

Yes, she had. Her thoughts clawed through the fog that wrapped her brain. She let go of her sweater and grasped her oldest's hand instead. "Thank you."

He tried to smile and squeeze back, but his eyes were glassy with terror and his scent even worse. Her soul howled in grief, grief, grief. A thousand shades and flavors of grief. The *silence*. The pure *silence*. Half her life there'd always been Magnes within her, his busy mind, his predatory deftness, the rumbling of his presence, and now there was *nothing*.

She stood and limped out of the room they were sharing. Every step felt like she dragged chains around her ankles, and the void kept trying to suck her back in. Her son, still holding her hand, led her into the hallway, and down stairs she didn't remember, through rooms, until she was outside on the house's porch.

"Here," he said softly. The littlest hugged onto her leg and buried his face. She rested a hand on his hair.

She listened for Magnes' howls from the shadows, but there was nothing except the void.

Magnes was not dead.

Magnes was *gone*.

One day she would fall into that chasm and cease to *be* as well. Because she had been his mate, his Luna, the love of his life, and she'd pledged her soul to his. And his soul was no more. One day she would be no more as well.

But not today.

Not now. Not while she had two sons who did not deserve this. If she died, if she failed, they'd inherit nothing but ashes and dust.

A growl rattled in her throat.

How long had Gabel known he was Magnes' bastard? Who had told him? Anita had sworn she had never revealed the truth to anyone. Magnes had sworn he had never spoken of the matter.

That Oracle was too powerful for her own good, and if Anita was to be believed, something called the Balance-Keeper, which Anita had not been able to define. The old Oracle had only known Gianna was powerful, special, and had a hole in her soul.

And that Magnes' bastard was the Destroyer, the Moon's Dark Comet.

"Not my pack, and not my sons," Adrianna whispered to herself. "It doesn't matter. My sons are all that matter."

A group of wolves had gathered in the yard behind the house, standing in the snow and waiting for her. There were many more standing at a respectful distance.

"Is it true?" her oldest asked. He was twelve, and old enough to understand that his future as the SableFur Alpha was in serious jeopardy.

"Is what true?" she asked.

"That Gabel of IronMoon is my brother," he said, reminding her too much of his father. "That's what they're saying. That Dad had another pup with a she-wolf that wasn't you. Before you. And it's Gabel of IronMoon."

Adrianna shoved down all the bile and howls. "It would seem he did."

"So you didn't know?"

"No." There was no reason to haunt her sons with the knowledge that the crazed spawn from the northern forests was their half-brother, or Magnes' relationship with that silvery-blue bitch. There was no strength for truth yet, or the questions that would come after. Magnes was still their father, this war wasn't over, and the truth could die when she ripped Gianna's head off and shoved it right through Gabel's chest.

Twelve and six. Why had she and Magnes put off having pups so long? Why had she mated with him so late?

She knew why.

She ran her tongue along her teeth as her jaw itched to bar her fangs and bite into a certain Oracle's neck. That careless, vapid, stupid silvery-blue whore and Magnes... Magnes had been such a fool.

Her oldest asked, "Are you going to talk to them?"

She looked sideways at him, rage tempering. Her oldest was so much like Magnes it hurt. Her sons could not afford her to indulge her anguish. She answered, "I have to."

They were old enough to realize something terrible was happening, but young enough to need her to protect them.

The Moon had made a foolish mistake: now Adrianna had *nothing* left to lose as long as her sons survived and sat on that throne Gabel wanted so much for himself.

"What are you going to tell them?" he asked.

"The truth."

"When can we go home?" her youngest asked.

Home. Back to the den she'd shared with a mate who no longer existed, to a thousand memories carved into the house and walls. How did she tell them they were homeless? That the den had been lost? "I don't know. Lucas has betrayed us. We have to be careful who we trust."

"Is Dad really dead?" the youngest asked, apparently needing to hear it again.

The chasm inside her soul yawned, and she almost lost her footing and fell inside it. She grabbed the porch railing. A splinter drove into her palm. "Yes. He's dead."

"Are you sure?"

"I'm sure," she rasped. She found the strength to roll up her sleeve and once again show them her arm. Their expressions fell to new lows as their little hands touched the fading Mark.

So cruel: the Mark faded, but the injury inside stayed.

The truth was more than she could name. Magnes wasn't dead. He was gone. Gone, gone, gone, and she'd never see him again and—

No. Her sons. Focus on her sons. Giving them their lives back, their legacy, their honor and dignity. Their *birthright* as SableFur.

Gianna was young, naïve, and untrained to rule, but she was cunning, far from stupid, and had endured and even tamed Gabel of IronMoon. She had tricked, lied, and snuck her way through Adrianna's own den. She'd proven a capacity for ruthlessness, and a stomach for killing.

But the Oracle, for all that she was, was also *very* young, and she'd had a terrible year. She'd lost her pack, her family, her mate, been betrayed, abused, bathed in death and blood. She'd start making mistakes and looking for a way out.

"She's been using a blue tourmaline and her nature as Balance-Keeper," Anita had told Adrianna. "She's been using a mirror. These aren't things she can do without consequence."

Adrianna cursed to herself. She'd told Magnes to not try to get Gianna away from Gabel—it was too flimsy. Kill her, trick her, something else, but this business with the Oracles had always been a mistake. Anita had promised she could control Gianna. That'd lasted less than a week.

Magnes had decided that Gianna was largely harmless, and when Aaron had shown up… Yes, it had seemed so neat, hadn't it, and like it would have worked out. Let Gianna vindicate herself and go to IceMaw. IronMoon's revenge on IceMaw would have been Gabel's sole concern, and when the IceMaw called on the SableFur for assistance, everything would have gone exactly as it needed to.

Adrianna told her pups, "Stay here. I'll be back soon."

The weak sun spoke of the lateness of the season. Spring would come soon.

The three leaders of this region bowed their knees to her.

She greeted each of them by name, and let her careful facade crack, and all her grief and anguish show. The chasm inside her opened a bit wider, grabbing for her, but she had to let them see her agony.

"We are loyal to you, Luna," Francis told her gravely.

"Thank you," she said, grateful to them. "What my mate

did was… I don't know how he kept it a secret from me all these years."

"It's a great shock to us as well," he replied.

"But Lucas betrayed me. He never—" She stopped talking. Lucas had always been stalwart, principled to the point he'd refused to mate Kiery. He'd always been absolutely committed to SableFur, even if he and Magnes had always been at odds with each other.

Magnes had enjoyed having the younger and brasher Lucas as First Beta. He'd enjoyed Lucas judging everything, watching, waiting, ready to snarl and bite.

Adrianna swallowed. "What is the word from SableFur?"

"Lucas gave the throne of SableFur to Gianna by right of conquest," Francis said.

Adrianna gasped and had to grab the railing to support herself. Lucas snarling at Magnes was one thing, Lucas betraying her another.

"Gianna claims you knew and covered Magnes' shame," Francis said. "Lucas acknowledges this as the truth. Bernhard attempted to challenge Gianna's authority, but Lucas forced him to kneel."

"And Bernhard didn't bite him in the knees?" Adrianna demanded.

"No, Luna," Thomas said, voice thick with disgust. "The First Beta and Oracle Kiery have Marks on their arms. You know who Lucas truly answers to now."

"How droll," Adrianna said sourly. She looked at the faces of her wolves, and she didn't know what to tell them. Everything about her felt so heavy, so aching. "And reports from IronMoon and IceMaw?"

Someone's voice said, "Alpha Aaron has returned to IceMaw. Alpha Gabel is amassing his forces in the old GleamingFang territory. We have refugees from his bloodbaths here. They have a story to tell."

Adrianna nodded. "I'll speak to them."

Francis brought a few wolves to her from the group beyond the ranked ones. They were cold, tired, and terrified. All females younger than her.

"You've seen the IronMoon recently?" Adrianna asked the oldest one, gently.

She nodded, biting her lower lip. Her voice shook with anger and fear. "I am—was—Shadowless."

Adrianna squeezed her shoulder. "You still are. Gabel didn't kill the pack if you won't accept it."

"He killed everything. Everyone." The she-wolf's voice trembled. "He made us all grovel in front of him, and anyone who didn't he killed. He was ranting about the Moon not keeping Her promises, and he was going to use our bones to build a tower to the Moon to punch out Her Eye."

She'd heard these stories before, but from the looks around her, many hadn't.

"The rest of us he told to get out. He turned us out into the winter. He didn't care about us." Her eyes brimmed with tears.

"I had heard that he offered everyone a choice of Iron-Moon or leaving," Adrianna said.

The she-wolf laughed. "Who wants to live in IronMoon under that monster? He killed everything, Luna. He killed innocents. He killed wolves who begged for mercy. They destroyed everything! It wasn't enough to kill us. They didn't take anything. They didn't loot anything. They just killed and destroyed."

"No looting?" Adrianna asked, frowning. "Are you sure? That can't be right."

When Gabel had originally appeared out of the forests, he had looted, but he'd stopped that quickly enough. His violence had become moderated and controlled. No looting, no rape, and only as much violence as needed to make his point. Adrianna had expected to hear that he'd at least started looting again, it tended to go hand in hand with destruction, but he'd burned everything of value?

"It's true, I swear it. They didn't take anything. Gabel's orders were to tear everything down and burn it, and his warriors did. He killed a warrior who tried to make off with a jewelry box. He made them rip everything down and drag it all into a huge pile and set fire to it."

She spoke to each of the refugees in turn and got similarly horrific stories—how Gabel had butchered the GleamingFang Luna and tortured Anders with her death, then taken her children to be raised within IronMoon, leaving Anders to die, he'd razed packs, exterminated entire bloodlines, and the only way to escape was to grovel before him.

Gabel had clearly lost what little mind he'd ever had.

This could be to her advantage.

Kiery and Anita had both seen a world where Gabel had been defeated, and yes, the world had been dark and burning, but of course it had been if Gabel was running around setting it on fire.

But Gabel *had* been defeated.

Gianna hadn't been in any of those visions. Both Kiery and Anita had confirmed there was no evidence Gianna had survived long enough for any version of the future to remember her. Kiery had especially seemed disturbed by the complete absence of anything indicating Gianna had ever been alive at all.

"What is Gianna's disposition towards Gabel?" Adrianna asked. With the forces of SableFur behind her, Gianna might like a little revenge against her old mate for his previous transgressions.

Francis said. "Gianna hasn't been seen since she left the hall."

Adrianna purred to herself. The Oracle's strength was at an end. Now to give her the rope with which to hang herself.

"Francis, your wolves will be the ones IronMoon attacks first. Gianna—or one of her slavering dogs—will contact you. Humor their pretensions that she is Luna."

"She isn't—" Francis growled.

Adrianna cut him off with a sharp gesture. "Gabel will come through that pass. Gianna will take revenge on the wolf who tortured her, then threw her away. When she orders you to fight, fight."

"Luna!" Francis protested, and there were howls of disagreement.

"Let her think she is Luna," Adrianna said with a sly, cold smile. "I want to see what she will do with it. Gianna was never raised to be a Luna, but she is an Oracle. Remember, this is the female who snuck into my pack, into my very den, and exposed my mate as a monster."

Adrianna clenched her jaw against the sudden howl of grief. In public she could not mourn Magnes. She had to despise him for the sake of her sons.

"She is just some she-pup," Francis snarled. "I will not call her Luna!"

"You will, because I've ordered you to." Adrianna leaned heavily on the railing, drawing deep breaths around her raw throat. "Do her bidding well, Francis. She is young and ignorant of being a Luna, but she is an Oracle, she is cunning, she is smart, and she was Gabel of IronMoon's mate until he threw her away. Remember that not even that forest-mongrel wanted her in the end. There is blood soaked through her silvery pelt, and if you are a fool, you will be her next victim. Do as I say and convince her you are obedient. It will make biting through her neck easier when the time comes."

CLOSE TO HOME

Magnes' map was now my map.

His office was eerie. He hadn't expected to die. There was a cup of cold tea on the desk. Some scrawled notes scattered about, letters and reports, a list of things to do over the next few days, and a few smooth pebbles his younger son had brought him as paperweights. Everything was painfully, neatly organized despite how much of it there all was, yet it all seemed comfortably lived in.

There was so much stuff on his desk, but part of it had nothing. That was where Adrianna had sat.

I glared at Ana and waved my mittens at her. "I am going to chew through these damn things."

I also had on a long-sleeved sweater to hide my Mark. The fibers constantly caught the crusty half-healed catastrophe of scabs.

"Go ahead. And when you swallow them, I'll just have to resection your bowel when you get an impaction." Ana plunked herself down in one of the chairs and kept tapping away on her phone.

"Why are you here?" Bernhard asked her.

"Because I know what's happening in IronMoon," Ana said sweetly.

I sat down in Magnes' chair, which caused Bernhard to flinch.

First question: "Where's Adrianna? Someone has to have tracked her down by now. Is she alive, or dead?"

Bernhard folded his arms across his chest. "She's alive."

"She *survived*?" I asked, although the reaction in the room said I was the last to know. "Are we sure? Is she *sane*? What's her condition?"

Lucas said, "We got word last night she's still alive, and sounds like she's sane."

"Why didn't anyone tell me?" I exclaimed.

"Doctor's orders it could wait and not to wake you." Kiery flicked a finger at Ana.

"Guilty." Ana smirked.

I bit down a growl. Fine. "Where is she?"

Lucas said, bristling with aggravation, "Unknown. We know she's a few hours north of here, but nobody's willing to tell us exactly where."

That was… not what I'd expected. "Does this pack not have Hunters?"

Nobody said anything. Not even Lucas.

"What about the regional leadership? Silence there too?"

SableFur was so large that each "area" of the territory was looked after by a group of senior wolves who administered it and provided local leadership. There were over a dozen such mini-territories. Magnes had been the closest thing to an Alpha-King the werewolves had seen in five hundred years.

Lucas' expression darkened. "Every single one denies having seen Adrianna, but all say they've spoken to her. She's contacted all of them to confirm she's alive."

So she was alive, *and* somewhat coherent, and gathering her allies. Introducing Gabel to SableFur was not my biggest problem. The previous Luna was. Somehow she'd survived. She *must* have the Seer gift and have had some basic training. "How did that go? What story did she give them?"

Lucas snorted. "The truth. She's not trying to say Magnes was innocent. She's claiming *she* is innocent, had absolutely no idea about Magnes, and that she is still the rightful Luna of SableFur and *I* betrayed her."

"*You* betrayed her," Ana said. "How the fuck does she come to that conclusion?"

Lucas gave Ana an impatient look. "I wouldn't expect a human to understand."

I pushed at a stray pen with one mitten. "How did *you* betray her?"

Bernhard said, dryly, "Because instead of defending Adrianna's claim to the throne, Lucas put you on it."

I shook my head. "That doesn't make any sense. Magnes was Adrianna's *mate*. He's a stain on an old wood floor, and she's cursed to eternal loneliness. Lucas' actions weren't high treason. *I* was the one with the starlight wolves."

"But it doesn't mean Adrianna knew about Magnes' sins," Bernhard said stiffly. "And you don't know if Adrianna's been condemned to eternal loneliness without Magnes. Maybe the Moon severed the Bond. Adrianna is *alive*, and she seems to be sane."

"That's not how it works," I said. "The Moon can't sever Bonds. They persist even if one wolf is damned, and the other goes to their reward."

"That can't be true," Bernhard argued. "The Moon forges them, She can break them. She wouldn't condemn one soul for the sins of another."

Kiery looked at me sideways, her expression warning me *shut up*. I bit the inside of my cheek. How many times had I snarled at Gabel to listen to me? I took my own advice and shut up when my Oracle told me to shut up.

Adrianna was alive. Pockets of wolves flocking to her and taking the fact she survived some blessed event made sense, but the majority of the pack outside the heart (and apparently a number inside it) believing she was *innocent* left me cold. Adrianna hadn't been there, *and* she had survived, *and* she was claiming she hadn't known anything about Gabel's mother… and everyone believed her.

In their eyes, Lucas was a traitor, and I was a pretender to the throne.

Magnes had defended her until his dying breath, saying he'd never endanger his mate by sharing such a dangerous secret. I had no proof to the contrary. It wasn't like lightening had struck down Adrianna, or the starlight wolves had dragged her carcass through the hall for me.

Bernhard's expression reminded me of molten glass.

Lucas' face pulled into a mask of stubborn resolve. "Just because Adrianna wasn't there for the starlight wolves doesn't mean she isn't complicit in Magnes' crimes. She knew all about how Magnes used the Oracles to get Gianna away from Gabel."

Bernhard shifted uncomfortably. "True."

"Do you really think she let Magnes do something like that without explanation?" Lucas barred his teeth at his Second Beta.

Bernhard growled. "He said he would never have endangered her by sharing the secret with her. I believe him."

"What if she already knew?" Lucas advanced a step.

"Then why hasn't there ever been so much as a rumor? *Nobody* knows anything about this!" Bernhard pointed to the door. "Go out there and ask every wolf in this heart if they remember even a small rumor about Magnes and a Seer."

"Maybe I will, now that it's in the open," I said. It had happened almost thirty years ago, so the wolves I would want to talk to would be at least… forty. More like fifty, sixty. The

younger ones—who had been kids at the time—might be
willing to talk. "Adrianna survived. It's not *impossible*, and a
female with young pups is the most likely to survive such a loss.
It doesn't mean she's innocent. It just means she's not dead."

Bernhard scowled at Lucas. "The Moon struck down
Magnes. Not Adrianna. Gianna took the vows to Gabel and let
him give her another Alpha's damned *head* as a gift, then
fucked him. Does that make her a monster like him?"

All eyes turned to me.

I'd left Gardenia to die the cruelest death I could think of for
her… the cruelest death I could think of for a wolf at all. To die
slowly and alone, forgotten, abandoned by the pack. The fate I'd
spared the RedWater wolves from was the exact same one I'd
left Gardenia to. And I still had no regrets. Not a single one.

Lucas said, stubbornly, "Gianna is our Luna. We were all in
that hall. We saw what we saw. Gabel does have a claim on the
SableFur throne—"

Bernhard growled, "I will not call that mongrel bastard
Alpha. He's rabid."

Lucas rolled his eyes and chuckled. "It's not going to
happen, Bernhard, and I don't know why Kiery is so worried
about it. We have a Luna. We need to prove Adrianna was
Magnes' accomplice in all things. Once we do that, SableFur
will accept Gianna as their Moon-ordained Luna."

"If," Bernhard said warily.

"You're being very optimistic," Kiery said from her place
against the wall.

Lucas gestured with his hands. "The next step to solidify
Gianna's rule is easy. She just has to choose a SableFur mate
and produce a pup as fast as possible. Everything will settle
down. Gabel can howl at the Moon all he wants but he won't
get his kingdom. As a bonus, Aaron won't have to wage war on
our southern border either. All our problems are solved."

Lucas dusted his hands and flicked his fingers and smiled at the Second Beta.

Lucas made it sound so nice and simple. I sighed from my very core.

"You have to take a mate, Luna," Lucas said. "SableFur isn't full of degenerates like IronMoon. We could make quick work of it by having them line up by the dozen and sniff you for lure-scent so we can speed up the process and weed out non-contenders."

If I'd been sipping coffee, it'd have come out of my nose and ended up all over the desk. Bernhard ventured, "That's not a bad plan. If we can find, say, five or six high-prestige males who can smell her lure-scent, it'd go a fair way to easing things. If they all think they're competing for a chance at being Alpha..."

"Exactly!" Lucas said. "A bunch of our better males knowing that their soul is compatible with hers? They have a chance at Alpha of SableFur, they won't be quick to speak badly of her, and we'll build her base of power."

Ana put her hand over her mouth and pressed her fingers down so hard on her lips the knuckles went white. Her huge eyes looked right at me, and her expression clearly said *uh-ho*.

The males in the room, though, all warmed considerably, and started to bandy around who to invite up first, and they'd have to be careful because it'd be very flattering to be first, as opposed to in a later group.

"Where should we cut off the age?" Lucas asked. "Thirty? Thirty-five?"

The Moon was laughing at me. Somewhere She was laughing at me. I sat in stunned silence, mind blank, frozen.

Ana twisted around and eyeballed Kiery. "Um, he's *your* husband."

"It's been a bit hectic," Kiery said helplessly.

"You mean you didn't know if Gianna was gonna die from her soul getting ripped up *again?*"

"Or her hands going septic, or the traces of silver…" Kiery admitted.

"You thought I was going to conveniently die?" I exclaimed.

"The thought did occur to me?" Kiery said. "You lost a lot of blood and you're half-dead now."

"Hey, she's not half-dead. She's at least three-quarters alive," Ana said defensively. "I do good work, okay?"

At this point I was half tempted to call Gabel and tell him to come on to SableFur and deal with this mess in person. I snarled at my stupid mittens. I swung them at Ana. "Roll up my sleeve."

Ana pulled the loose sleeve of my sweater up over the Mark carved into my arm. It sat blue-black-red against my skin, the scabs a deep horrible color and shiny like obsidian.

"The fuck is *that*," Lucas demanded.

"It appeared after she dealt with Magnes," Kiery told him. "It's a Mark."

"Are you sure that's a Mark?" Bernhard asked. "Because I don't think that's a Mark."

Ana said, "Whatever it is, Gabel's got a matching one on the opposite arm. I saw it right after it ripped itself into his skin. He screamed. We all came running. Well, some of us ran in the opposite direction."

Kiery said, quietly, "I was with Gianna when the Moon did it. I watched it rip itself out of her arm. I thought she was going to die."

"But why?" Lucas asked, staring at me. "That wolf gave you up. He's insane. He took you against your will. He humiliated you. You know what kind of monster he is."

"You say that like she got a choice in it, asshole," Ana snapped.

As Lucas seethed, I breathed a silent sigh of relief that I'd never told Kiery the truth about how Gabel really *hadn't* repudiated me, and how our Bond had never actually been severed. She and Lucas already had so many struggles with Oracles and their secrets. The only souls who knew the truth were Gabel, Flint, and myself. This was one I'd been smart to keep to myself. I'd tried to tell Aaron, but he hadn't listened, and I hadn't given him the details.

It also meant that Aaron and Gabel's little alliance was a secret, too, although Lucas and Kiery had suspected it.

"Gianna is the Balance-Keeper," Kiery said. "Gabel is the Moon's Dark Comet, Her Destroyer. We don't understand why the Moon has bound them together, but She has."

"That doesn't look like any Mark I've ever seen." Lucas eyed the thick black scabs.

It was so crusted that I couldn't tell if it was going to be beautiful or disgusting once the scabs fell off. It hadn't occurred to me, though, people would doubt what it actually was.

Lucas remained skeptical. "Are you sure? Is there a Bond?"

"Yes, Lucas, I'm sure this is a Mark." I sighed. First Betas sometimes…

"The pack can't know," Bernhard said instantly, almost panicked. "We have to keep it a secret. If Aaron finds out, it will cause a war in the south."

"Yeahhh," Ana said, "I'm just a human, but the way I see it, Aaron's the least of your problems. Call me crazy, but mate of current ruler plus son of previous ruler sounds like Gabel is the Alpha of SableFur."

"If not an uncrowned King," Kiery said softly.

Will you make him King?

"It means the only thing standing between him and being King-Alpha is Adrianna and Aaron," Lucas said dully. He laughed once. "Maybe we should let Adrianna live."

"You know what I've seen and you're saying that!" Kiery exclaimed while I tried not to faint from shock.

"I know what Anita has seen too! What does it matter, Kiery? Adrianna wearing a crown of bones, or Gabel crowning Gianna with obsidian?" Lucas shouted. "It all ends the same way: in death and fire! I am *not* accepting Gabel as my King, and I'll take my chances with Adrianna and her sons first!"

Kiery stiffened as if he'd struck her. "You idiot. The Moon sent Her Destroyer. Adrianna will lead us all to hell!"

"You don't know that! You've seen her, and you've heard SableFur's howls of joy at her rule!"

"No," I said suddenly, understanding. "No, no, Kiery, when you had the dream of Adrianna wearing Gabel's skull. The bone-cathedral. It was in the bone-cathedral, wasn't it?"

Kiery froze, and her eyes widened impossibly large, and she went completely gray. "Dear Moon, it *was*. You're right. Anita saw Gabel crown you under the sky. At some kind of cele-bration."

"So death all around. You Oracles never tell us anything so we can choose for ourselves. We just get dragged along with your damn Tides!" Lucas raged.

Kiery set her jaw. A few stray tears shone on her cheeks. "They aren't *our* Tides."

I'd hoped I could have dealt with Adrianna like Gabel had dealt with Anders' scheming: it was a threat to be monitored, might require the occasional discipline. Now I realized the awful truth: I didn't just need Adrianna dead. I needed her disgraced.

She had to be *destroyed*.

And the result would be two pups who weren't just orphans, but grew up as the sons of wolves the Moon Herself had marked for the highest of punishments. And they'd have to know their parents were in the Moon's Void, where She did not see.

My eye pounded with my heartbeat. The Bond writhed, dark and gasping, and the bones in my right hand shifted.

The Mark clamped down on my arm like a shackle, and the weight of chains bound me to the stupid chair upon which I sat.

SableFur needed an outlet for their frustration and anger, and I needed to see what sort of pack I had.

I drew in a breath, the Bond warming and rising in my awareness, like a smoldering ember. "Gabel is coming, First Beta. He'll come for SableFur's heart, and whoever is on the throne when he arrives. You've been eager to face him and test your SableFur claws against his IronMoon hide. Now is your chance. Go meet him and try to hold back the Tides."

OH, BY THE WAY...

With the Betas distracted by IronMoon, it was time to go down to the kitchen and speak with Cook.

The SableFur kitchen was not like the Iron-Moon one—it was a huge commercial type kitchen with an army of assistants and whirling knives and pans hanging from racks and prepared to feed an army. Which it probably had done over the generations, at one time or another.

"Luna," the head Cook—Walter—greeted me as he diced large amounts of green onions.

"You asked to see me?" I inquired. I hoped the kitchen's needs were a little less dire than the rest of the pack's.

He set down his knife, wiped off his hands, and led me to a quiet part of the kitchen, tucked away in a little alcove with a messy desk with menus scribbled on papers tacked to the walls. Dinner looked like it was going to be excellent. Although I was so used to eating the congealed left-overs and frozen food pockets that the SableFur deigned to toss my way that anything fresh sounded delicious.

"Did you want to make changes?" Cook asked.

"What? No. I was just looking. I'm sure you know how to

feed these wolves better than I ever will pretend to," I said honestly. "I'm grateful to have you keep doing as you have been."

The silence went a bit awkward, then Cook said, formally, "We're loyal to you, Luna. Hungry wolves are dangerous wolves, so we're going to make sure the SableFur here are fat and happy."

Now this was some unexpected good news. "My Second Beta threatens me out of the corner of his mouth, but the kitchen staff support me. Why?"

"Because kitchen staff knows and hears things," he said, a flicker of discomfort over his face. "Please don't ask me to say more. I don't want to be put in the middle. I have family. We all do."

I asked, bluntly, "Do you know anything about Gabel's mother, the Oracle of Mirrors?"

Cook twisted his fingers together. Then he said in a low tone, "I know there was a she-wolf that they fought about a long time ago, but I never heard anything about an Oracle, Seer, or pup."

If starlight wolves ripping their former Alpha into pieces couldn't scare the wolves of SableFur's heart firmly onto my side, juicy household gossip probably couldn't either. I'd take the quiet loyalty and forgo digging further. "What's on your mind?"

"Beltane, Luna," Cook said.

Beltane. The upcoming spring holiday had completely slipped my mind. "It's in about six weeks, isn't it?"

"Yes, and SableFur always has a large celebration for it. Wolves come in from all over."

Werewolves celebrated three major holidays: Beltane, Hallow, and Solstice. Some packs celebrated the summer solstice as well, and there were a sprinkling of other festivals and the like. Every pack celebrated Solstice, most celebrated

Beltane and Hallow. Beltane was the Festival of Fire: Earth was alive again, flowers blooming, prey bountiful, fertility, new life, purging the darkness of winter.

IronMoon hadn't formally celebrated Hallow the previous year, as the events of the time coincided with Gabel and I's own courtship celebrations, and the ceremonial Hunt to announce our decision to take the vows had matched up nicely with it. I doubted they celebrated Beltane either, considering the pack was almost entirely bachelor males, and Beltane was a festival celebrating birth, mating, and the hunt.

The SableFur had had Beltane festivities while I'd been in the pack training with Kiery and Anita, but I obviously hadn't been invited. I'd only heard Beltane was an *extra* big to-do in SableFur. "Any chance we can skip it? I don't think anyone's in the mood for a party this year."

Cook's eyes widened. "If you cancelled it, the whole pack would be shocked. Beltane is the Luna's holiday, Hallow is the Alpha's, and Solstice is the Pack's."

That was bad news. "So here in SableFur it's *my* holiday?" Cook nodded.

Shit. I couldn't cancel my own holiday.

"In a pack this large," Cook added, trying to be helpful, "we celebrate the three major holidays because it's a way for everyone to come together."

"The whole of *SableFur* attends?" I asked.

"Well, no, but many get invited to the heart for the festivities. It's an honor to be invited. The tradition is to invite the local leadership from each area of SableFur, and then unmated females and prestigious young warriors, or pairs that are going to make an announcement, and Marks are exchanged."

There was *no way* I could skip this. I also couldn't plan it. Could Platinum manifest out of the abyss and handle this for me? "I can't plan it, Cook. I'm an Oracle by training. I haven't been to a Beltane celebration since forever."

Most of my younger years I'd been in training, and because acolytes weren't pack members and didn't need the distraction, we hadn't been invited. When I'd become an adult, I'd stayed away because I had no interest in finding a mate, and I'd worried that if I'd partaken of the usual Beltane partying, it'd have made my being an Oracle awkward.

I knew nothing about Beltane celebrations. I could have muddled through for IronMoon, but SableFur had *expectations*.

Cook tried to reassure me. "We can do most of it, but I will need you to help with some of it. It can't be avoided. Things need to be purchased, procured. The invitations went out two weeks ago, so that is done, but the party itself is six weeks away. The ceremonial hunt needs to be planned, the dancers chosen, the placement of the fires—"

My *Mark*.

Beltane was held in late afternoon and as the sun set the fires got lit, but I'd have to be in wolf form and my Mark visible.

There was no way around it. I was the Luna. I *had* to officiate. I couldn't *not*.

Cook added, "Because you're unmated, it's also where Lunas historically have been courted. The invitations have already gone out, but you might want to consider sending a second round to potential suiters. Just to flatter them."

I felt myself go very, very pale. Green, even. "I'll think about it. I have a lot of things on my mind."

"I know you just got out of a relationship," Cook pressed, "but it'd—"

"That's what you call being mated? A *relationship*?" I asked, stunned.

"I mean he wasn't the one you chose," Cook said awkwardly. "I know the matebond is no small thing, but… wasn't it a relief to get free of Gabel? Now you're free. You're the Luna of the most powerful pack in the world. You never have to go back to him."

He needed to stop talking. My last nerve frayed to nothing. "I will do my duty, Cook, but the Moon dictates how I serve."

"We'll help you," Cook said.

I laughed miserably. "Cook, I think I'm far beyond any help at this point. The Moon wants what She wants, no matter what it costs any of us."

GAMES QUEENS PLAY

"**Y**ou don't need to be showing the pack how weak you are," Lucas said.

I managed a dry laugh. "Why not? Let them think I'm dying. Nobody's going to bother to overthrow a Luna who will be dead soon."

Lucas shortened his stride to match mine, his body tense and movements sharp, his kilt swishing around his knees and barely sashed. He expected to have to rip it off within the next few hours. "You are not safe outside the heart."

"I am barely safe *in* the heart."

"And you want to risk dying out here? These wolves think you're a pretender and I'm a traitor. They might stab me in the back on the field and then turn on you. At least if I died on the field you'd know because of Kiery and have time to run to the south to Aaron."

That wasn't going to happen. My Marked arm felt heavy, like I was dragging thick chains all the way from SableFur's heart, and the Moon seemed to croon in the distant back of my mind. "You think I'll run south to *Aaron*? Do you hear what you're saying?"

"At worst, he'd hold you hostage."

"At best, you can collect another throne," Evan, walking on Lucas' other side, said. He was wearing a red kilt with bright orange paisley print all over it.

"Let's not even joke about that," I said, feeling faint and gutted as the vision of the crown of bleeding bone punched my brain.

Their brains were on the battle, not me. The IronMoon had advanced far enough into SableFur it was time for Lucas to get the fight he'd been hungering for. I'd insisted on coming along to observe. Lucas had only relented when I'd pointed out, in private, that I had nothing to fear from the IronMoon, and technically SableFur shouldn't murder me. I didn't plan on being anywhere close to the battlefield. You know, just in case a claw *accidentally* found its way into my back.

Lucas had brought up a small selection of warriors he (more or less) trusted from the heart to lead the fight, but the bulk of the warriors were being supplied by the wolves in this region. The fight wasn't a surprise for them, and as far as I knew, they were eager to meet the IronMoon.

Gabel wasn't exactly where they'd expected. Everyone had thought he'd take the direct route to SableFur's heart, but he'd bent in a more northern route, and now were to the west, not south.

"I still want to know why he chose *here*," Lucas rumbled, with Evan at his side, who nodded curtly. "There isn't even that much to burn out that way. Why hasn't he come *here* to take this hamlet?"

Evan grunted and shook his head. "He's an idiot thinking he can sneak in."

"He's a lupine, not an idiot," Lucas said gruffly. "He's picked this northern route for a reason."

"Strategically it's worthless." Evan nodded. "His supply lines will be cut off soon, he'll be in rough territory, and enemies on all sides. No element of surprise. When he loses today, he'll have no choice but to fall back to the north. We could just chase him across the open steppes. There's nothing out there."

"That lupine brain of his is up to something."

"That lupine brain is broken," Evan said.

Lucas grunted. "That too. When he loses today, we'll let them retreat just to see what he's planning. But if he leads his warriors off a cliff and they all drown like a sack of kittens, I'll howl the Moon's praises for the next seven years."

Evan laughed.

Lucas preferred to live in some fantasy land where Gabel could die and I'd survive. Adrianna had given him some unrealistic expectations.

We had turned onto a gravel road that quickly turned into packed dirt and half-thawed icy muck. This ended at a small cluster of buildings, all centered around an ancient stone well. Three dozen skeptical SableFur warriors had formed up near it, with the male who ran the show down this way standing on the edge. They were all in kilts, barefoot, and ready for a fight. Any she-wolves, pups, and non-warriors watched from the various buildings.

The wolf standing on the edge of the well folded his arms across his strong chest. He was something of a specimen, I'd grant him that. He said, "We are here. As ordered."

He didn't jump down off the well. Kept his head above mine, and he spoke to Lucas, not me.

Evan growled under his breath.

"Francis," Lucas murmured.

I'd turned Gabel's own cheap malevolence against him. Time-proven strategy. I couldn't suddenly look healthy, but fat chance I was going to let any of these wolves think I was weak. I'd had Ana take off my wraps so my tattered hands were on display. My sweater's low neckline revealed my necklace of silver scars, while the long sleeves hid my scabbed Mark. I'd found some black eyeliner to rim my eyes to make the pale mark in my iris stand out more.

Nobody got to think I was a timid weakling who might *possibly* be impressed with a warrior who kept his head above mine. His sad display of dominance was exactly that: sad.

And I was going to give him exactly what he wanted, but he'd have to eat it straight from my stitched-up palm.

I raised my voice. "Wolves of SableFur, Alpha Gabel of IronMoon has come through the pass. He is Magnes' biological son. This fact is not disputed by anyone, and Magnes paid for the wrongs of his past with his soul. Which, if you care to come see it, is melted into the wooden floor of the SableFur Hall."

The warriors shifted nervously.

"Gabel claims to be the rightful heir to SableFur," I went on, "and intends to enforce his claim."

"Why would he think SableFur is his just because he's Magnes' bastard?" Francis spit a wad of phlegm. It landed close to my boot.

Because that was how it worked, and Francis knew it. "Because Adrianna was Magnes' accomplice. This terminated her right to rule and her line of succession. I am the Luna by right of conquest. Gabel is the only one with an unsullied blood claim to the throne, bastard or not."

"Adrianna knew nothing!" Francis barked, and some of the wolves howled.

"Magnes' soul is less than nothing, and Adrianna's reward is eternal despair. Sounds like damnation to me. She's just getting started while she's still alive," I said.

Francis scowled, and a low tremor of growls echoed through the clearing. "The Moon didn't strike her down or set the starlight wolves on her trail."

I feigned boredom and casually pointed one lazy finger

towards the north. "No, but the Moon has put me on her trail. That's not really your concern. There's a battle with IronMoon that way. Fight for me, or fight for Adrianna, or because you're bored. You're still going to fight."

Francis leaned over and spat again.

I shrugged. "Or don't fight, and I'm sure he'll show up here, rip this place to pieces, leave your mates and pups in the cold, and you can explain to the Moon how you abandoned your Luna when your territory was invaded."

They all snarled and barred their teeth at me. Francis scoffed, "Perhaps we should just let Gabel take the throne back. What do you think he's going to do to your scarred neck when he gets his hands on you?"

I chuckled. "I imagine he'll put his Mark back on my arm and declare himself King."

Point made, I walked away.

"Way to tell them their place in the order of things," Ana said upon my return.

My hands throbbed from the brittle cold. Posturing was exhausting, and I had no idea what I was doing, which made it doubly not fun. "It's the only way. If they're fighting Iron-Moon, they're not fighting me."

"You're getting a little crazy out there. All it's gonna take is one of them remembering where he left his balls and come right at you to start a riot. You aren't Gabel—physically, I mean—and you're about as sturdy as a wet paper bag."

"I know, I know, I know," I said.

Ana lowered her voice. "You ever consider just saying fuck this and letting Gabel take it all to hell while you have tea and babies? He's the Destroyer. This is sort of his scene."

My Mark squeezed again, and my arm pulled under the weight of thick chains. "I can't do that. Come on, I have somewhere to be."

One of the loyal (sort of) Hunters had scouted me a place

where I could more or less watch the IronMoon face off against SableFur. The vantage point was the dirt shoulder of a hillside road intended to catch vehicles that drifted too far to the outside of the bend. In spring, trees would have obscured the fields below, but in winter, it was a pretty good view.

Ana re-wrapped my fingers in a few layers of gauze and pads. I tried to ignore the bodies clashing into each other and the distant sound of snarls and scent of blood on the wind.

The phone in my long coat's pocket buzzed. It was Hix's phone still. Wolf had never put a passcode on it.

Gabel >> I smell you, buttercup.

Half an hour later three wolves loped around the asphalt bend. The claws of one made a distinctive *click-scratch click-scratch click-scratch.*

"What the——" Bernhard rasped as Gabel's nightmare form came closer, his eyes ichor-yellow and his oily pelt oozing out of the freezing mist, and his massive claws scratching into the asphalt, yellow and hideous. With him were my Original Goons: A and B.

Gabel melted up into his human form with the smooth, inky swiftness of the most powerful combat shifters. Fresh scratches and bruises marred his toned body, and the stab wounds from Aaron still flushed pink on his powerful thigh.

Carved into his arm in all its raw, scabbed glory was our new Mark.

FOR A MOMENT

Seeing the Mark slashed across the curves of his arm, the cruel lines and the blue-black-red-smoldering glory of it, and the way his shifting had torn and pulled at the scabs and trickles of blood traced down his arm—

He was glorious, he was terrible, and he was mine.

"Buttercup." Gabel clicked his tongue as he walked into the small clearing careless of the mist sliding off his naked body, his bare feet crunching small pieces of sharp gravel and road debris. "Does your ambition know no end?"

Ana grabbed Bernhard and hissed, "Let's find somewhere else to be for ten minutes."

Bernhard didn't move. His eyes were transfixed on Gabel's Marked arm. Ana yanked him by the hair this time. "You never seen a Mark before, wolf? You knew it'd be there. Let's *go*."

The others reluctantly fell back about fifteen feet. There wasn't much place to go on this particular curve of dangerous road, but even a few yards of breathing room was enough. I inhaled, drawing in Gabel's scent of ash and burning.

He slid his hands over my hips, and pressed his face into my neck, then inhaled my scent.

I brushed my hand against him. His face was clean shaven, but he had fresh scars along his jaw, as if he'd peeled up layers of skin shaving himself down to the quick. His cheeks were drawn, circles under his eyes, a haunted pallor.

He pulled at the collar of my sweater, and his fingertips brushed each scar around my neck in turn, counting, then he took each hand, pressed my palms to his lips, inhaled the scent of pain and blood from each.

"I cannot leave you unattended a moment, can I?" His voice rumbled low and smoldering in my ears. "I turn my back and you've made yourself a Luna. If I place that necklace of obsidian around your neck," he drew a line with one finger along my scars, "will I wake up to find you strangling me with it?"

Beyond us in the valley, a howl went up. A call to fall back. An IronMoon howl.

He captured my right hand and gently brushed his lips over my bandaged palm. His other hand still held me steady against his naked, warm strength. "If you are here on a battlefield, you are not safe in your den. So, a victory for you. To feed your warriors tonight."

The shape of his body fit perfectly against mine. Thinner, perhaps, more raw than it had been a month ago. New scars too. But it was still him. "My warriors will hate me all the more for it."

Gabel's smile intensified a bit, his scent burning and cruel mischief. "I expected Adrianna to be howling the orders, and yet here you are, throwing fangs and claws at me. Are you going to make me tear SableFur apart to have you? To seal our new Mark in an appropriate amount of blood?" His dark presence engulfed me, and he murmured, "I will do it to please you. I will build that tower to the Moon if you wish to claw out

Her eye. I will hold you above my head so you may have the honor of reaching Her first."

My throat became impossibly dry, and the Bond throbbed between us like a second heart.

He bent lower. "You are not well. How much silver did they use?"

"I've been beyond the Tides too much this month," I said, bracing myself against his strength. "I have to find a way to destroy Adrianna. SableFur doesn't believe she knew about your mother, and they're going to revolt under me. It's not a negotiable situation."

Gabel chuckled. "There is no negotiation needed. I am the rightful heir to the SableFur throne as the oldest son, and I happen to be mated to the Luna currently upon it."

"You aren't legitimate until I de-legitimize Adrianna," I said. "SableFur doesn't know about the Mark. They think Lucas betrayed them and I'm a pretender. I need time to—"

Gabel released me and stepped back. "I played along with the Moon's designs. It is time for us to be together again."

"If I leave, or falter, Adrianna will take my place, and she will conquer all of us. Kiery has seen her wearing your skull as a crown." And in SableFur, who liked to either burn or inter their dead, Adrianna wearing Gabel's skull took on a whole new level of meaning.

He grit his teeth, and his whole body clenched. "You are mine, and I am yours. We made promises to each other."

"And those promises have been kept! Our Bond and Marks have been restored."

"If I leave here without you how is that *restored*? You are asking me to entrust your safety to wolves who you have admitted will kill you at the slightest provocation, and you expect me to let you return there?"

"Yes," I said. "I have to handle it. My power is fragile. If you try to come now, you'll destroy us both."

He seethed, shifted like a restless Tide against my senses, the Bond churning, and a strange, smoldering ache manifested deep within me. "The Moon destroyed Magnes. Why leave Adrianna behind?"

I laughed and flung up my hands. "I don't know, but it doesn't matter. She has an army of thousands of wolves, and I've got a chair."

Gabel's lip curled. "Fine. I'll humor our separation for a short time, but *only* a short time. I *am* prepared to walk into SableFur and claim you as my own and inform them who their true Alpha is and kill every single wolf who challenges that. I am the Alpha of SableFur. My mate conquered it and solidi-fied my birthright." He seized my face in his hands. "I will not let them have you. I will not let the Moon have you. She gave us to each other when She forged our Bond, when She heard our vows, and when She put these Marks back on us. I will force Her to honor that, or I will tear this world apart."

Anguish threatened to suffocate me. "I don't want more blood, and I don't want the world ruined. You are the Comet, but I'm the Balance-Keeper. I want the day when we don't have to be monsters."

"Do you really think that day will come?" he asked, one brow raised.

"It has to! Otherwise none of this matters, and it never did, and there is absolutely no legacy to leave to my pups except a pile of bones and a puddle of blood." I rested my forehead against his chest for a moment. "Aaron says you are the Alpha who doesn't know what he has, or how to keep it, right up to your very own head. And I wonder if he's right. You're the Destroyer, and I'm afraid you'll destroy yourself in the end."

"There is a shadow on your scent," he said, peering intently at me. He smoothed one hand over my head, and gripped my hair tightly, and pulled back, exposing my throat. "What have you seen?"

"Beltane," I rasped.

"In six weeks time, I believe."

"No, it's the Luna's festival in SableFur. I won't be able to hide my Mark."

His ocean-colored eyes illuminated with a fell light, and the Bond surged with his thrill. "Six weeks to shed enough blood worthy of you. The Moon lays a challenge at my paws. The sky-bitch will find me equal to it, and you."

He bent and kissed me deeply. His fierce ardor and the thrill of coming conquest surged through the Bond, which sighed like an exhausted muscle no longer required to hold up its own weight.

He shifted his grip on me, and bent low, his lips brushing mine in the cold. "I shouldn't linger. I don't care to risk getting a pup on you. I need you at my side with fangs barred."

I swallowed, remembering what had happened in the grove. He had no way of knowing that I'd returned with what had to have been him on my thighs, and inside me.

"Or did that happen before you left?" he asked, focusing on me with sudden intensity. "Is there something to tell me? Is that why you are so unwell? Did you have a pup in your belly when you left?"

"That night in the grove. When I came back, you were on my thighs. It's only been two weeks, so it's too early to know…" My voice trailed off.

He bent forward and nipped my neck. "So it was not my imagination waking up with a wet cock and the scent of you on me. I had thought it was a most wonderful dream."

I whispered, "Don't get too hopeful. The silver."

He released me and stepped back. "Goodbye, my Queen. We will rule together yet."

He shifted down into wolf-form and loped away with the goons.

ALONE, TOGETHER

I arrived back in SableFur to a guest.

He was with his wolves in the dining room he and Magnes had destroyed, sitting on the one chair that had managed to stay intact, casually reading something on his phone, one knee over the other, with a coffee cup on a make-shift table of debris. He also wasn't in a suit, or anything casual: he was in a bright blue kilt, and his feet were bare. His warriors—an angrier, more prestigious group than his previous entourage—were also in kilts and barefoot.

I'd changed clothes on the hillside and Ana had stamped my other clothing into the muck and debris so I wouldn't smell like Gabel. I wasn't as clean and presentable as I could be, and I didn't appreciate Alphas randomly wandering into my den.

This one, though, I owed a favor to. And he knew it.

"Luna Gianna," he greeted me with his usual arrogant grin, like it was such a surprise I had come home. "They told me you were in the field. Here I thought that coming to see you while Gabel was occupied would be polite timing on my part."

"In another context, Aaron, that would sound scandalous,"

I said as Bernhard took my coat off my shoulders. "What brings you back to SableFur?"

"Well, I previously had left on rather bad terms, but considering that was on *your* account, I thought you may be interested in renewing SableFur and IceMaw's reasonable relationship." Arrogance and prestige oozed from every syllable, and he practically licked his teeth after every word.

"Oh *hey*." Ana shoved her way around the wall into the remains of the dining room. "Whoa, what happened in here?"

"Magnes and I had a disagreement," Aaron said. "I recognize your voice, human."

"Gianna, you didn't tell me he was *hot*," Ana said.

I sighed at her. "Ana. He is a visiting Alpha."

"Looks like he knows how to get dirty. Ain't much left of this room. I've got to deal with your hands. You've been in a literal combat zone." She turned to Aaron and smiled sweetly. "You don't mind waiting a bit longer do you, Alpha?"

"I will wait as long as necessary," Aaron said, gaze never leaving my face.

Ana curtsied primly and dragged me off to her clinic.

She hauled me up onto a metal table meant for wolf-forms and dead bodies. "Alpha FriendZone there looks at you like you're dessert. You going to tell him about your arm? Because *I* didn't tell him. I just said you'd been cut up and had lost a lot of blood and silver and all that. Which is technically true."

I shook my head. "I don't trust what he'd do with the knowledge. Aaron's dangerous."

"Dangerous like Gabel or dangerous like…?"

"He killed his family to make himself Alpha of IceMaw," I said. "He did it—according to him—to free his pack from corrupt leadership. But he challenged his uncle, the Alpha, and by association it killed the Luna, and his father also challenged him, so… he killed a lot of his kin."

She didn't pause as she set out bandages and scissors and

the like. "There've been rumors you and him are maybe sort of a thing."

"He wants us to be."

"Can that be a thing? You've got two arms."

"A female's lure-scent disappears once she has a Mark. And I don't want to be stuck between Aaron and Gabel. They despise each other."

"Oh, come on, what are a few stab wounds between friends?" She dragged the metal tray over and started to cut off my bandages.

"Are you serious?" I was *not* interested. I wouldn't lie and say I couldn't feel Aaron's prestige, and admire him, but I was Gabel's mate, and I had *his* Mark on my arm, and I had taken the vows with *him*.

"Well, if he could smell your lure-scent, he's in for a rude surprise now that it's gone. That's how it works, right? He's going to know about your Mark."

"Crap, I hadn't thought of that."

"Yeah, because you're half-dead." She pulled off the bandages and tossed them aside.

"Didn't you already replace my bandages when we were in the field?"

"That was sixteen hours ago." She dangled one length of gauze that was bloody and gross. "You *wanna* keep these nasty finger-nappies on?"

My hands were flushed red and had so many stitches my fingers looked like candy canes and my palms patchwork quilts. "I'd like to have my hands when I'm dealing with Aaron."

She glanced up, a wry comment passing across her face, then said, "Yeah, mittens for you."

"If you want to make a pass at him, I won't object," I teased weakly. "Go ahead and distract him for me."

She cracked a grin and ran her tongue over her teeth. "You want a shower while these are unwrapped?"

"Hell, yes."

"Okies. Come on then. I'll wash your hair." Ana began to strap plastic bags over my hands and duct-tape them to my wrists. I couldn't wash my hair, but at least I could soap my own butt. Kiery had offered to help me bathe (as we were both Oracles, and technically sisters) but I was more comfortable with Ana doing it. Ana was a human, so prestige and rank meant nothing to her, and my fragile physical state was her business anyway.

As I stood under the hot water and Ana squirted shampoo into my hair, I said, "Anyone offers you money to stab me, let me know. I'll make a better offer."

"Hah, joke would be on them. I'd take their money and then tattle."

"Why? You're in it for the money. Won't blame you."

"Nah," Ana said. "You got me out of my life. Where you go, I go."

"That wasn't our deal," I said. "You *liked* your life before you got mixed up with this."

"I don't want to go back to my strip mall and getting paid in hams. I want to stay with the wolves and looks like I'm going to have to pick a side. Your star seems the best of the lot to hitch my wagon to. I'm kind of hoping this Moon Goddess of yours is recruiting. She seems to get results."

"Wait, you want to be a wolf?"

"Yeah, can you just bite me or something?"

"We're a species, not a disease."

"Boo."

About ninety minutes later I was finally in my office, and Aaron was still around. A young and nervous wolf, obviously cowed by the Alpha that had smashed around his previous Alpha, showed him in.

Something hit my guts. I squished my strange knot of feelings aside. Another thing to juggle. Another current to ride. I hadn't been prepared to face Aaron. I'd told him there'd never be anything between us, I hadn't led him on, but as he stepped into my office, his expression was—well, there wasn't a word to describe the expression buried underneath Aaron's Alpha mask.

"What did you really come for, Aaron?" I asked warily.

"To see you," Aaron answered. "You didn't leave with me before. Did you know what you were going to do? If you did, you are the supreme actress. I am almost offended at feeling played."

I managed a single laugh. "I am only the Moon's puppet, it seems."

He eyed me. "I have never doubted what I did to become Alpha of IceMaw until this moment, Gianna. Now I wonder if I have offended the Moon."

"Why?" I had never led him on, he was the one who had thrown himself into all of this. And I still felt absolutely terrible. Like I *had* betrayed him somehow. And that was a stupid way to feel because I'd never, not even for a *second*, entertained the thought of a life with Aaron.

"Your lure-scent fills this room. The Moon seems determined to torment me with you, yet keep you out of my reach. I have sworn I will call no wolf King, including myself, yet here you sit, the SableFur Luna, and I am an Alpha. The SableFur gem isn't a trinket. It's a crown jewel."

That was impossible. But he'd smelled it through my Mark the first time we'd met—I hadn't understood it then, and I didn't understand it now. "You're lying about my lure-scent, Aaron."

"If anything, it's stronger now. Cereus, the night-blooming flower."

I wanted to scream *you're lying, you're lying!* But Aaron had no reason to lie. He'd identified my lure-scent back at Anders' party, much to Gabel's fury.

Aaron had been in my last vision before Magnes had died.
Three sets of runes, three runes, three—
Obsidian, tourmaline, quartz.
IronMoon, SableFur, IceMaw.
Aaron had been the wolf Anders had spoken to in the
jungle vision, he'd been the MeatMan, and then he'd been a
voice in a chorus telling me to believe.

The grotto, the house, the temple. Those were consistent,
as were the runes. Another Oracle might have concluded
Aaron was Gabel's littermate, or Aaron was another lost
Magnes bastard, but both of those were impossible. Gabel was
a lupine, Aaron wasn't. Aaron was two years older, and there
was no question who his father had been. If there was any
blood relation between Gabel and Aaron, it was distant.

"You smell of the Moon, the cereus, blood and…" He
sniffed the air. "Why blood?"

I held up my hands. Easy explanation.

He nodded, then said, "Burning. Very faintly like burning.
Like a summer storm."

I wanted to rip off my sweater and show him what a liar he
was, but Aaron wasn't lying, and the truth of that gripped my
liver and squeezed until I couldn't breathe. "Do you dream?"

Males didn't get the Seer Gift, but the Moon could speak to
males, and send them dreams too. And She made them into
Her Servants, like Flint.

Aaron said, grimly, "I always dream. In my dreams I
always feel the silver claw-tips going into my spine, but in my
nightmares, they cut too deep, my legs go numb, and I am
broken, and fail. What I did didn't come without cost. It's a
cost I don't count, but there was a cost."

"Have your dreams changed at all?" I asked, a strange part
of me aching. The Bond panged, thrumming like a piece of
strummed wire.

He picked up one of the pebbles from the desk. I hadn't

had the heart to clear off Magnes' desk. Not really. There were still two kids who had lost their father. It didn't seem right, somehow, to just erase everything of their father before they had a chance to say goodbye.

Aaron set the stone down. "I dream I am on a small, rocky island in a stormy ocean. The storm itself hasn't broken, just some breeze and mist, but all the light rain turns to blood and runs into the ocean. The moon is huge and setting in the distance, this huge white sliver, like a scythe coming down onto the horizon."

I kept my expression neutral. "Were you alone on the island?"

"Yes."

"Did you notice anything else? On the ground? On your body? What form were you in? Smell anything?"

"War-form," he said after a moment to ponder it. "Just a rocky island as the Moon set. I see the Moon setting and feel those claws going into my spine."

"So you felt the claws in your spine too."

"I always feel claws in my spine."

My entire ribcage had turned into a tuning fork of anguish.

Aaron had risen up against the sort of corruption that the Moon had just destroyed! She didn't need a Comet when She had Aaron! Hell, She didn't need *me* when She had Aaron.

Except Aaron wasn't willing to build an empire. Aaron didn't want to be King. He didn't want to dismantle the world.

"Gianna?" Aaron's quiet voice prodded me.

I shook off the stormy thoughts. "Were you bleeding in the dream? Do you remember?"

"I always bleed in my dreams. In all my dreams the wounds on my spine are open and unhealed." He tried to say it easily, as if it was nothing at all, but I recognized that haunted gleam in his expression. I'd seen it before in petitioners: dreams that were too vivid to just be dreams.

"How long have you been dreaming that way?"

"Eight years." He smiled. "Since it happened. I've learned to ignore them. I've asked two Oracles, but they tell me there's nothing to the dreams."

"Wait, you've been dreaming of the island for eight years? It's a reoccurring nightmare?"

"That's right."

"And always on that island."

"The scythe-Moon has sunk progressively lower over the years," Aaron said. "Now it's just above the horizon. The Oracles have told me over and over it is just a dream."

Gabel's IronMoon had emerged out of their forests about eight years earlier. I had left for my Oracle training about eight years earlier as well. I pulled nervously at one lip, insides squirming in fear. "Did you ask SableFur Oracles?"

"No. Oracles in the south. It's not a dream, is it?"

"I've been to that island."

"You have?" He raised a brow, skeptical.

"It's an island at the Edge of the Tides."

"The Tides have an edge?"

"Apparently," I said, shuddering all over. "And I've been to a Place Beyond the Tides. I don't know what else to call it. The Moon has never given it a name. I don't know what or where or even *when* it is—"

"Did you say *when*?"

"Yes." I shuddered again. "It's terrifying. But the island you've been to is at the Edge of the Tides."

"Have you been seeing the island as long as I have?"

"No." That was another frightening implication. Aaron had seen it before all of us.

"Why would the Moon show me that place?"

His guess was probably better than mine at this point. "Do you wake up normally from these dreams?"

"What's normal?" he asked with that cagey, handsome grin of his. Only it was tinged with sadness and self-hatred.

"No headache, disorientation. You wake up and you're fine."

"They're nightmares. I usually wake up as one does from nightmares."

So he wasn't *going* to the Island. Not like I did.

Aaron didn't deserve heartbreak. He was the wolf who had done all the right things. Why would the Moon punish him with loneliness and no pups? Why would the Moon not let *him* —the most obviously worthy male I'd ever met—leave a legacy? Raise more pups in his image?

That was not right. "Why do you think the Moon is torturing you? It sounds to me like you have a rare soul. Stands to reason your potential mates would be few and far between too."

"I'm flattered," he said, but the feral grin on his lips was tormented. "When I was young, before I was Alpha, and was just another poorly fed flea-ridden dog in my Alpha's service, I smelled the lure-scent often. Frequently. In fact, as I made my plans to challenge my uncle, I had already been courting one she-wolf. I resolved if I survived I'd ask her to be my Luna."

"She refused?" I asked. "Did you have to kill her?"

"If only," Aaron said grimly. "If only. No, I became Alpha, went to her, and no scent. Gone. Every she-wolf I'd smelled before? Gone."

"What?" I blurted out. That didn't happen. The Bond could only form between compatible souls. That meant that Aaron's soul had *changed* after his challenge. That wasn't even possible! Souls were *souls*!

Aaron gestured to his head with an elegant flick of his fingers, but his eyes were dark and sharp, like obsidian knives. "I've always told myself that of course what I did changed me, but I did the *right* thing, and my mate would appear in time. And here she is."

Without another word, he half-bowed, and showed himself out.

I put my head down on my desk and wept.

DISCIPLINE

I had six weeks to destroy Adrianna and prevent the world from exploding under me. My personal life was already a fiery mess.

Not that I knew where Adrianna was, and there was zero chance any of the outlying wolves would help me find her, and even if I did find her, she wasn't going to confess.

So six weeks to unearth answers that had been buried for thirty years.

Sure. No problem.

"Luna," Lucas said, stepping into the office. He was wearing just a kilt, as usual, his feet were bare and dirty, and a bruise from an IronMoon warrior's bite on his shoulder, and a couple of stitches scattered throughout.

"Close the door." I pushed a small piece of paper at him. "Gabel's number. Beltane is coming. You forgot to mention it was the Luna's holiday, and I'd be leading the ceremonial hunt."

Lucas looked confused.

"Certain secrets aren't going to keep once I'm in wolf-form, Lucas," I said, annoyed. After Aaron's little visit, I needed to put a hard stop on all this matchmaking nonsense. "So take all your ideas about courtships and bachelors and shove them. They're not happening."

Lucas' expression washed over with shocked realization. "I—I—"

"We're all overwhelmed, but Cook remembered to talk to me. Now we've got to plan for the inevitable," I said.

Lucas looked, blankly, at the note. "So why did you give me this?"

"Coordinate a series of skirmishes with Gabel that will keep SableFur occupied, but bring Gabel here to SableFur by Beltane. I don't really care who wins or loses, or the form it takes. I don't really care why he's decided to arc north instead of come directly. You two figure out what's going to be most palatable to SableFur."

"You would send wolves to fight and die for a *farce*?!"

Guilt poked me in the liver. I swallowed the sour taste that bubbled up my throat. "Unless you think Gabel just showing up at Beltane would go better?"

Lucas shifted on his feet and his face darkened with a scowl. "We already defeated the IronMoon once. We can drive them back across the border. You can't expect me to start throwing fights."

"Gabel gave us that victory. He met me on the hillside to tell me himself. He said it was to feed my army."

"He did what!"

"Without it, you would have been defeated. The SableFur underestimated the IronMoon. So arrogant and convinced that because you—"

"*We*. You're SableFur now, too," Lucas growled.

Oh, so he wanted to snarl at me? I could deal with that. "Fine, then as the newest member of SableFur, it's time for this pack to stop thinking just howling *SableFur* means anything. In six weeks this pack finds out who their new Alpha is."

Lucas crumpled up the paper in his fist and threw it to the side. "I will never call that wolf Alpha."

I paced around the desk. "He is the Moon's Dark Comet, and my mate. You will—"

"He took you by force and you don't owe him anything!"

"Keep your voice down! The *Moon* did this!" I jabbed my finger at my arm. "So go howl at Her if you think it'll do any good!"

"You *have choices*!" Lucas snarled. "Repudiate him! Reject it! You're the Balance-Keeper. Maybe that's how you stop him— by not being his goddamn victim!"

I almost laughed. It was like talking to Anita. "Don't you think I *tried* to get free of him? I'm the Balance-Keeper and the Moon isn't going to let me get free of him."

"No. You have a choice. Reject him. The Moon might have put that on your arm but you don't *have* to be with him. It doesn't even look like a Mark. Why would the Moon give you a Mark that doesn't *look* like a damned Mark? Why have it be blue-gloss?"

"Gabel will never, ever let me go, and he will destroy the world to have me."

"Then we will stop him. I am not calling that wolf Alpha, and he doesn't get to have you just because he Marked you first. This isn't a game of mating tag."

The Moon had put this Mark on my arm and bound me to Gabel. "Do as you are told, or I will find someone who will."

"You need me," Lucas snarled. "If you get rid of me, this is over for you. SableFur will consume you, and your death will kill Gabel, so I'm not sure what the loss is. I made a mistake putting you on the throne. I should have—"

"Your courage failing you now, First Beta?" I mocked him. "Go run back to Adrianna. Your mate won't go with you."

"You leave Kiery out of this!" He roared and lunged towards me.

I scampered to the side and slid over the desk, scattering papers and pens. I tumbled onto the floor and scrambled under the desk to the other side as Lucas spun. I backed towards the door, hands straining against their stitches and my fingernails burning in their beds. "Kiery's in this up to her neck, and you're too weak to go into the Tides with her, you coward. You were never worthy of an Oracle's unfailing love."

"And Gabel was worthy of yours?!" Lucas advanced, backing me out into the hallway.

"Gabel had the courage to say what he was and not look away from the void like a weak-willed wolf." I continued to back towards the stairs.

"Because Gabel's a monster. You haven't seen what he's done. You don't know what he's turned into since you left him." Lucas matched me stair for stair, snarling, his face not entirely human anymore and his teeth sharp, bright fangs.

"I know what he's done. I know *exactly* what he's capable of, and *exactly* what he is." I knew all about Gabel. I felt him within me now, dark and burning.

Lucas lunged forward. I ducked out of the way, wishing I could shift into wolf form but not daring. He missed me deliberately, sending me almost stumbling down the remainder of the stairs, and his fist went through the wall.

Great. More household repairs. As if the dining room wasn't still a calamity.

I circled around him in the foyer, watching his shoulders and eyes like Flint had taught me.

Lucas matched me pace for pace. "I am not following those orders. I will not do what you've told me to do."

I laughed at him as bitterly as I'd ever laughed at Gabel. "You want to be in that cathedral of bones, but you're going to be burned and forgotten. Hix was my First Beta, and you aren't worthy of the title!"

Lucas growled, but retreated an uncertain half-step.

"That's right." I ground it deeper. "Hix defied his Alpha to save the wolf he believed was his Luna. He died in that court-yard like an animal, singing *my* song, and he *never* hesitated. Not for one minute!" My voice cracked. "I left him to die in that pit because he begged me not to save him, and he gave his life to vindicate me and expose Magnes and Adrianna for the cowards they are, and what are you doing? You're not even ankle-deep in the Tides and you're crying about being wet."

I jerked up my chin to expose my throat. "If you believe Adrianna is your true Luna, do your duty and kill me."

Lucas didn't move.

I walked towards him, neck still exposed. "Here is my throat. You know what I am. Do your duty to your Luna and kill me. Rip out my throat and lay it at her feet."

The veins in his throat stood out against his skin.

"Do it. Decide what kind of First Beta you are. Decide which future you serve."

The Moon spun in my awareness, passing through all Her phases as She too waited for Lucas' choice, hot and red like the blood moon in the autumn sky.

Do it. Kill me. Do it.

Lucas, slowly and very stiffly, like a machine that hadn't been oiled in years, bent one knee, then the next. He placed his hands on his knees and bowed his head, all slowly, one joint at a time.

I stared down at him for a full minute, watching every breath that moved his shoulders.

Good.

I walked past him. "You will do as I have ordered, Beta."

"Yes, Luna," he murmured.

"And you will do it *well*, Beta, with the best interests of this pack at heart, no matter how much it may cost you." I stopped on the second step. He knelt there on the floor back bent and head bowed, reeking of brokenness and grief. The ridge of his spine stood out against the muscled thickness of his back. "The next time we argue about the strength of your spine, one of us will die."

His shoulders dipped further as if being pummeled by driving rain. "Yes, Luna."

LUCAS : FURBALLS

"Tell me," Kiery said, sliding onto the couch next to him.

"About how I ended up on my knees?"

"Obviously. I've seen you fight with Magnes a dozen times, but this was different."

"She wants me to coordinate a farce with Gabel to keep SableFur's attention elsewhere while she looks for proof against Adrianna," Lucas said. "She wants to have our warriors fight in… rigged matches!"

Kiery retrieved a bottle of beer for herself from the little mini-fridge, then returned to the couch. Lucas grumbled and shifted as she tucked herself against his side. "You refused?"

"I've never menaced a she-wolf before," Lucas said quietly, smacking the bottom of his beer bottle against his forehead while staring blankly at the twenty-four-hour weather channel. "But I *did*. I snarled at her and backed her out of that office like she was a male. Practically shoved her down the stairs. What the hell is happening to me?"

"Oh, please, you and Magnes clawed each other up on occasion."

"And me beating up some fragile half-dead she-wolf with stitches in her hands is such a fair fight," Lucas muttered.

"Is that why you gave in?"

"She hit me with Hix. She's right. Hix would have gone along with her crazy plan. She's trying to save everyone. But asking warriors to go out and fight and die like this?"

"It keeps her in control of her warriors," Kiery said. "She knows they're all loyal to Adrianna, but they'll fight IronMoon under her banner all the same, and the IronMoon can handle them."

"It's all going to get exposed in what, a month, anyway?"

Kiery drank half her beer and put her feet up across his thighs. He clamped his hand down over her and sighed. Kiery said, "You know, Gianna's not wrong with trying to direct SableFur's energy and nerves, but maybe she's got the wrong idea about how."

Lucas cracked open one eye.

She shrugged. "He's going to be your Alpha, so you're going to have to talk to him eventually."

Lucas blew out a long breath and nodded. "After I finish this beer, and after you help me forget all about how to shit everything has gone."

She grinned, set her own bottle down, and pulled her top over her head. "We're still alive, right? That's automatically better than how we thought it was going to end."

"According to you and Anita, there's no happy ending at all."

"Then I guess I'm going to have to give you one..."

LUCAS TYPED IN THE NUMBERS, but each one made him feel ill. He didn't have the stomach to call Gabel.

Much less call him *Alpha*. Or put him into his phone as *Gabel*.

He rubbed his thumb along the glass lip of his beer bottle.

Lucas [Furballs] >> Gianna wants us to talk.

He turned on the twenty-four-hour weather channel. Good background noise.

An hour later, someone replied to his text.

Furballs >> Who are you?

Lucas [Furballs] >> Lucas.

Five minutes later, his phone rang. Furballs. He almost didn't answer, then grit his teeth and brought the phone to his ear. "This is her idea."

"You may be *her* First Beta," a voice like ash and honey said on the other end, laced with amusement and darkness that made Lucas' skin crawl up and down his spine, "but you are not *mine*."

"That suits me fine. I haven't even decided if I will actually call you Alpha or not. For now you're in my phone as Furballs. I don't want anyone to overhear me say your name."

"Afraid I will invoke bad luck?"

"Exactly, Furballs, exactly."

"Yes, they are, in wolf-form. Are you somehow exceptional, like a baboon?"

Lucas rubbed his forehead.

A chuckle like the rumble from the back of a deep, dark cave. "What do you want, Baboon? My time is limited. I am in the field on my four paws, and my pack is restless."

"How convenient. She wants us to coordinate a series of… engagements." Lucas grit his teeth.

Quiet.

"Are you there?" Lucas asked after two minutes had passed.

"To what purpose?"

"Keeping SableFur entertained. I'm not sure how it's going to go well. If I let you burn a path down here, she looks weak.

If we fight you back, then she can't welcome you. But she knows Adrianna's got a grip on most of them, and Adrianna hates you as much as she hates Gianna."

"I see," Gabel said.

Another maddeningly long pause. Lucas bit down a snarl of frustration. Nobody had taught this wolf phone skills. "I'm not sure what resources you have in the field."

"Do you have wolves in the heart you can trust?"

"Some."

"How many know about her Mark?"

"It's a closely guarded secret. For now."

"You may have noticed we are not burning our way through SableFur. I don't believe causing needless violence and destruction will ingratiate me to my eventual pack."

Gabel, not wanting bloodshed? "After the past four weeks of the terror you've wrecked on your side of the mountains, I find that hard to believe."

"My vassals were disloyal to me," Gabel said flatly. "They conspired against me and made false promises. Explain to me why the Moon needed to take my mate from me instead of simply striking down my father and his whore."

Lucas flinched instinctively at Adrianna being called a whore. "You didn't need to butcher Anders' mate in front of him and his kids."

"The Moon wants destruction," Gabel murmured. "The Comet is the instrument of Her Wrath."

Lucas' blood ran cold. "And that gives you the right to act like a complete and total monster?"

"I don't use more force than is required to make a point," Gabel said, his tone like he was studying his fingernails. "Anders had betrayed me. Of course I destroyed what he loved most in the world to punish him for his cowardice and duplicity. His Luna—he was *not* worthy of such a creature. I broke her body, shattered her jaw, and she *still* fought me."

"Where are her pups?" Lucas asked.

"In IronMoon being cared for. Did you know her?"

Lucas closed his eyes. "You are a monster, Furballs. A monster from the void."

A dark, bone-rattling chuckle. "I also have an idea. One that I think even your delicate SableFur palette will find palatable. Tell me what you think…"

AN OFFERING

Bernhard jogged across the half-thawed muck. He presented me with a red leather binder. "Luna, this just arrived."

I looked away from supervising a training session, and said, "Oracle Kiery is in her workroom."

"No, Luna, it's for you."

"Who delivered it?" I took the binder. It stank. While this one had been wiped off, it had obviously had a very rough trip and was heavily stained and well… moist. Had Anita sent me a token of her affection?

I'd be seeing the old Oracle soon enough. How amusing if she'd sent me an invitation. Had there ever been a Luna-Oracle in our history? I might have been the first. At the rate I was going, I might just be the last.

"A Hunter," Bernhard said. "I've never seen her before. She said she'd been paid for discretion, and that the binder's contents will explain themselves."

The binders were almost always delivered by Oracles or acolytes and not handed off. The contents of the binder felt like a small lump. I turned it over a few more times, contemplating it. It did stink. "Think Anita sent me the Oracle equivalent of a flaming bag of dog shit?"

Bernhard cracked a smile and chortled. "It's pretty ripe, but everything is ripe and rotting this time of year."

Hey, I got Bernhard to smile. Lucas had taken our little confrontation on the chin—a First Beta getting out of line and having to be disciplined by the Alpha was nothing new, and pretty much expected, and Lucas and Magnes had come to blows on more than one occasion—but Bernhard had been nothing but traumatized since seeing Gabel for the first time.

I unfolded the binder.

"Oh, Moon," I gasped.

Inside the binder was a finger. An index finger, from a female hand. Not nearly decomposed enough to be putrid. Oh, and flattened from being smashed into the binder.

Bernhard grabbed the binder (and finger) from me. "Don't touch it, Luna. Let me take that. Your hands."

On it, written in black, permanent ink in small, weathered lettering was the name *Anita of SableFur.*

So was it Anita's binder, Anita's finger… or both?

Bernhard bellowed for Lucas and Kiery, and we all retreated up to the office. Kiery took one look at the defiled binder and dutifully went into her own silvery-blue wolf form to sniff the finger. She hacked once, then was gagging as she melted back into human form, and turned her face into Lucas' chest, shaking with silent sobs.

"Is it Anita's?" I asked immediately.

"It's Thessa's," she managed to choke out.

Thessa. The third SableFur Oracle. The one who had come to IronMoon to deliver the edict to Gabel and I. Anita had implied that Thessa—but not Kiery—knew the truth about the Oracle of Mirrors.

There was no note or demand. Just Thessa's decomposing finger.

"How old is it?" Kiery found her voice first.

Lucas crouched down and picked up the appendage. He gave it a once-over and a sniff. "Looks like three or four days to me. It wasn't bitten off. Hacked off clean. A cleaver, and I'll bet she was alive at the time. Might still be."

"Why would anyone hurt Thessa?" one of the wolves who had come up asked nobody in particular.

"Because Thessa knows something about Gabel's mother," Kiery said softly.

"Why would Thessa know something and you don't know anything, Elder Oracle?" that wolf asked with an edge to his voice.

"If you know something—" Evan said.

"I don't know anything about it," Kiery snapped.

"Gabel's cleaning house," Lucas said, disgusted.

Now Lucas was pissing me off. "You know that's not true."

"How do I know that's not true? It'd explain his northern route if he decided to kill some Oracles on his way here."

"Gabel wouldn't have used a damn *cleaver* or some unknown Hunter. He's not a belly-crawling snake like Magnes." I grabbed the binder and threw it at him. "If Gabel had sent it, Donovan would have brought it with a damn bow around it."

Lucas snarled. "He said he'd send Thessa back to SableFur in pieces. I guess he is making good on it."

"Gabel would have included a card," I retorted. "Adrianna, on the other hand, needs everyone who may know her secret dead, and she doesn't want to get caught with her paws bloody. We have to get to Anita before Adrianna does. Bernhard—"

"We are not rushing north like a bunch of idiots. We don't even know if Thessa's dead. That's just a finger. Gabel may have taken her back to IronMoon to interrogate." Lucas cut me off.

Evan broke into the conversation with a snort. "Everyone's forgetting someone else."

"Who?" one of the other wolves asked.

"Alpha Aaron," Evan said dryly.

Bernhard glowered at Evan. "Aaron isn't dumb enough to murder Oracles when he's trying to court an Oracle."

"Then I agree with Luna Gianna. When has Gabel *ever* hidden what he's capable of? It doesn't make sense. Adrianna did it," Evan said, like he was ringing a giant gong that was going to break a bunch of fragile china and he was out of fucks to give.

"Adrianna wouldn't have murdered Thessa," someone snapped. "If Anita's house is the mark, then Gabel's northern bending route makes perfect sense. He's heading for Anita."

Everyone descended into arguing over who had the spine and motive to mutilate an Oracle, and what the best way was to go about finding Thessa. Gabel's looping north-westerly route now made perfect sense. Anita's cottage was on the lee side of a ridge of bluffs that ran north to south. Coming at the cottage from the north, south, or east meant going through some heavily patrolled bits of SableFur. But by heading north, then west, he could loop south down the spine and come at Anita from the west. The terrain was tough going, with no roads and difficult to patrol, and dangerous in the winter and spring thaw, but none of that would stop the IronMoon.

"But he's still going to have to go fifteen miles overland once they're out of the ridge," I said. They hadn't even been spotted at the foot of the bluffs either. It was possible that Gabel had killed any handful of scouts, but enough scouts missing would have sent up alarms.

"Bernhard," I said. "You and I are going to Anita's. We're dragging her back here to SableFur's heart for her protection. And perhaps some conversation."

If Gabel had killed Thessa, I'd be pissed. I had questions for Thessa. He could have murdered her later.

I'd despised Thessa. I didn't care beyond damnit, someone had sent me a fucking finger in a stolen Oracle binder just to ruin my day. I rubbed the corner of my marked eye. "Get this out of here. Put it in a freezer somewhere. If we ever find the rest of Thessa, we'll give her a proper funeral."

"And if we don't?" Lucas asked.

"Then let's hope someone else gave her a proper funeral," I said darkly. "Bernhard, come get me when we're ready to leave."

I waited until they were all out of my office, then fished Hix's phone out of a drawer. I dialed Gabel's number. It rang, and rang, and rang some more. Voicemail. Tried again. And again.

"Gianna," he said, very slightly breathless, and a brook babbled in the background. Or a lot of traffic.

I slid down so I sat on the floor by my desk. "Do you have Oracle Thessa?"

A pause. He'd been running and was still catching his breath. "No. Why?"

"Because I just got one of her fingers shipped to me in a red binder, and everyone here is convinced *you* did it."

"As flattered as I am that they would instantly think I killed her, I didn't. It was on my list of things to do but I wanted to have enough time to enjoy it."

I shuddered. "Did you maim her?"

"I haven't seen her since the day she came to take you from me. Although I would like to find her. As intact and alive as possible." He purred, tone low and dark and very hungry. "Come now, my love, you know that we are *both* owed something from the Oracles of SableFur. I would not presume to destroy them without you to watch."

"Leave Kiery out of this."

"Why should I? She was Magnes' Oracle."

"And now she's mine. We can trust her."

"I will meet her and agree to nothing more than that. You will not have to be patient long. We will be together again soon."

CARNAGE

I stepped out of the car. The cold air hit me, along with the sight of the cottage I'd never wanted to see again.

Not much longer than a month earlier I'd been dumped here and left to Anita's tender mercies. She'd probably conspired with Magnes and Adrianna, promising them she'd keep me buried and out of sight for the rest of my natural life. Until I'd convinced her I was dangerously insane, and she'd promptly packed me off to Kiery's care.

I'd never call any Oracle a coward, but Anita was as close to gutless and self-serving as we came.

Bernhard's eyes scanned the area. It was a brilliant, sunny day, damp and chilly, but the sun was warm. "Be quick, Luna. I'm sure Adrianna has scouts keeping an eye on Anita."

Bernhard would make a great First Beta one day. He had stiff asshole down to a fine art.

Bernhard sniffed the air. "Something smells wrong. Like death. Are you sure there's no fighting here?"

One of the wolves said, "Yes, Second Beta. Certain."

Bernhard scanned the area once more. This area was

remote by design. Anita wanted her acolytes to have no distractions.

And no escape.

I stalked up the path to the house and tapped the door with the toe of my shoe. Instead of the door rattling, it creaked open.

I stumbled back and gagged.

A rush of warm air from the cottage blasted out into the cold. I cried out, yanked my scarf around my face, and plunged into the cottage as Bernhard shouted for me to stop.

The inside was a bloodbath. Blood smeared the walls, gouges from war-form claws had torn patterns into the wood floors, gouges and dents in the walls. Clots and lumps of things, shiny bits—

The blood had dried into something horrible days earlier. The heat was on, encouraging the bodies to rot, and the smell was beyond imagining.

The kitchen seemed curiously devoid of blood, but the front room housed what was left of what I guessed was Anita's body. It looked like an under-stuffed cuddle toy, all broken and diminished while also being swollen and bloated from death. Blood soaked everything. The head was missing. In its place was a teacup placed on the stump of her neck.

The mangled corpse of an acolyte lay crumbled in the corner of the living room. There was a large dent in the blood-soaked wall just above her. Blood had spread in a gummy puddle.

The upstairs was no better. Blood had flowed down the stairs. A desperate acolyte had tried to crawl upstairs and left handprints and loops of entrails. I stepped over all of it to find where she'd ultimately died in the hallway. Another one had been butchered while she showered. The fourth I barely recognized. Blood soaked everything. The killers had located every bowl, mirror, and rhinestone in the place and shattered them.

The blood mingled with splinters and shards and crushed stones, and Anita's stock of obsidian and quartz chunks had been piled onto her bed and crushed with a hammer.

At least, I hoped it had been a hammer.

I stood in the bathroom, trying to take it all in. My sisters. My little sisters. Dead. Murdered. Slaughtered.

I knelt down. This acolyte was mostly intact, except for the things crawling in her mouth.

Bernhard took my elbow. "We can't stay here, Luna. They're dead. We have to go."

I staggered free of him and stumbled to Anita's bedroom. Someone had already ripped open all the drawers in her side table, tossed the contents of her closet. I pawed through it, looking for something or *anything*, but everything was gone, destroyed, or impossibly soaked with gore.

"We can't stay here, Luna." Bernhard hauled me back with more force.

"Wait—" I pleaded. My fingers caught the edge of a wall slippery and sticky with blood.

Bernhard yanked. "We have to *go*. Now. They're dead. There's nothing you can do for them. This place needs to be burned."

"No! We aren't going to burn it." If it was burned, there was no hope of ever recovering any clues at all. This place stank of blood and death and wolves—many male wolves, but the scents were so confused and jumbled with so much of everything else, I couldn't identify a single one.

"We *must* burn it. It's full of death and disease, and we can't stay here to clean it or let humans find it. There's *nothing here*, Luna, but death!"

He dragged me out of the house through sheer muscle and dropped me to my knees halfway down the stone walkway. I tried to bolt, he grabbed me. He barked at Goon A, "Burn this. Now. All of it. Raze it."

His voice trailed off as I sobbed again, without tears, just a huge spasm.

"What's it like inside?" Goon B asked.

"Slaughterhouse. Fucking Gabel beat us here," Bernhard said, disgusted.

I climbed to my feet. "Gabel didn't do this."

Bernhard ignored me.

I snarled, "Adrianna did."

"Gianna, stop," Ana murmured as Bernhard flicked his gaze at me to acknowledge I'd spoken, but he didn't correct himself and his dark expression was a thousand miles away on the other side of a cavern I couldn't cross.

I balled my fingers into fists. The stitches pulled and sent sharp pains through my fingers. "Gabel didn't do this. Adrianna did, and she butchered them to make it look like Gabel! Gabel would never have killed the acolytes!"

"Come on, you're going to fuck up all those pretty stitches." Ana urged me back towards the car. "You can fight about it later."

"Gabel's scent isn't in there," I snapped.

Ana pulled on me. "Gianna, they're *dead*. Bloated, rotting. You're not going to get any evidence off them."

The stank settled into my skin like the oily sheen on Gabel's fur. Gabel hadn't done it. Gabel would have killed Anita, but he'd never have permitted the wholesale slaughter of four innocent acolytes.

"He wouldn't have," I whispered.

Ana, her arm around me, whispered, "Gianna... these days, I think he would have."

~*~ *Gianna's Dream* ~*~

I was back on the hilltop path.

I looked behind me: the little village was there, and ahead of me, the forest with the three paths: bog, river, thicket.

The sun set in the west, and the night rose in the east as I faced north. A storm crawled along the western horizon, and a strong breeze carrying the scent of rain, salt, and storm pulled at my hair. Behind me the villagers ran around boarding up windows, hurrying livestock into structures, and every minute or so one peeked at the storm, then shouted back about how it was going to be a bad one, get below ground.

"Get inside!" a voice shouted behind me.

She was an older female warrior, stern, with dark hair and a scar across her face that had taken one eye. The pale, cloudy globe was still in the socket, although cut through and split diagonally, leaving a deep crevice. "You crazy pup, get inside!"

"Why, auntie?" I asked, bewildered by her eye and choosing a term of respect. I'd never met her or seen her, no idea who she was, but no reason to be rude. I approached her with caution, briefly turning my back on the coming storm.

The warrior pointed at the storm coming. "That's why. Come on, there's room below."

My torso had been cut all over, engraved with runes carved deep into my flesh. They were a mix of half-healed and still weeping blood. Balance, Faith, Love, Mate, Pack, Dark Comet, Luna, and some I didn't recognize.

"Do I know you, auntie, have we met before?" I asked.

"Come on!" the warrior howled as the wind increased.

"No, auntie," I said, backing away from her. "I will stay up here."

She turned and ran back into the little cluster of buildings. She rounded a corner, and as she did, the town went completely still and dim.

The sky darkened. On the west side of the meadow a form moved, striding across the grass towards the dirt path, and a similar one came from the east, pulling the storm behind him with cords of smoke and cloud and burning. The grass around him withered and died, and the world burned and charred behind him.

Gabel brought the storm with him, burning smoke rising off his skin *in tendrils that spiraled back towards the storm front. Or was he making the storm? My horror didn't have time to process, because the eastern man came close enough I recognized his frame, and carriage: Aaron, alone, naked, and his right arm covered in blood as if it had been flayed, and blood streamed down his back, and he limped, but he still came.*

Smoke tendrils rose off my Mark, and blood wept out of it, dripping down my hand and off my fingers.

"It is over, IceMaw," Gabel rumbled with the voice of the storm, blue eyes wild and gleaming with triumph. "The scythe-Moon has fallen, and the Sun has set."

Aaron stepped up to the edge of the road. "It stops here, Comet. I will not let you destroy everything."

"You cannot stop me."

"What is the fate of comets? And what is the fate of the planets they plow into? You are destroyed, and the surface cracked, but the planet continues. You have no idea what you have, and even less idea how to keep it, but for a comet, what can you keep—not even your own head. That is how I will stop you."

Gabel grinned as the storm shattered around us, and every molecule in the air splintered—

~*~

I woke up gasping for air that had ceased to exist.

"Fuck," I whispered in the dim light of my little room, heart pounding so hard my breasts twitched. The Mark throbbed under the strain.

Gabel.

I rolled over onto my back and stared at the ceiling for a very long time, the weight of the Mark on my arm too much to move alone.

THE MONSTER IS ME

I went into the kitchen with Lucas in tow. Cook wiped his hands off on his apron as we entered. "May I make you something, Luna? You didn't eat breakfast."

After the grisly scene at the cottage my stomach wasn't interested in food. "After yesterday it's difficult to eat."

Cook's face fell. "Yes, we heard."

I didn't have a single tear for Anita, but my poor little sisters. Two of them had been still technically children. I turned my face to get hold of my emotions, my brain all clogged up with the vision of Aaron and Gabel colliding, but what frightened me the most was Gabel bringing that storm with him.

The scythe-Moon has fallen, and the Sun has set.

The sun, in my jungle visions, had not set. It had been that exact moment in evening before night overtook day, when everything hung in perfect balance for that one instant.

When I'd gone to the island at the edge of the Tides, the Moon had always been a thin crescent. Hanging like a scythe in the sky, descending towards the horizon while the storm blew in.

"Luna?" Cook asked.

"Bad dreams," I said, gathering myself and shaking it off. I couldn't let my Gift get ahead of me. I needed to stay focused on *this* world for now. "Anyway, I wanted to speak with you and Lucas about Beltane."

We crowded into his little pantry-sized office. Actually, the pantry was bigger. There were more papers taped to the wall as he had scribbled and scrawled menus, and a large master list of items needed for Beltane. "I want you two," I gestured between Lucas and Cook, "but mostly you, Cook, to think of names of SableFur who wouldn't normally get Beltane invitations, but you both feel *should*."

"You mean the ones who are good wolves but maybe pissed off the wrong people?" Lucas asked, tone guarded.

"Exactly." The way I figured it SableFur had to have at least a few wolves that were good wolves, but the sort of good that didn't get invited to fancy parties because their good was the same sort of good that Hix and Ana had. The sort of good that knew how to say *no* and *you're an asshole* and *shut up*. "Wolves you two would give an invitation to, but Magnes and Adrianna wouldn't."

Lucas and Cook exchanged looks. They weren't used to working with each other this way.

"Ask around, figure it out. Maybe… twenty or thirty? Males or females." From the glint in Lucas' eye, he already had some names in mind, and Cook looked thoughtful. "Any prestige. Give me a list, I'll write up the invitations, and send them out."

"Can I ask why?" Lucas asked.

"I'm sure there are wolves in SableFur who have been given a raw deal and not made the right friends," I said, thinking back to my first day in IronMoon, where Gabel had told me that all those combat shifters had been thrown away by their previous packs.

There were opportunities in my SableFur, and an ambitious wolf who had had a raw deal under the old leadership might be interested in supporting a Luna who was going to give everything a fresh look. I needed to be careful, but throwing an extra twenty invitations into a two-hundred-name party wasn't exactly tossing over a table.

Lucas crossed his arms and stared at the existing guest list tacked to the wall. "I can think of some names that haven't been on that list the past few years, but should be."

"Same," Cook said. "Gossip comes through the kitchen."

"Gossip *lives* in the kitchen." Lucas snorted.

"A wolf has to eat." Cook grinned. "And we feed all the pages and messengers."

"Great," I said with relief. The even both agreed this was a good idea. Or at least not a bad idea. Best news I'd had in weeks.

KIERY WAS IN HER WORKROOM: a large room facing east on the uppermost floor, quiet and still and so, so peaceful. She had her tools arranged on shelves along one wall, an array of velvet bags filled with the familiar shapes of bowls and runestones.

The weight of the Mark on my arm pulled down my shoulder. "I come with a question."

"The Moon hasn't had Her Eye open to me. You cast a large shadow," Kiery said.

"Will you try?" I asked.

She nodded.

I took a very deep breath. "Why do I keep seeing Aaron of IceMaw in my visions? Is he the white quartz?"

She nodded again and didn't ask further questions. It wasn't her question: it was mine, and whatever answer the Moon gave was mine too.

I didn't expect the Moon to actually answer, but I had to try.

"We should talk." Kiery set down the bag of salt she was holding. "As Oracle and Luna."

"About?" I wasn't in the mood to talk, but I'd yelled at Gabel and groused at Jermain often enough about not listening to me. I was already a murderer, killer, and Moon knew what else, so hypocrite wasn't a feather I wanted for my hat.

How long ago had that been? A year? Not even?

It had been a lifetime ago.

My father was dead, and my birthpack scattered like ashes. Because I'd told Gabel to do it.

Guilt saturated me.

I was a monster.

"You."

Me. Obviously. I asked, "Is this about Lucas?"

"No, it's about how hard you're pushing this pack."

She said that like I had a choice in any of this. "Starlight wolves turned Magnes into a puddle, and everyone around me wants to live in some fantasy land where Adrianna didn't know, I am some pretender and your mate is a traitor, and you want to tell me to back off? Why is everyone in this pack so determined to be dense?"

"That's why we're talking. Otherwise *you* will turn into the Destroyer, Balance-Keeper."

I cocked my head to the side. "Has the Moon shown you something?"

"No, I've lived in this pack longer than you, and I'm mated to the First Beta you're torturing."

I narrowed my eyes. "If by torture you mean I expect him to do his job."

Kiery didn't flinch under her flawless Oracle mask. "Lucas wasn't born into status or privilege. He played by the rules and was rewarded. He believed he had built something our pups could inherit with pride. Then the Moon changed the rules. Showed him his Alpha and Luna are the living damned. That his new Alpha is a monster from the Moon's Void. This is hard for him."

"I do not want to hear anything about what is *hard*," I said, something like acid coating my throat with all its bitterness and anger. "Do not tell me what is hard, or terrifying, or difficult, or unfair, or unjust, or what it is like to be trapped in a situation from which you cannot escape."

Kiery sighed. "They are not you."

"I don't expect them to be."

She sighed again, heavier this time. "You don't see how broken you are. How much damage you've suffered. What the past year has done to you. You see what's happened to you, but you look right through it."

"I have a complete understanding of what is happening now," I said, anger increasing and the burning coal of the neglected Bond waking from its slumber to grumble about the distance between Gabel and I.

"Not in this pack you don't. The Moon just shoved Sable-Fur's nose into their own shit like they were bad dogs."

"I'm not blaming anyone that isn't named Adrianna and Magnes. I just want everyone to realize *they* were the problem."

"Fuck all, you are dense as a box of rocks. And a single-minded self-righteous bitch to boot."

"You were ready to die right alongside Lucas, so don't call *me* the self-righteous bitch."

Kiery gestured in frustration. "You're asking for more than they can give. You and I spent years training to look into the void, and we both know Seers who didn't survive. These SableFur have *no* training, and every single damn day the Moon is holding their head over the rim telling them to look. They aren't allowed to look away, wake up, or come out of the vision."

Oh. When she put it like that…

"Would that scare the ever-loving fuck out of you?" Kiery growled. "You'll scream and flail and try to chew your way free. That's *exactly* how and why Seers go insane. This is why I told Anita you'd never be an Elder Oracle, and we should never give you your own students."

"Because I'm not chewing my way free?"

Kiery sighed. "Exactly. You're a shitty teacher. And what makes you a shitty teacher is going to make you a shitty Luna, and you being a shitty Luna is going to have a direct impact on how long I live."

"You think I'm a bad Luna?" It was a little early to tell me I was *bad*. Lackluster, lacking, incompetent, ignorant, sure. But *bad*? That stung.

Kiery shrugged and rolled her eyes. "I see a lot of the same things in Luna Gianna that I saw in Seer Gianna. We managed to tame it for Oracle Gianna. Baby Seers have to *learn* to be brave, but not you. You came brave. You arrived scared of your gift, but ready to do battle with it and win. Anita said it was that warrior breeding in you. You know how much ass your mother had to kick to have her own prestige? She must have had fangs as big as Lucas' dick. If you hadn't been a Seer, you'd have probably been a First Beta. You aren't physically gifted enough for that job, but you know how to rip a male's spine out and beat him to death with it, and I don't see you letting anyone boss you around just because he's got a hundred pounds on you."

Kiery's expression turned dour. "When you were an acolyte, we got to watch the Tides batter you, throw you, nearly drown you, and you never flinched or faltered. You *became* a careful Oracle because we trained you to be one. You'd charge right off towards the Tides, just like you used that stupid mirror without thinking about it."

"But cowards don't make Oracles," I said. She said it like I

had just pranced off and used a mirror like an idiot. I hadn't
had a *choice*. It was the mirror or failure. "The weak drown. I
remember being scared. I remember *bad* times."

Kiery threw up her hands and laughed. "You keep thinking
like you're just some golly-gee random Oracle that drew the
short straw. You're the Balance-Keeper. The Moon made you
what you are, the same as She made Gabel. Everyone else
here? Literally *everyone* else? We're all just wolves that *did* draw
the short straw. What's happening here is a nightmare, and
they aren't Seers trained to face nightmares and come out the
other side. As far as they're concerned, you're just another part
of their nightmare."

"Kiery, I'd be lying to them if I patted them on the head
and said there, there, everything will be fine. We both know it's
bullshit. It's *not* going to be fine."

Kiery's tone softened. "I know that, and I know your inten-
tions are good. I've seen the future where Adrianna wins. Anita
saw the future where Gabel crowns you with obsidian shards.
Adrianna brings damnation, but you bring the destruction of
everything the SableFur have ever known. That kind of difference is just academic."

Her point chilled me and washed all the blood out of my
cheeks.

Kiery came over to me, and she touched my hair, coiling
one of the dull locks around her finger. "Gabel is a lupine. He
sees the world as a lupine does. You see the world as an Oracle.
SableFur doesn't need an Oracle. They have *me*. They need a
Luna to see them through this nightmare."

All must believe. Even you must doubt.

IN PIECES (LITERALLY)

Over the next three days more pieces of Thessa arrived: the other index finger, two big toes, and, on the fourth day a vertebra. Complete with rotting spinal cord still in the channel. The pieces didn't arrive in binders, but red boxes, and each delivered by an unknown Hunter who refused to give their name or disclose who had sent them.

Thessa was dead.

I had the green-tinged page who had brought the last gift pass it to Ana for deep-freeze storage at the clinic. Kiery said, grimly, "So Thessa is dead."

"Adrianna has cleaned house," I said, despondent. I cradled the envelopes for the last round of Beltane invitations in my hands. Ana had removed the stitches, but the skin was still sore and tender. There was the possibility I wouldn't be able to run at Beltane at all with my hands as they were—my paw pads would not have toughened up enough—but I couldn't very well wear a long-sleeved sweater either.

"Do you think Anita's head will show up next?" Kiery asked.

"I hope not." I had no use for Anita's head unless it was still attached to her body and able to talk.

Kiery sat down in one of the chairs. For the first time I noticed she was drawn. She rocked her head back and stared at the ceiling. "I have your answer."

I set the envelopes down. "The Moon opened Her Eye to you?"

She raised her head. "Sort of. I was meditating, and She gave me the vision. No doubt it was intended as the answer for your question. I guess She was not willing to wait for me to formally ask."

Confused, I slowly sank down into my own chair. Why hadn't the Moon just showed me directly if it was that urgent? I rubbed my marked eye as if it itched, but it didn't. Something else did.

She said, "I was on a rocky island in the middle of an ocean. A very small island. It's mounded at the top enough you can't see from shore to shore, but it's easy enough to walk around. There's a path that winds from the top to a cavern, but the tides are too high to enter the cavern itself. The ocean is completely still, and so dark and flat it's like a mirror. In the distance, there's a storm coming, and the Moon is just a waning crescent, like a scythe, and it's almost set."

I managed a bare nod.

"There's nothing on the island except an old stone altar and Aaron." She swallowed, hard, and took a moment to gather herself. "He's in his war-form, and he's been burned. Where he hasn't been burned, he's been cut and sliced down to his bones. His skin and muscle and pelt are just hanging. Stabbed into the small of his back are four silver claw-tips. He oozes blood, and it's draining down him onto the island, and I realize I can't be sure if that island is a rock, or a huge scab. He's just staring at the Moon."

I put my hand over my mouth.

"I walk over to him. He doesn't acknowledge me. I can see his bones and organs. On the bone of his left arm, here," she gestured to her own Mark, "there's this rune carved into the bone itself, and the bone is bleeding. The drops of blood are welling up like sweat and trickling down the bone."

I had to focus on what she was saying, but it was hard to breathe. Like the crown of bone I'd held. The crown for the she-wolf's head. "Do you know the rune?"

She shook her head. "He walks into the water, except where he steps on the water it hardens into more rocks... or scabs, I guess, and he walks towards the storm."

I shuddered all over. I gulped and then doodled the rune I'd seen on Aaron's arm in my own vision with the crown. I turned over the paper, and told Kiery, "Draw the design you saw on his bone."

Neither of us were artists, and I'd seen mine on skin, and she'd seen hers on bone, but there was no doubt: they were the same rune.

"You've seen it too," she said instantly.

"Not only that, but I've seen it on his arm, on that very island." I stopped short of revealing what Aaron had told me. He would not have wanted his personal anguish trotted out for even another Oracle. "We need to track down this rune and what it means."

Kiery glanced between the two drawings. "The only person who might know is Flint. He has those blue-gloss tattoos that nobody within the last three hundred years has had."

Easier said than done. "If Gabel thinks I'm helping Aaron, he'll go ballistic."

Kiery rolled her eyes. "You realize you having to molly-coddle your mate's unreasonable jealousy is, itself, unreasonable, right? You're a Luna. You're allowed to talk with other Alphas. It's part of your job."

Aaron wasn't other Alphas. "Other Alphas haven't sworn I belong to them."

"Don't put up with this bullshit behavior. You're not trying to get with Aaron or help IceMaw, you're trying to figure out what the Moon wants."

Gabel wouldn't see it that way, and he'd fly off into a misdirected rage. The same as when he wanted to go rip into SaltPaw just because they'd tricked him, even if it was probably some kind of trap set up by Magnes or Aaron. "Aaron's a special case."

"Is he *really* the only male Gabel has been jealous about?"

"Well, there was Hix," I admitted, but that had been stupid too.

"Tell your mate to grow the fuck up. We're dealing with divine wrath and your mate is going to get bent because you're trying to figure out which way the hellfire is burning? Tell him, *yeah, thanks, it's burning in my general direction, now will you put Flint on the phone?*"

My mate *was* divine wrath the last time I checked, but Kiery had made her point.

Kiery picked up Hix's phone—which had become my phone—and handed it to me. "You'd rather do the tourmaline than expect your mate to act right? Think about that for a minute."

I took the phone, sighed, and took a picture of the rune.

HER INSTRUMENT

"What is this? Pictures of doodles? Gianna, I didn't know we had a pup who had matured on to fingerpainting already." Gabel's voice strummed my skin from a far distance.

I shivered with pleasure at hearing his voice, and the Bond between us thumped like a second heart. I said, "Show it to Flint and hand him your phone."

"Why?"

"Oracle reasons," I said. The Bond stung like dry, cracked skin that had been salted.

"Oracle reasons?"

I set the phone down and put it on speaker. "Kiery had a dream, and I've gotten a few more pieces of Thessa. Promise me you have not been sending me pieces of Thessa."

"I would not presume to know which pieces you would want. I am a lupine, not ill-bred." Gabel clucked his tongue.

Kiery visibly shuddered.

"Flint is in IronMoon. Let me have a moment."

The line went dead.

"Should I be concerned he was so reasonable?" Kiery asked dryly.

"Gabel is always reasonable in preparation for being unreasonable," I said, chewing on my lip. I felt the tension brewing at the far end of the Bond. Gabel paced at the end of his chain.

My phone rang. A number I didn't recognize, but Flint's voice. "Where did you see this rune, Luna?"

"I didn't. Kiery did. In a dream offered in response to my question," I said.

"You misunderstand. I mean *where*. It's an old rune, obscure even by my understanding, but I know that the meaning varies depending on where and how it is carved."

Kiery said, "I saw it carved into living bone that was bleeding."

"And I've seen it carved into flesh," I supplied.

"On a living body?"

"The left arm, both times," Kiery said.

"Ah. You may or may not have noticed it on *my* arm, Luna. It is entwined with all the others."

I tried to recall the writhing tangle of tattoos. Many of the designs seemed abstract, or personal to him, like the lines now cut into my own arm.

"It means *instrument*," Flint said. "An instrument the Moon has chosen for Herself."

Instrument. That was goddamn useless. Everyone seemed to be the Moon's instruments. Kiery and I were Oracles, Gabel was the Comet, Flint was Her Servant, and Aaron was already involved so him being an *instrument* was a useless piece of information. That told me exactly nothing I didn't already know. "Is there anything else to know about it?"

"Who did you see it carved on?"

"Aaron of IceMaw. Kiery saw him flayed to his bone, and the bone was bleeding, and the rune was—"

"Burned," Kiery supplied. "It was burned into his arm."

"And I saw it cut into his skin, but like a tattoo. Like the needle had carved him the same time it inked him." Not that that exactly made sense in literal terms.

A pause, then, "Yes, that is how these tattoos are done."

"It is?" Kiery leaned forward with interest.

"Yes," Flint said, reluctantly. "Did Aaron make a bargain with the Moon?"

"No, I'm fairly sure he didn't."

"That rune, inked into the arm," Flint said, cautiously, heavily, weighed down with the memory of something, "it does not mean *chosen* or… it means *possession.*"

Possession? "You're Her Servant. You serve out of penance," I said, speaking carefully because I didn't want to offend him. "I am very sure Aaron did not make a bargain with the Moon like you did. We're all Her instruments. I'm an Oracle, Gabel is the Comet. We're all Her possessions, aren't we?"

"What were the other marks on him?"

"I saw some, but Kiery did not."

Kiery paused, and said, "His skin was flayed. Maybe there were more marks on the skin that had been peeled down? I can't be sure."

"That is… disturbing," Flint said. "The marks will tell you. The blue-gloss tattoos always tell the wolf's story."

"Always?" I asked.

A grim chuckle. "Always. For some, it is a mark of glory, for others, like myself, it is a brand. A confession."

Kiery and I exchanged looks. Aaron didn't have blue-gloss tattoos. He didn't have a single one.

"He is Her possession." Flint broke into our thoughts. "She has a use for him. Be careful when you're dealing with him until you divine what purpose he serves. The Moon has many faces. She has proven She is willing to use you, Gianna, with unspeakable cruelty to achieve Her ends. The future is always changing, but it is obvious that She will not let you escape the purpose She has created you for. I was sent to keep-safe Gabel. Perhaps Aaron is here to safeguard Her interests in you."

Flint hung up.

"What am I even hearing," Kiery said.

I rested my hands on the desk, and said, quietly, "I've been to that island. I've been calling it the island at the Edge of the Tides. When the tide is low, the path leads to a grotto that leads to a place beyond the Tides. I've seen the storm. I saw the storm the other night in a dream. But I was in a village—I've been to it before too—and Gabel came from the west, and Aaron from the east, also bloody and flayed apart. Aaron swore to stop him, but Gabel told him it was too late. *The scythe-Moon has fallen, and the sun has set.*"

Had the sun set at the jungle temple? "I have to go to the temple."

"What temple?"

"The jungle temple. It's a place the Moon keeps taking me. I have to go see if the sun has set."

"Gianna, you don't have tools—"

"I have a mirror and a blue tourmaline."

"Are you insane?" Kiery shot to her feet.

"The Temple isn't beyond the Tides," I argued.

"You are *Luna*. This is what I'm talking about when I told you you're too brave for your own good."

"I *have* to go," I said. "I have to know if the sun has set!"

"Who cares if it has? You can't summon it to rise again! Do you really need to see the sun to know *bad* things are happening?"

"I suppose not," I muttered.

Kiery grabbed the papers and tore them into little shreds. "This is why the Moon won't open Her Eye to me. If I could see it, we might be able to change it, and She doesn't want it changed. It's too late for that. There are two outcomes, and only two, and in both, the world burns."

"No," I said, feeling more stubborn than usual. "There has to be another way."

"What would it look like?" Kiery pressed. "Even if we beat Adrianna, Aaron will never let Gabel crown himself King. If you leave SableFur, Adrianna will take the throne back, she'll rally the western packs, and crown herself Queen. I don't even think if you can tie Adrianna to Gabel's mother SableFur will care. If their choice is Adrianna or Gabel, I think half of them will choose Adrianna."

"We have to try," I told her. "I don't have these answers, but I know we have to defeat Adrianna. We can worry about Aaron later. The Moon has a use for him. It wasn't a shock to me. He can still smell my lure-scent. Even now."

"That's impossible."

"I know."

She looked at me sideways.

In my hands I still felt the warm, bleeding bone crown for a female's head.

"We have to find my bowls," I said, making a decision. "I know you don't agree with it, but we need to. I have to see if the sun has set. I want to see what's on the island. The Moon might not show you, but She may not deny me a glimpse."

THE FIRST, THE LAST

A few days later, Kiery came into my office as I tried to make sense of the newest reports from the north. Gabel had turned his attentions on Adrianna and the IronMoon were burning a path due west, clearly not attempting to conquer anything. There were also reports of some nasty barfights and scuffles breaking out, with a few dives getting completely trashed.

"He's going for Adrianna," I murmured to myself. Must have been what Lucas and Gabel had worked out between them. I didn't want the details. The less I knew, the better. I needed Adrianna disgraced, but dead would do too. If Gabel was chasing Adrianna, my wolves wouldn't be wondering when he'd come for them.

Kiery was carrying two things: another red box and a velvet bag. She looked nauseated.

"Oh no," I said softly. "Another piece of Thessa?"

"No," she said. She put the box down on my desk. "This one was addressed to me."

Inside was a finger with shards of consecrated obsidian shoved under the fingernail. Given the bruising in the nailbed, it'd been done while her heart had still been beating. There was a small card in the box. I fished it out and read it: *Beatrice.*

"Beatrice? Who is Beatrice?" I asked Kiery.

"The only other Elder Oracle I know of," Kiery said softly, visibly trying not to vomit. She put a hand to her mouth and looked away. "She's from a pack called AspenBark, southwest of Aaron's influence. She was my first teacher."

I stared down at the finger in horror. "How many Oracles are in that part of the world?"

"Two others, I think."

For our entire history there hadn't been a time without Oracles. There had never been a time when Seers had had to re-discover how to ride the Tides. The Seer gift wasn't rare, but Oracles *were.* Without Oracles to train Seers, an unknown number of Seers would go insane and die horrific deaths, while our species also lost access to the Tides.

The Oracle traditions were oral. There were no books or parchments or scrolls. There were books that had the runes in them, and texts with descriptions of the various herbs or oils you could use, but there was no how-to guide on how to *be* an Oracle. That was all passed from Oracle to Seer. It'd been that way for thousands of years. An unbroken line, hundreds of generations, about to die.

"Adrianna is killing us," I said.

Kiery hung her head and sobbed once. "You and I may be the only ones left. There are only two other Oracles I know of, and they're probably dead."

I rushed around the desk and hugged her tightly. "We'll warn them. Tell them to go to IceMaw. Aaron will protect them. You're from the south. Can you find a way to contact them?"

"I've already tried," she said, eyes leaking tears. "No one has seen them for a week."

I held her tighter.

"You and I are all that's left," Kiery said. "And she'll kill us too if she can. And there's this."

She untangled herself from me and set the velvet bag down on my desk. It made an awful, broken sound. The bulk of the sack sagged.

"Your obsidian chunks," she said softly.

I yanked the bag's neck open. Nothing but glossy, shiny black sand and powder. I reached inside to scoop up a handful.

"Don't touch it!" Kiery shoved my hands away. "You have no sense around glass. How did you grow up and still have your damn hands?"

"I should have known Magnes would have ordered it destroyed." I shoved it onto the ground and flinched at the sound it made. Or Anita had ordered it destroyed. I would have been told it had met with "an accident," then put off getting a replacement. And off. And off. Until I would have had to grovel at Anita's feet to please, please, please let me have another set of bowls, I wouldn't break this set.

"It's worse than that," Kiery said.

"How can it *possibly* be worse? How can this day get any worse?" I exclaimed.

"The stonecutter did it."

"What?"

Kiery rubbed her head. "To protest you on the throne. He shattered everything. So did the other cutters."

"Everything? What do you mean *everything*?" I asked. "What is *everything*?"

"*Everything*. All the bowls they were making, raw chunks, stones. *Everything*. They even destroyed their tools and workshops!"

"But we're *Oracles*," I said. "The stones and bowls have nothing to do with who is and isn't Alpha."

"Gianna, maybe you aren't paying attention, but you're a Luna and an Oracle, and your First Beta's mate is an Oracle,"

Kiery said. "The same First Beta that Adrianna has been saying betrayed her? We're being exterminated, and they don't even realize it."

"Why would the stonecutters do it?" I asked, not following.

"Anita was guilty as hell keeping Magnes' secret, and no matter if you're Team Gianna or Team Adrianna, she could have prevented all of this. Another Oracle got involved and had a pup she shouldn't have. You have done this to SableFur. I'm a First Beta's mate. We keep secrets by design. If I was a nervous person thinking Oracles had gotten a bit too powerful…"

I had to sit down. "But the Moon made us what we are."

"And the Moon made Magnes what he is, which is now a puddle." She sat down as well.

I couldn't know if Kiery and I were the last Oracles in the world. It seemed impossible, but if she was right: we *were*.

I had to protect Kiery. Adrianna could get to both of us here in the heart. She had spies and informants. Beltane would be the perfect time to stab both of us.

"You and Lucas have to leave," I said.

"I'm not leaving. Lucas is your First Beta."

"And you are the last Elder Oracle. I don't even have tools I can use," I said, thinking quickly. "Lucas is your mate. Preserving the Oracles takes precedence. Go to IceMaw, or go to IronMoon. Your choice. Flint can protect you in IronMoon, Aaron can protect you in the south."

"I am *not* leaving you, and neither is Lucas."

"Kiery, if we both die the Oracles are *lost*. You *have* to leave. It's not safe for you here as long as Adrianna is alive."

Kiery straightened. "Then it's the Moon's doing," she said sharply. "Lucas and I aren't abandoning you. If we die, the Moon can figure it out. You and I just have to live until Beltane."

"I'm also sure if Adrianna's going to kill us, she'll do it at Beltane."

"You know what Anita and I have both seen. There is not a single vision any of us have had where any of this ends well."

I dropped my hand to my side. "It seems like every move I make drags me further down a path I don't want to go. We're supposed to be able to change the future. That's why Oracles exist, and now we're dying and powerless, and the Moon seems implacable."

Kiery said, "Gabel is the destroyer. He's doing his job. You are the only thing in this world he loves more than being King. The problem is those two things aren't mutually exclusive, and the Moon's made it clear your place is at his side."

I rubbed my Mark. Some of the scabs crumbled and flaked against my sleeve. "I'm frightened what he will turn the world into."

"So am I," Kiery said. "And what scares me even more is we know the day our world ends."

"How ironic," I said. "Beltane. The fire festival and instead of new life, we're going to set everything on fire."

"I guess." Kiery wiped at her eyes.

"Go on," I told her. "You don't have to stick around if you don't want to. Go find Lucas."

"I'm going to go find a beer and crawl into bed to cry," she admitted.

After she left, I picked up my phone. My thumb hesitated over one entry. After a few moments, I hit *call*.

Two rings later. "Luna Gianna, what an unexpected surprise."

"Who gave you my number?" I asked dryly.

"Your First Beta, of course," Aaron said.

I ran one hand through my hair, then regretted it as strands pulled at barely healed flesh. "I... need your help."

"Anything."

Could he not say *anything*? I didn't want to hear *anything*. *Anything* made it obvious why he'd help me. "You've heard about the dead Oracles?"

"I've heard Anita and four acolytes died an exceptionally grisly death, presumably at Gabel's claws, and that you have gotten a few pieces of Thessa delivered to your door."

Of course Aaron would have spies in my pack. I didn't even bother to get pissed about it. It wasn't exactly like the bodyparts were a state secret. "Do you know an Elder Oracle Beatrice?"

"She's one of the ones I asked about my dreams."

"She's dead."

"How do you know?"

"Someone brought Kiery a finger with shards of what I believe is an obsidian bowl under her fingernail. She was Kiery's first teacher. Kiery recognized the scent."

Quiet.

"Kiery tried to reach the other two Oracles in that region and no one has seen them for a week. The south is your area of influence, Aaron, and there are some dead Oracles being carved up under your nose," I said, heart aching. I hung my head. "And, Aaron… Kiery thinks she and I are the last Oracles in the world. You have to find the other two southern Oracles and keep them safe."

"I will send out wolves right away," Aaron said.

"Thank you," I whispered. Gabel was going to gnash his teeth that I asked Aaron for help, but my mate could just get over it. Preserving the last remaining Oracles was more important. I gulped down the cottony lump in my throat. "If you find them—"

"I will bring them here to IceMaw and keep them safe," he said.

"Thank you," I whispered again. "I hope Kiery is wrong about…"

"I believe she's right. There may be another Oracle far to the north and west, but I don't know their name. If these two remaining Oracles are dead, you two are likely the last."

Tears slid out of my eyes. My sisters. The world falling into darkness around us. Was the Moon closing Her Eye to us now? Were we all being landlocked, unable to reach Her?

The Oracles had always been the ones who kept secrets. We were the most trusted. Our purpose had been to see down the path of existence to where any given set of choices may lead, or what may have led to a point. The Moon let us see the future, and sometimes the past, so we could change course. But how long had wolves been ignoring the Moon's warning, and how long had Oracles been protecting powerful wolves from consequences?

I had tools so dangerous they'd nearly killed me. Kiery was the last Oracle qualified to teach. The stonecutters had thrown down their tools. Were we going to be forced to start over from nothing but ash and glints of light?

The scythe-Moon has fallen, and the Sun has set.

STARS & STORIES

At dinner, Lucas and Bernhard discussed details of things that had been happening beyond SableFur's heart that I had no knowledge of. Nothing too serious, stuff like who was living where, minor disputes about housing and land and hunting, human encroachment and concerns, upcoming Beltane preparations, summer training sessions, potential complications with the war brewing in the north, Aaron lurking around in the south.

They didn't talk about the dead Oracles, or how Gabel marched westward towards Adrianna, while fights broke out all up and down the stretch of road that ran straight to SableFur's heart, past Anita's old cottage, and into the northern hills.

Kiery picked at her food. She'd been close to Beatrice—her first teacher—and she'd been grieving. There were whispers another box had arrived. I probably needed to address it.

"I don't think Alpha Aaron is going to be a problem," Bernhard was saying.

Lucas pointed his fork at Bernhard. "That's what that wolf *wants* you to think. He butchered his entire family. Never underestimate what that wolf will do."

"Aaron eats out of Luna Gianna's hand."

I coughed politely. Bernhard knew damn well that I had a Mark on my arm, although… Aaron didn't know that. And neither did the SableFur nearby who overheard, noted it, and murmured it to their tablemates.

Lucas grunted. "So you're suggesting she make *him* Lord-Alpha and not choose a SableFur?"

Could these two shut up? They needed to shut up.

Bernhard rolled his eyes. "No. I'm saying he's so moon-eyed over our Luna that he's not going to piss her off by attacking us."

I gave up silently willing them to shut up. It seemed to give them something cheerful to chat about and made me seem all the more desirable. Lucas was right: Aaron wasn't where he was because he was a nice guy who had sweet-talked his way to power. The Moon had a use for him, and the Alpha of IceMaw was in his den biding his time, not writing forlorn love letters he never intended to send.

"Wolves," I said, and I stood up, drawing silence from them. All attention turned to me. I squished down my nerves. I wasn't one for speeches, but I was going to have to fake it. "Today, as you may have heard, another red box arrived. This one was addressed to Elder Oracle Kiery."

Lucas placed his hand over Kiery's thigh.

"In it was a finger," I went on. "It was to Elder Oracle Beatrice, who lives far to the south and west, and was Kiery's first teacher. We have not been able to make contact with the other two Oracles in that region, and their packs do not know where they are."

Now the quiet became a hush. The scent of the room thickened.

"I have asked Alpha Aaron to try to find the two other Oracles," I said. "But it's far outside his own territory and influence. At this time, we should consider the gravest outcome: that the two southern Oracles are dead."

"How did Gabel kill them from so far away?" someone at one of the low tables asked.

Instead of saying *obviously, he didn't,* I sat down and shut my mouth. Dinner conversation picked back up, although more somber than before. I also didn't include about how Kiery and I may be the last Oracles. That was a can of worms best left closed, and one too many nightmares for either of us to consider.

After dinner as I was leaving, Evan approached me and asked, "Would you like to go for a walk, Luna?"

My jaw tried to unhinge.

Evan was about Aaron's age, if I had to guess, tall, good-looking, and had a smooth, confident voice and asked the question in such a neutral way I couldn't quite tell what the hell he was offering. He didn't know about my Mark. Could he smell my lure-scent like Aaron could? But I *was* Luna, and power was attractive, and Evan was ambitious. He wasn't First or Second Beta, but he had one eye on Bernhard and knew what side his bread was buttered on.

Luckily, Ana saw the situation, poked Kiery, who poked Lucas, and Lucas came up behind the warrior, clapped him around the shoulder, and said, "I can vouch for this one, Luna. He is a bit of an ass, but he also can point out interesting constellations. He enjoys star-gazing."

What! Lucas was supposed to get me out of this, not push me deeper.

Evan gave me a grin. "Guilty."

I cringed, then looked to Kiery and Ana, who flashed me a thumb's up each, and then a shoo motion. What was going on? All of them knew I wasn't available! I gulped, recovered, and told Evan, "Let me speak to Lucas very quickly. I have something I need him to do."

Like stop trying to hook me up with random males.

Evan gave me an easy grin and stepped to the side while I dragged Lucas off towards the pantry.

"You know about my arm!" I hissed to him.

"Exactly, I know," he hissed back. "He doesn't. Play along."

"Can he smell my lure-scent?" I shouldn't have a scent, but Aaron said I did. I'd never been approached by another male (Romero didn't count) so if Evan could still smell my scent then…

Then things got weird. Very weird. I did not need more weirdness and to be emitting a scent that told all males within a mile *VACANCY. APPLY WITHIN.*

"I don't know, why don't you ask him? He's one of the most prestigious warriors here, so you need his support," Lucas retorted in a low growl. "You don't have to fuck him, just let him show you Saturn or something."

Zero chance of getting into bed with Evan. "And he's not going to get pissed when he finds out the truth?"

"I'll tell him he protected his Luna." Lucas waved it off. "Play along. You're *supposed* to be single. Give Evan thirty minutes. He's leaving for the front tomorrow anyway."

I *had* a mate. "Did you put him up to this?"

"I may have suggested you'd like to feel welcome in your own pack, and because you're a Seer, the only male attention you've ever had is Gabel. He figured out what he wanted to do with that information. Get used to it, because I've got to curate suitors for you."

"Oh for fuck's sake, do you *want* Gabel to come through here and start murdering all the best warriors?" I hissed.

"*You* deal with the bastard's jealousy. My loyalty is to *you* and this pack and keeping it in one piece. *You're* the Luna, so *you* figure out how to manage your mate. He's not my Alpha yet, so he's not my fucking problem."

"You *want* me to look like I'm betraying my mate?"

"I want all of us to live long enough for it to matter," he snapped.

I fumed, but bit my tongue. Lucas had sold me out for a simple walk on the terrace. I'd handle that first, keep it short, and in plain sight so everyone would just think (hopefully) I was being polite to a decorated warrior in my service. I *did* need allies, but not if the price was pretending I'd pay them with my vagina.

"Fine," I hissed. "But as soon as I'm done with him this evening, you tell him the truth. I'm not leading him on, especially not if you're going to send him into the field."

"Are you sure about that?" Lucas whispered back.

"If you think the only reason he's going to be loyal to me is he wants to get laid, I don't want him within breathing distance of me. *I* can tell him, or you can break it to him gently."

Lucas grumbled and said he'd deal with it.

Evan took me around the back of the house to a small, private porch that I strongly suspected from the smell had been Magnes' and Adrianna's private haunt. Uneasily, I went with him, trying to keep to the edge of the porch so I was more or less within line of sight of snoopers despite his attempts to lure me away with claims the darkness on the other side made for better star-gazing.

He pointed out several constellations and told me some of the stories about them.

Was this my awkward first date? My father would have teased me unmercifully. Good-natured ribbing, but he'd still have teased me.

Hell. It *was*. This was my first date.

And I was already mated.

What even was my life sometimes.

I almost asked him if he could smell my lure-scent, but that seemed like terrible etiquette. Was that poor etiquette? The scent just said a soul was compatible and the Bond could take root, but plenty of wolves dated around, or didn't want to get mated at all. Very occasionally, Lunas took consorts to father offspring, and sometimes Alphas had had concubines, and those illegitimate pups, if recognized, entered the line of succession.

So Evan didn't even need to be gunning for a place as Alpha, he just might be trying to make himself consort material.

I needed out of here, because this was pretty firmly in the realm of *Things Gabel Won't Understand*.

Ana appeared with a pair of scissors in her hand. She clicked them back and forth. "Time to check your hands, Luna. Make sure you haven't torn them up again."

Evan eyed the scissors. "You sound like you're going to enjoy that, Doctor."

"The name's *Ana*. Doctor is my dad. Don't make me feel old. And yeah, I enjoy my patients healing. I've got a hot date, so can we hurry this up?"

"Bernhard?" Evan asked with a grin.

"Hey, I don't tell." Ana clacked the scissors at him, then pointed them towards the stairs. Evan chuckled and obeyed.

Grateful, I followed her down the lane to the small cottage that was the SableFur clinic. Nobody was there this time of night. "You don't waste time lining up entertainment."

"I lied." Ana flicked on the lights and directed me to sit down at a metal table. She gathered up some trays of items she'd already prepared and then straddled the stool on the other side of the table.

"Why?" I asked.

"You needed rescue, and Bernhard? Please. Not a chance. He is not my type."

"Why not?"

"Have you seen the size of the stick up his butt? Heck, no.

These SableFur wolves are wayyyy too precious for my taste. I feel like I'm corrupting them."

"So is your father really a doctor?" I asked.

Ana took my hands and examined them casually. They'd healed up nicely, even if they were criss-crossed with red scars and the new skin tender and soft. "Hmm-hmm. Does for humans what I do for critters. Have a mess of siblings too. We don't talk much. They wanted me to become a doctor and were not happy I became a vet, or that I ended up at a shitty strip mall being paid in hams."

"How did you end up in that mall?" I asked.

"Told my bosses to fuck off when they tried to get me to up-sell traumatized patient owners on pricey procedures that wouldn't work for shit in favor of the pink brew."

"The pink brew?"

She raised her eyes to me, and for the first time, I saw something haunted in her expression. "Yeah, the pink brew. You didn't know the drug that does the final deed is bright fucking pink?"

The deed? Oh. She meant… "It is?"

"Yep. You will never look at candy pink the same way again." After a few minutes of quiet, she asked, "So how are you feeling?"

"Better," I said. Heck, I'd even venture to say despite every-thing I'd started to feel alive again. I flexed my healing hands. "These are still bothering me a bit."

"Yeah, you sliced 'em deep. The nerves and tiny fibers are going to need a few months to heal all the way, but the mittens did their job."

"I hated those stupid mittens." Then I sighed. "I've got my hands back at least. Never wanted to be Luna, though."

"Sorry, don't have a drug to unfuck your life. But I do have some whiskey and ice-cream in my room."

"How did you score ice cream? Not even I've been able to

score ice cream." There was a notable lack of ice cream in SableFur. I would have to have a talk with Cook about that. There'd been pie.

"You have to know who to ask. Come on, you can be my hot date. It'll confuse the fuck out of all of them."

EVAN : LET THE GAMES BEGIN

Evan appraised the small, dingy structure, and the gravel lot around it. It smelled of wolves, and a few humans as well. An isolated stretch of blacktop, but not too isolated—there were a few more structures clinging to the road up a short distance, and the scent of homes on the hillside nearby.

Outside the bar waited a group of three wolves. They looked less like degenerates than he'd expected, but that was not saying much.

The things one did for the pack.

He approached.

"You're late," a tall, lanky one said.

"I'm here, aren't I?" Evan shot back.

"Renzo. Hunter," he said. The others introduced themselves as Kevin and Tim. Warriors.

"You got told how the game's getting played?" Evan asked.

Renzo nodded. "Good thing about a pack this large. Nobody knows everyone."

"Try to smell a little happier to be here." Tim curled his lip and showed a flash of teeth.

"Fuck you," Evan said in a withering tone. "I'm a first-rank warrior and I'm here getting my paws filthy with you fucking degenerates."

"So run along home if you've not got the stomach for it."

"This isn't what I thought my stomach would get used for, but if it works, it works," Evan growled. Adrianna still being alive was a serious problem. Too much talk about what the Moon really intended to happen, and which side was blessed and which side was damned. Adrianna shouldn't be alive, but Gianna shouldn't have starlight wolves. It was a stupid argument with an obvious answer for anyone willing to engage their brains.

Anyone who had spent more than a few weeks in the main house under Adrianna's service knew *nothing* happened in her den she didn't know about. She'd known about Magnes and Gabel and Gabel's mother. Maybe she hadn't known thirty years ago, but she'd known about it the instant Gianna had been dragged to IronMoon and the Oracles had allowed it. She'd known *exactly* why SableFur had abandoned Shadowless, and she'd known *exactly* why Magnes had used spies and the Oracles to get Gianna away from Gabel. She'd *never* have let Magnes do those things without an explanation.

She'd known *exactly* what she was doing when she'd killed the IronMoon First Beta.

Killing Hix had not been to send a warning to IronMoon. Having some worthless wolf shove a knife into his back hadn't been an insult to IronMoon. It'd been a warning to SableFur. To the prestigious wolves like him: do not ask questions.

Decades of smoke, human, piss, and sweat clung to every surface in the bar, obfuscating scents. It was dimly lit as well, and a tired jukebox rattled out tinny songs from a corner. Through the haze of scent and dimness, Evan determined the group playing darts was human, but the wolves were playing pool. He didn't recognize the wolves. Renzo was right:

SableFur was so large even two hours outside its heart Evan couldn't be sure who all the wolves were. Those weren't warriors, so he didn't know them.

His senses sharpened, his ears straining to hear, and his nose useless. Especially by the bar, where he was compelled to take inventory of the spilled beer and splashed liquor, the dishwater that hadn't been changed in hours, and the onion-laced sweat of the bartender undercut with a sweetness that revealed a certain degree of diabetes and liver woes, as well as a bitter, tarry scent that indicated a lifetime affection for cigars.

He ordered something—it didn't matter, he wasn't going to drink it, human booze held little appeal to him, and he wanted all his senses. He pulled up a stool close to the pool table while the IronMoon negotiated who had next.

One of the local wolves asked, "Who are you, friend?"

Friend being the customary greeting among SableFur who recognized another wolf. It could be a threat, or an actual greeting.

"Evan," Evan answered after a mouthful of the terrible beer. He tilted his bottle towards the IronMoon. "They're coming from east."

"Mountain-side-more-than-not," Renzo said, eyeing the pool table and arrangement of balls.

Grunts from the locals. *Mountain-side-more-than-not* meant the long, narrow region to the far east that ran north-south along the shadows of the eastern mountains. Only a local SableFur would refer to it that way. Renzo had done his research.

Tim grunted something non-specific.

"Is there fighting out that way?" one of the local SableFur asked.

Renzo chucked the chalk at the local. "Not enough for our liking. That's why we came out this way. Going to head down to the heart and see if Luna Gianna's got a use for us."

Evan rested the butt of his cue on the floor.

"That's the wrong way, pup," one of the locals said. "Luna Adrianna is to the north."

The cue went thunk against the ball, then *clack!* as it struck the solid orange five ball. The ball thunked softly against the lip, then spun into the pocket. Renzo chuckled. "I'll just pretend you didn't say that, friend."

The two locals puffed a bit. The one said, "You're on the IronMoon bitch's side?"

Tim tossed the chalk to the third IronMoon, Kevin. "She turned Magnes into a puddle. Just a matter of time before she gets her claws on Adrianna and boom!"

Renzo chuckled. The SableFur who hadn't spoken yet downed the remainder of his beer and chucked the can at a bin. "Luna Adrianna didn't know anything about it."

"If I was Adrianna, I'd be insulted you thought I was so dumb I didn't know where my mate stuck his dick," Renzo said. "She knew all about Magnes' little love-child. Magnes couldn't shit without Adrianna knowing."

"She *didn't* know," was the growled reply.

Another wolf, sitting a table over, slammed his beer bottle down. "Who cares? You two are arguing like either of them'd know you on sight, or that who's Luna matters outside the heart."

"You heard what the IronMoon did the past month? It matters," one of the SableFur growled.

"You dumbass, Adrianna wouldn't know who you were if you bled on her, and Gianna wouldn't either," the surly SableFur rolled his eyes and downed his drink. "Who cares who the Luna is. Maybe in some other pack it matters, but here? Come on, can anyone here say they've actually *met* either of them?"

Evan kept his hand firmly on his thigh, even as he itched to raise it and say *I have.* Because he had, and he was proud of it, but he had to gulp it down like the shitty beer. The IronMoon —who had *all* met Gianna, and served under her—just leaned on pool sticks or the table, drinks in hand. The SableFur shuffled their feet and grimaced and growled.

Renzo rolled his tongue in his mouth, and grinned a lazy, feral smile. "I'd like to be the sort of wolf the Luna knows who exists. My choice is the Oracle who they say's got the Moon in her eye and starlight wolves at her command *orrrr* the old bitch who either knew, or was too stupid to figure it out. I'm gonna go with the divine hero, thanks."

One of the SableFur leapt at Renzo and smashed the pool cue down over the Hunter's shoulder. Renzo snarled, ducked, and punched the SableFur clean in the jaw.

Tim grabbed the solid yellow ball and punched the second SableFur. Something cracked. Didn't sound like the ball broke.

"Hey! Hey!" the bartender shouted, slapping his filthy rag down on the counter and storming around. Humans jumped into the fray and wolves howled and punched each other, while Evan shouted *Gianna!* and one of the SableFur shouted *Adrianna!* A few other wolves that had been watching joined the fray.

"Hey, hey!" Evan shouted, ducking out from under the wolves and tackling the IronMoon. "Don't *kill* them!"

The IronMoon flipped under him, nearly clocked Evan with the poolball, Evan smashed his hand down into the floor. Three SableFur piled onto them and clocked Evan in the back of the head.

The IronMoon warrior belatedly remembered Evan was on *their* side, and shrimped out from under the rattled warrior, grabbed two SableFur by the hair, and smashed their heads together. Blood spurted as scalps split.

The bartender was shouting and kicking and smacking

them with that filthy towel. "Stop it, you crazy fucks! I'm going to call the cops!"

Evan got back on his feet, shoved the bleeding SableFur back against the pool table (leaving a fan of blood droplets on the green felt), and decked one last ambitious SableFur with his fist.

"All of you get out!" The bartender howled, waving his towel around like a banner. "Out, damnit! Get out!"

"Dumb assholes," the surly wolf grabbed two SableFur by the collars and dragged them out after him, "stop making trouble. It won't matter who the hell sits on that throne!"

It *would* matter. Evan shrugged his shoulders and stalked out anyway, head held high. Renzo picked up the errant ball and smacked it onto the table, grinning as he did so, and the IronMoon-SableFur sauntered out, chortling to themselves.

"Fuck you!" One of the SableFur picked up a ball and flung it at Renzo's head. It smashed harmlessly into the wall.

Evan crunched into the parking lot and pulled out his phone.

Evan *[Lucas] >> They took the bait. Moving on to the next bar.*

Lucas >> How many injuries?

Evan [Lucas] >> Nothing serious. Surprise tho: one wolf was talking about he didn't care who the Luna was.

Lucas >> Why not?

Evan [Lucas] >> Because he'd never meet her and it doesn't affect him either way. Do you think it's true?

A long pause.

Lucas >> I haven't thought about it that way in a long time, but yeah. Probably?

Evan [Lucas] >> I don't get that.

Lucas >> We'll talk about it later. Move to the next target and report back. Try not to bash out too many teeth.

Evan pocketed his phone. The IronMoon had shuffled out

of the bar and around the side, flicking blood off their lips and wiping their hands on their pants. Evan went to join them.

"Ready for more?" Renzo asked, grinning. His teeth were stained with blood. Tim and Kevin slammed into each other and punched each other in the gut.

Was Gianna *really* the Luna of this pack? Evan hid his grimace as best he could. "Yes."

"If you don't have the spine for it, go back to the heart and sit at her paws," Renzo needled him.

Damn Hunters. Evan scowled. "I do. I don't like the taste of my packmates' blood. They can't help that they're idiots."

"Then we'll knock some sense into them before Gabel shows up to scratch it into their bones." Renzo grinned. The two warriors howled.

Evan winced. "Would you two idiots knock it off? You're going to get us noticed. And whichever one of you assholes used the poolball, don't. If you can't get the job done with your bare hands, go back to the front and have him send me two wolves who can."

"We're allowed to celebrate," Tim said shortly, pushing his way up into Evan's space.

"Don't, or I will send you back to Gabel in large chunks." Evan growled. "And we both know he'll be angry at the stupid way you died, not that you're dead."

The warrior slunk backwards.

"So *why* are we doing this again?" Kevin asked. "Brawling seems like a waste of time if we can't break bones."

Evan winced. These were *not* the brightest tools in the shed. At least the Hunter looked pained as well. "Because the wolves of SableFur don't support Gianna as Luna. We're going around pretending to be SableFur loyal to Gianna and picking fights so it seems like SableFur is divided and willing to shed blood over the Luna they support. First Beta Lucas believes that if we demonstrate not everyone has the same opinion, it makes it easier to have *different* opinions. Although I wasn't expecting a wolf to just not care."

"Then that wolf can't complain when shit doesn't go his way," Renzo said, licking blood off his teeth. "Let's go. We've got a place to be. You know, SableFur, Gabel doesn't have a First Beta right now. Maybe you should apply for the job. You kind of remind me of the last one."

ADRIANNA : PLAY DATE

Adrianna contemplated the messenger in front of her. Her fingers itched to cut into the wolf's neck and peel back his head. What he was telling her was impossible. She just didn't know what part of it offended her more: that it had happened at all, or that one of the voices had said they didn't care.

Shocks of grey had appeared at her temples in the past few weeks, and as she warred with her own claws, the gauntness of her hands was obvious, the way the bones of her wrist strained against her skin and muscle. Her nightmares refused to abate.

Her only solace was her pups, and the Moon wouldn't take them away from her.

My life doesn't matter. I'll weather this, Moon. We've argued before.

Something shifted in the back of her mind—a strange warning she'd sensed before. The weight of the Moon. The goddess heard her.

If you wanted to smite me, you would have done it by now. You won't do it. You have limits.

She suppressed a snarl, but turned her frayed nerves on the messenger. "Tell me. Again."

"There was a fight a day ago," the messenger said, sidling out of range of her claws. "Just a brawl at a bar. Some local wolves. They were going to the heart to join Gianna's side."

"And?" Adrianna hissed.

"They said she was the rightful Luna," the messenger said. "That's what the fight was about. Tore up a bar. Blood everywhere. Real nasty."

Thomas added, "We've gotten another report of a similar brawl closer to the heart. Doesn't seem to be anything serious."

"Except for the wolves who say they don't want to get involved and don't care *who* is Luna," the messenger said, noting each word with care. The messenger was smart enough to know that last point was salient.

Adrianna's eyes narrowed. What idiot pack did not care who the Luna was? Apathy was disgusting news, and disturbing. Wolves who simply didn't want to get involved, and would flock to whichever Luna least disrupted their lives.

Reports also told her additional Beltane invitations had gone out. She didn't know how many, but she did know a few names—not wolves she'd have invited, but Gianna had passed out favors, and no doubt had Lucas whispering in her ear which ass to sniff.

The little Oracle was more deft than expected. Kiery had even contacted IronMoon to have them send Gianna's personal doctor, not trusting the SableFur doctors to look after the newly-minted Luna. No one attended Gianna save Kiery and an obnoxious, foul-mouthed, low-class *human* veterinarian.

Adrianna snarled to herself. Gianna's poor health would have made killing her easy, except none of the doctors could get close enough. She'd already tried that. The veterinarian was too paranoid, kept her medications under lock and key, and as a human, didn't give a fuck about prestige or rank, and wasn't afraid of making a spectacle of herself.

Now she had IronMoon dancing around to the north,

gnawing on her sentries, stealing, pissing, and howling, and refusing to meet her on the battlefield. She advanced, they retreated. She struck, they dodged. Her sanity and patience with those degenerate bottom-feeding toads frayed to its last fibers. "Who were these local wolves? I want names."

"No names given. Two of them said they'd come from the eastern front to join up," the messenger said.

"Find out who these wolves are," Adrianna snapped at Thomas.

"Luna, it's not important, they're just random males. They probably see Gianna as a way to make some prestige for themselves," Thomas said. "They're just fleas hopping dogs."

No, they were important, because it meant that support for Gianna was stronger than she'd realized. Reports until now had said that all of SableFur except the heart—the *critical* part of SableFur that held the entire pack together—had remained loyal to Adrianna, and that the wolves in the heart were shaky in their loyalty to Gianna. She'd hoped someone would just kill Gianna in a fit of inspired pique, but even an unpopular Luna was a reluctant kill.

But if these reports were right, Gianna had more popularity than expected. A *serious* problem. Gabel hadn't gone for the heart like Adrianna had thought he would. She'd expected him to try to press south to the heart. Instead the damn fool had come after *her*, leaving Gianna unchallenged.

So much for thinking the IronMoon would try to overthrow his ex-mate. The beast wanted *her* instead. Adrianna's hopes that Gabel would press Gianna and fracture what little support the bitch had had proven wrong.

"There are rumors Gabel is going to attempt to reconcile with Gianna," the messenger said in a tiny voice.

Adrianna turned a hairy eyeball to him. "*What?*"

"He's still in love with her," the messenger whispered. "That's what he's been howling about. A lot of wolves are thinking he's not going to attack her. He's already tried to conquer her once and failed and killing her pack isn't going to make her happy."

Adrianna gnashed her teeth together. So the wolves were so afraid of Gabel coming and burning their hamlets would flock to Gianna for protection because she could protect them from Gabel's monstrosity.

The IronMoon Alpha's forces were small, and if all of SableFur united (or even half), they could crush IronMoon. But Gabel's fearsome reputation as a creature from nightmares preceded him, and she was trapped up here, trying to accumulate supporters and resources.

It was hard to think through the haze of pain and the emptiness of Magnes simply not *being there*. He wasn't there. Nothing was except a void that consumed her thoughts and her mind if she stared at it too long. Her thoughts rattled around in her head with no where else to go. For all these years he'd been there, her heart, her soul, her friend, her closest confidant, sharer of burdens and now he was gone, gone, gone...

She yanked herself back from the edge of the void.

She curled mental fingers into the waking world. Gabel wanted Gianna back. Did Gianna want *Gabel* back? The she-wolf would be a fool to reconsider it, but Anita had always said Gianna was The Balance-Keeper, the point on which light and dark turned. Gabel was the Moon's Dark Comet. Gianna had somehow known to look for Gabel's mother, the starlight wolves... Gianna had always known where Gabel was going to be.

"They're working together," Adrianna said.

"That's impossible," Thomas said.

"No, no it's not," Adrianna insisted, hating how the edges of her mind incinerated. The grief was killing her and robbing her of her sanity.

"Why?"

"I don't know, but we'll watch and wait for our opportunity. Gabel will make a mistake," Adrianna hissed. "He *always* makes a mistake where Gianna is concerned. She is his one blindspot, his one weakness, and he is such a fool he doesn't realize it."

"Or he won't admit it," Thomas said.

Adrianna grinned. "Even better. Magnes was arrogant to a fault as well, and his lupine bastard has that trait. Send out scouts. Track the IronMoon Alpha's movements exactly. I don't care what the rest of his army is doing, monitor *him*."

Adrianna's frozen soul warmed and the predatory hunger raced along her gums, sharpening her teeth, and the Moon watched, silent.

You will do nothing, Silvery Sky Bitch. Nothing at all. Watch your pets play.

GABEL : HOW FORTUNATE

"They're ready, Lord-Alpha," Eroth said.

Gabel inhaled the breeze. Fear, blood, death, but resentment and anger. He smiled. His fingers twitched as his anger pushed against his skin. His mate's soul howled for his. In his sleep he woke to the scent of the night-blooming cereus pulling him into the darkness, drawing him from his bed to pursue her.

We will be together soon.

He rolled his neck on his shoulders. Out of the corner of his eye Flint watched, silent. Flint had come from IronMoon for this, tried briefly to talk him out of it, and failing that, now watched, mindful and refusing to let Gabel out of his sight for more than a few moments. "Advice, old man?"

Flint cocked a brow. "To be careful. You're not Alpha here. You are not here to take. You are not here to possess. This is already yours. You must tame it without endangering her further, but carve out the cancer that infests it. If you lose this ground, she will be lost with it. The situation is more complicated than you are permitting yourself to see."

Gabel took another moment to settle his mind before he entered the small hamlet.

As expected, a cluster of wolves waited for him. Fear. Disgust. Violence simmering under the edges. The gift of a few scouts' heads had gotten their attention.

The leader of the group, a wolf in his thirties, stood at the front, shaking with fury. "What do you want, dog?"

Gabel glanced around. He gave his fingers something to do by straightening the cuff at his wrist. His attire in these situations always sent the other wolves onto their heels. "I am here to inquire where your loyalties lie."

"Not with you! You will have to kill us all," he snarled. Growls and howls in response.

"Of course your allegiance does not lie with me. That is not what I asked. I asked if you claim allegiance to Gianna or Adrianna?"

The wolf shifted back on his heel. Fool. Not a polished negotiator, nor particularly strong-spined. The group suddenly smelled of nerves, but no further clue as to why. Gabel waited, and upon getting no answer, said, "It's not a difficult question unless you are trying to decide what the correct answer is."

The tension increased.

"What pack does not declare their loyalty to their Luna proudly?" Gabel asked. "Your lack of appreciation disgusts me. I should divide the pile of carcasses you would produce evenly between the two of them."

"Luna Gianna," Francis said in a great, tortured gust.

That was a lie, but a useful one. "How fortuitous. I am going to see Luna Gianna. You will not mind if we pass through, hmm? I am bringing her a gift."

Francis stiffened. "I—she doesn't want to see you! She doesn't want your gift!"

"But she *needs* the gift I bring," Gabel said as he

approached the leader. "And, Francis, she has something that belongs to me."

The SableFur pushed together, but Gabel kept coming, pressing into the cluster, inhaling their scent, carrying ash and burning on his shoulders. "She has my crown."

Gabel pressed closer into their bulk, eyes never leaving Francis' face. "I am Magnes' oldest son, and there are two ways we can do this. One is the violent way, where I start killing you one by one by one and you may shed your blood defending Luna Gianna's claim to my crown. I will tell her how bravely you died defending her, and she and I will sing of your bravery."

Gabel leaned closer and whispered, "Or you can accept that you are small creatures that will *always* be ruled, by guile or by might or by a gentle hand, and that that is how you like your lives, and that it is best and safest and most clever to simply kneel."

He straightened, and half-looked over his shoulder. "IronMoon!"

The warriors behind him straightened.

"Will you die for your Luna?!" Gabel shouted.

Howls singing the Luna's Song.

"They wait for me to bring her back to them," Gabel told Francis, eyes bright and too blue, and his scent of ash intensifying. "They wait for me to bring back their future. Their Luna came here to destroy my father, and she triumphed. Now. Shall I throw your bones on my tower, or will you *kneel?!*"

Some of the cluster mewled and dropped to their knees. Some others trembled and staggered down onto one knee. Then, slowly, the remainder bent, except for three defiant she-wolves who clutched their pups against them and snarled at him.

Gabel placed a hand over his heart, half-bowed to them, and stepped away from the cluster. To his warriors, he shouted,

"We go forward. Touch nothing, disturb nothing. There are no bones for us here. Pay proper respect to the she-wolves who would rather fight than kneel. And be gentle with my Luna's gift. I don't wish to break it. More than it has already been broken."

COMING

I pressed *call.*

"Did you just want to hear my voice?" Gabel murmured on the other end.

I leaned back against my pillows. "Perhaps I knew you wanted to hear mine."

A chuckle like warm embers. "Always. How does your pack enjoy learning there are wolves willing to fight and die for you?"

"You mean bar brawls?" I said, keeping my voice down so any prying ears wouldn't hear. I slid out of bed and locked myself in the bathroom and sat on the edge of the tub.

"A bar brawl is a prelude to war," he murmured, amused.

"Was that your idea or Lucas'?" I asked, warming with fondness.

"I will give the First Beta credit for refining my idea and supplying Evan."

"So that's where Evan got off to. Lucas was cryptic about it."

"Don't ask questions you don't want answered. He is tolerable only because he is smart. These old packs disappoint. Fat, bloated, lost their mettle, forgot what it was to defend what they've been sitting on unchallenged so long."

"Don't think Adrianna can't put the whip to them," I said.

"That would make for a very interesting war. Very satisfying."

"SableFur believes you killed Anita. That you killed her acolytes. They believe you are killing the Oracles for your mother's sake. They want every reason to believe Adrianna is innocent, and you are a monster." I sighed and hung my head.

"I *am* a monster, but I agree that SableFur needs a reason to believe I am innocent of that particular crime. We cannot make them think kindly of me, but we can make them think badly of my father's whore."

I sighed again. "Tell me about your mother. I need to connect her to Adrianna, somehow, and no one here knows anything. Kiery suggested perhaps there is a link to NightScent."

I heard him settle himself somewhere to sit. "She was beautiful. Silvery-blue, like you. I never saw her human form. I never knew her human name. She only told me my father had died in the winter, and my littermates had died as well. Now I'm not sure how much of that is a lie."

"You think some of your littermates may have survived?" I asked, sitting up straight.

"She told me there had been six of us. Perhaps the others died before I could remember them. We were very young. Born in the winter. I don't know how we survived. I have the memories of a pup, and they are difficult to put into words."

I asked, "So when did your mother die?"

Gabel thought a moment. "My third Solstice. Deep in that winter."

A wild wolf would have been a young adult by their third birthday, but a lupine was still a child. "How?"

An aggravated sound, and then, "Wolves. Lone wolves. I'd

been scouting a few miles east, tracking a deer, and by the time I arrived, there was not much left. I tracked their scents, but only found one of them a few years later. He was my first kill."

His tone caused me to shudder and cringe. I still had so many questions, but I didn't dare ask them. The Bond writhed on my loneliness and despair, and I stared at the ugly tile flooring of the bathroom.

"There is just you and I now," he said. His voice was low-lying darkness, like fog in the evening.

I closed my eyes. I'd had him attack Shadowless. I'd turned him loose on my own flesh and blood. My head dropped to my chest under the impossible weight of what I'd done to get this far, and how far I still had to go.

"I must go," he murmured. "Beltane is almost here, and I have something to do to prepare for it."

"We both do."

His voice warmed, slid through the phone into my ear as if a hand slid along our Bond, as if up my thigh. "I am coming for you, buttercup."

I closed my eyes. "I know."

A TOKEN OF MY AFFECTION

"What do you mean Gabel is coming *here?*"

"He's been spotted traveling with a wolf with blue-gloss tattoos, and possibly another wolf," Lucas said.

"Fuck, I didn't realize he meant *literally...*" I fumed, and I rubbed my head. When Gabel had said *I'm coming for you* I'd thought he'd meant like... in a few weeks. For Beltane. Not *right now, I'm on my way, meet me outside.*

"They have white tied around their wrists. It's parlay," Bernhard said, annoyed. "He's passing relatively unmolested. Should we turn him back and tell him we aren't interested in what he has to say?"

"How are we going to keep his arm concealed?" Kiery said.

"Gabel can be trusted to keep his clothes on. He's not *that* feral," I said.

"Things happen, Gianna. Like what you're going to smell like around him, what he'll smell—"

"Who cares what he smells like. He's up to something. He was aggravated when he found out that he's getting blamed for killing the Oracles. That sounded personal," I said, aggravated and pacing.

"You think he's got some proof of his innocence?" Kiery asked.

"I can't imagine what he'd have," Lucas said.

"We should tell him to go back home," Bernhard said.

I wanted to agree, but Gabel wouldn't listen. The stubborn wolf was going to show up. "He's got Flint with him. That means he's bringing an advisor we can all trust. And a handler."

Kiery nodded. "I still don't like this."

I didn't either. I didn't trust Gabel, but I did trust Flint. If Gabel had come to claim me and announce he was the SableFur Alpha, I'd gut him.

———

GABEL STRODE into the hall wearing his usual civilized conquest attire—pants and a button-down shirt in a startling shade, this one a pale white-violet that was decidedly unnatural and seemed to make him shine. An ironic color choice to be sure. He was barefoot, cuffs unbuttoned and flicked twice over his wrists, no tie.

His scowl said everything he cared to say about that. And his sharp, angry stride, and the tension in his shoulders, and the throb in my arm got worse with every step he took.

Flint walked just a half-step behind him, in a kilt low over his hips, his blue-gloss tattoos swimming in the light. Around Flint's wrist was a white strip of cloth to indicate they were there under parlay.

Another wolf—one of the more senior IronMoon warriors —came on the other side, also in a kilt. And dragging something behind him.

My Mark throbbed and thudded, the Bond pulsing warm but strained and weak, like it was dying of thirst.

The SableFur studied Gabel, a soft breath moving through all of them as they noted what I'd seen: his resemblance to Magnes, from the frame to the shoulders, the shade of hair, the jaw, the height, but where Magnes had been imposing, domineering, Gabel was dark, smoldering, dangerous, inexorable.

And then there were gasps of horror that went through the collected SableFur as they beheld what the warrior had brought. I couldn't quite make it out, but it looked like a body. Knowing Gabel, it was probably a body.

Gabel stopped at the end of the runner. He noted Kiery with a curl of his upper lip, and then Lucas, then me. "Gianna," he said, and he said it such that my skin prickled so painfully I almost arched and gasped, "I have brought you a gift."

"*Luna* Gianna," Lucas corrected sharply, stepping forward. "You will give her the respect she deserves, or I will throw you out."

"Your Luna and I are on very familiar terms," Gabel said.

"You repudiated her."

"The Moon compelled me to do so. Now I am here to reclaim what has always been mine: the throne of SableFur and the Luna that sits upon it."

SableFur collectively inhaled and swelled with tension.

I sat myself down in Adrianna's chair. Magnes' had been removed. "I'm humoring your presence here, Gabel. If you believe I am your Luna, then you will respect that this is *my* den. You threw me out of my den. I'm not inclined to share this one with you. Especially since you are killing my Oracle sisters."

"No." Gabel held up one finger. "I am not the one responsible for that butchery. And I will prove it with a gift for you."

The warrior dragging the body strode forward. What he

was dragging left a damp trail up the runner and carried a
rotting scent with it. It was a pulpy, ruined mass of a human
form, covered in awful black bruises and wounds, swollen and
mangled. She had on a single sleeveless shift. She'd been
washed, her hair combed back and carefully braided, and the
shift, while bloody from wounds that were still open, was otherwise clean.

It was Anita.

And she was somehow alive.

Lucas' brow raised. "You do play with your prey, don't you,
you sick bastard."

Kiery and I both stepped down off the dais and knelt
beside the old Elder Oracle. I touched one of Anita's strange,
square-shaped bruises. They weren't bruises. Gabel had shoved
the shards of her shattered bowl under her skin.

Anita's eyes opened. They were bloodshot. One pupil
blown and dilated. She trembled and moved as if to grab one
of us with one of her ruined hands, but flinched on the pain
and froze instead. Each of her fingers had been methodically
broken at each joint. He'd taken the time to wash her, dress
her, braid her hair—or someone had. The shift afforded her a
modesty that Gabel had no respect for.

I leaned closer as she focused on me. I said, softly, "Did he
show you the place he has, where the Moon does not deign to
look? Did he show you the void whence Comets come? The
void beyond the Tides the Moon granted him?"

Her eyes shone bright with shock and pure terror, but she
was still in there. I rose from my crouch. "Her mind is intact.
Did you break her will? Did she tell you who your mother is?
Did she confess that Adrianna knew all along?"

"No," Gabel said, annoyed. "She is as stubborn and
beholden to her vows as you are. She is the first I have not been
able to break. I am… impressed. But perhaps not surprised."

"I swore I would never speak it," Anita rasped.

"It is somewhat comforting an Oracle's word is good for something," Bernhard said.

"That name is your only chance at redemption," I told her. "Tell us the truth. Tell us what happened."

A bone-clacking laugh. "You offer nothing. The Moon does not forgive. I swore I would never speak the name. I won't."

Anita's breathless cackle echoed through the silent hall.

If Gabel couldn't break her, she could not be broken. "Keep your secret then. It seems fitting to me that the instrument of your destruction is the Comet you summoned from the abyss all those years ago."

"Adrianna still lives," Anita wheezed.

I didn't need the old bat to tell me that. I turned my attention to Gabel. "You abducted her from the cottage?"

Gabel chuckled. "No. I stood outside and shouted that if she did not come out, I'd dismantle the cottage and use the door as the final piece of my tower. She came out to tell me to get off her lawn. From there I abducted her."

"Then I would very much like to know who the dead SableFur crone was in that house, and who put her there," I said.

A murmur and ripple through the Hall.

I glanced at Bernhard. "But *you* insisted we burn the cottage."

Bernhard stiffened.

"Are you not as loyal as you should be, Second Beta?" Gabel asked in a delicate tone. Delicate like a claw drawing a line of blood across a throat.

"The cottage was full of disease and death. I ordered it burned for safety reasons," Bernhard snapped.

"And we never even verified who the headless body was," I said, letting Bernhard squirm a bit in front of the pack.

Nobody had reported an old she-wolf having gone missing, so maybe it had been a volunteer.

"He could have killed the acolytes and—" Bernhard pointed at Gabel.

"Be quiet," Evan said from the front row, annoyed. "You are embarrassing us. He didn't kill the Oracles. Move on."

Gabel straightened one of his cuffs. "We have come a far distance. You and I have matters to discuss."

"We have nothing to discuss," I said, although it was a lie for everyone's benefit.

He smirked. "I am Magnes' eldest son and Alpha by right of birth. You are Luna by right of conquest. We have a mutual enemy in Adrianna. She will be a thorn in both our paws for as long as she is alive. Once we ruled IronMoon. Who is to say you will not rule it again? The crown, and I, am yours to have."

Lucas stood at my side practically jumping out of his skin. The ground seemed to be a thin sheet of ice under my feet, creaking and groaning under the weight of all of us.

Gabel needed to shut up. I told him, "We'll show you a degree of hospitality, since, if nothing else, this pack is the birthright your father denied you."

Gabel walked over to the yellow blot on the floor. He used his heel to push Anita away from it and then rubbed the ball of his foot on it. "This is what's left of him?"

"The Moon melted his fangs."

Gabel crouched down by Anita. She moaned as she looked up at him.

"That is all that is left of him," Gabel told her gently. "All your secrets are worthless, old wolf. You cannot stop what is coming. You are the one who ensured it would come to pass."

Anita's guttural, damned moan came from the void itself.

"We do not need your secrets." Gabel cradled her shard-inlaid chin in his hand. "We never have. I merely wanted them. They would make things easier, but they won't stop anything."

"She deserves punishment," Kiery said, voice trembling in anger. "This is her fault! She could have stopped all of it!"

"You were the one who ripped my Luna from me," Gabel told Anita. "I will get her back, but it doesn't change the suffering and humiliation she had to endure."

The Mark on my arm weighed very heavy. I said, "My hands haven't healed enough to shift. Since I cannot kill her with my own claws, I leave it to you, IronMoon, for what she did to us. Make it quick."

Gabel lifted his left arm, and his hand twisted into a dark, leathery claw with yellow talons. Anita managed a scream. "No! No!"

"What did you think was going to happen, you old rotting bitch?" Kiery demanded. "Did you think the Moon would save you? The Moon has come to claim you!"

Gabel's claw stabbed through her neck into the wood beneath her.

He pulled down, shredding her neck from jaw to collar, and drawing deep grooves in the ancient wood.

Blood splattered him, then flooded the floor.

The blue-black-red blood slowly pooled under Anita. Her head, attached by ribbons to her shoulders, rolled ghoulishly a few inches to the right.

"Evan," I told the wolf standing in the first row. "Find somewhere for Lord-Alpha Gabel and Master of Arms Flint to stay this evening. Bernhard, find a detail to clean up that mess. Throw her into a bog for the scavengers."

UNAPOLOGETIC

Evan had given Gabel and Flint two rooms at a far end of the house, on the third floor, by Kiery's workroom. It was a quiet, untravelled part of the house, which made it perfect for me to sneak upstairs and see them.

"Are you going to go see them?" Lucas asked in a corner of the kitchen while Cook muttered over his menus. Lucas loomed over me with his thick arms folded, reeking of general pissed-off-ness.

"I imagine I should talk to them, yes," I replied. Cook's little corner was one of the few places we could talk in the house without ears listening in. I trusted Cook—even though Cook didn't know the truth—and his kitchen staff were so busy chopping and banging and pots boiling and things burning they couldn't overhear or smell us.

"You know what I meant," Lucas grumbled.

"I don't have specific plans. Things are happening quickly. I didn't expect him to show up dragging a corpse. That sort of punches a wrench in Bernhard's idea of Adrianna being innocent, doesn't it."

Poor Bernhard. I liked Bernhard. Bernhard was just

squirmy, squeamish, and not nearly as loyal as he should have been. He didn't want to ride this ride. Too bad he was strapped in and someone had already pressed the start button.

Lucas rubbed his head and winced. "I'll be honest, even I thought it was Gabel. Now I don't know if it's Adrianna or Aaron, and now we don't know who the old woman was. Nobody's reported a missing old she-wolf."

I sighed. "I've considered it was a volunteer."

Lucas grumbled. "You might be right."

"We should find out who she was. If there's a chance we can tie it back to Adrianna, all the better. Explains why the head was removed. We'd have realized immediately it wasn't Anita."

Lucas nodded.

"How's Kiery?" I asked, my eyes drawn to the Mark on Lucas' arm. It had already faded to a pale creamy color. It'd healed quickly and well, like it'd been there for ten years. Which it probably should have been.

"She went with Bernhard to piss on Anita's corpse."

Kiery was a mild-mannered, aloof, reserved Oracle except when she wasn't.

"Kiery was the SableFur Oracle, but Anita always pulled the strings and Kiery hated it. Kiery never picked the fight because she thought squabbling between Oracles was disgraceful," Lucas elaborated. "Now we see that Anita was just setting Kiery up to do her dirty work and be her puppet. What's got her really upset is the two of you being the last Oracles."

"That terrifies both of us," I said worriedly. Aaron was rounding up the acolytes in the south—if there had been any —to ship them to IceMaw, and hopefully (maybe) they'd come to SableFur for Kiery to train when things became more stable.

The problem was Seers couldn't put training on hold. Depending on their age they may be advanced enough to keep themselves safe, but unable to develop further. If they were younger, they'd be at their most vulnerable.

I scratched my arm. Some of the scabs flaked off under my sleeve. Damn thing had started to itch-hurt. "I'd like for the pack to get a look at Gabel, and for Gabel to get a look at SableFur. I'm thinking a warrior presentation and inspection tomorrow."

Lucas shifted unhappily. "You want to put a group of questionably loyal warriors in ranks and you walk around them?"

"Yes. Gabel can just watch, and they can watch him. He's got his arm to conceal for now."

"You think he's going to keep it bound up? Because that wolf is at the end of his chain and he's gnawed halfway through it."

"He'll play along for now," I said, eyes narrowing. "He wants Adrianna. Round up a collection of warriors. Some good ones, and some that might growl at me. I want everyone to get a look at Gabel, not just the wolves of the heart. And I'd like Flint to get some time too. Those blue-gloss tattoos are not just for show."

"Who is Flint to this?" Lucas asked, brow furrowing.

"I only know bits and pieces, even now. What I know is that he's a Moon's Servant, and that he was sent to find and raise Gabel, and if Gabel couldn't be managed, to kill him."

Lucas barked a laugh. "So he hasn't killed Gabel yet? What's the Moon's definition of 'not managed'?"

"Hell if I know," I said, thinking back to my first couple of months in IronMoon. "But I have seen Flint literally rip warforms down the middle into two pieces so…"

"Fuck," Lucas said eloquently.

I nodded and pushed off the wall. "I'll talk to you later, Lucas."

"Should I even ask where you're going?"

"Not if you want to be able to say you have no idea where I am."

GABEL WAS STARING out the window onto the groomed lawn.

I closed the door behind me with a soft click.

"Buttercup," Gabel said, yanking the curtains shut.

He swept me up in his arms and kissed me hungrily.

Then it dissolved into slow and hot, his tongue against mine, his hands curled into my skin, crushing me against him. The Mark on my arm seared like a brand, and I was drowning in him again, his hands pulling me deeper and deeper into the Tides.

He released me and started to unbutton his shirt.

Well, this wasn't what I had planned, but...

"I was just about to shower. You will join me," he said as he pulled the shirt over his head and threw it away. Then he reached for the hem of my sweater, and with a smooth motion, pulled it over my head.

"We have to be quiet," I whispered. And pray nobody smelled us... but especially nobody heard us.

He smiled wickedly. "The SableFur Luna cannot use me for her pleasure? They expect you to remain chaste?"

"It's the *you* part of it that's the problem."

He pulled me after him into the bathroom, and that shower water was blistering cold, even if he used his naked body to shield mine. He braced himself on the tile wall behind me, and leaned close, the cold water searing him as he loomed over me, breathing heavy and thick.

I pulled away from the kiss to trace his Mark. He'd pulled off the scabs, exposing not the raised threading of a regular scar, but blue-gloss limned with fainter blue, like a halo around the Moon on a winter's night, when the sky is full of ice crystals. The blue clung to each curve and hollow and ridge of his muscled arm, from the softness of his elbow to beyond the cap of his shoulder, the tail edges of the design reaching towards his throat like questing claws.

"It's blue-gloss," I whispered, placing three fingers against the slash marks that had comprised our original Mark. "Not exactly like Flint's but…"

"For us," he said, voice as raw as the warming water. He pulled at the last of the scabs on my arm. Sharp pull, a kiss on my neck, his breath raw and heavy, over and over until my matching Mark was completely exposed to his gaze in its blue, wicked glory. I leaned my head to the side as he pushed fingers down into the trailing edges at my collar, and he bent and bit down over the blue.

He kissed each of the silver scars around my neck. "One, two, three…"

He counted each one as his strong hands ran over my ribs.

"They are nothing," I said.

He turned me around. His cock pressed against the cleft of my ass, but his broad palms ran down my spine, smoothed over my hips, tugging me against him. He drew his tongue over the scar where the silver buckle of the collar had burned into the base of my neck. "The scars of a Queen."

His hands slipped forward and cupped my breasts, lifting the flesh and squeezing. His body hardened further, and the scent of desire engulfed me through the steam.

I looked down at his hands, enjoying the sight of his broad palms holding my breasts.

He pinched one nipple, sending a shock right to my core, and then the other, and I suppressed a whimper.

Gabel whispered in my ear, "Not here."

"Why not?" I breathed, because right here sounded excellent. "They won't hear us over the water."

"But I want them to hear us, and smell us, and know

exactly what I am doing to their Luna." He bit my ear, and I gasped as his teeth broke the first layer of skin.

"I'd rather not——"

He chuckled, and stepped away from me, and out of the shower.

Beast.

"Fine," I said, joining him on the bed and straddling him, both of us dripping wet, and the water sluicing down my skin and onto his body. "But not a sound."

He laughed, his big hands tugging me forward so the tip of his cock pressed dangerously against my eager, moist opening, and his hips shifted just enough to tease me with what was on offer, and what I'd been missing. The connection between our souls howled its happiness.

"That sounds like a challenge."

I leaned over him. "It's not, but take it as one if you like."

He slipped downward—how the hell did he move so quickly over the sheets?—until his face was right where his hips had been. He pulled my hips down, and I ended up sitting on his face.

I suppressed a moan as his tongue moved between my folds, slow and infinitely patient, like he had all the time in the world to torture me.

I dug my fingers into his hair and twisted. He hissed in pain —sending shivers of delight through my most delicate flesh— and rewarded me with a bite on one fold that made me jump, and a nip of my jewel, which was too delicate for such abuse.

His tongue resumed its slow, careful work, exploring every fold and ridge of my body, and I arched my spine, silently pleading for release as the pressure built. I gasped and suppressed anything louder, keening in my throat as I tore at his hair, grinding myself onto his face.

He spanked my ass at one point, but his fingers dug into my hips and pulled me into him. I tried to squirm free to turn around so I could return the favor, but he held me pinned to him until I thought I couldn't take it any longer and my thighs trembled.

His grip eased, and we shifted, giving him breathing room and my body backing away from the beautiful edge. He licked me once, slowly, and then his tongue darted inside me, and I moaned, then clamped my hands over my mouth to hold in any other sounds.

He flipped me onto my back on the blankets. I squeaked. He kissed me deeply, silencing me and his tongue tasting of me.

"Taste yourself," he murmured, offering me his tongue. I sucked on it eagerly, bathing it with my own, and felt him smile.

"I hate you," I whispered, poised on the edge between pleasure and defeat, and he nipped my ear again.

"Sticks and stones," he teased, biting my earlobe, and I heard myself laugh before he shoved his hand over my mouth to silence me. "Silence. That was my Luna's command, was it not?"

I squirmed under him, inviting him closer.

"If you cannot be silent," he whispered by my ear, "I will have to take care of myself. While you watch."

His body pressed into my thigh, slick and eager. I raked my fingernails across his broad shoulders, sending him trembling with fierce desire. "Empty threats, IronMoon. Empty threats."

I loved his scent in moments like this. I arched up to him as he came into me, my entire body wracked with a rictus of pleasure in that moment of completion. I dug my fingernails into him again. The connection between our souls surged, and I laughed as I met his thrust again, and again, and again, driving me farther and farther until I arched one last time under him, my entire body clenching around his, and my nails digging into his skin.

We tumbled together into the blankets, sweat-slick and panting.

"For all your talk about not making a sound," Gabel's breath was raw and full of laughter as he kissed me, "you left marks no one will mistake."

"Then I guess you'll have to wear a shirt," I whispered back. I sat up, and traced the blue-black Mark on his arm idly, admiring the intricate pattern.

He snorted impatiently and pulled me back down against him.

"No one will think it's a Mark," I mused.

"The IronMoon know it is one, but no one else seems to assume that is what it is. It is a blue-gloss tattoo as far as everyone else is concerned."

Flint had said that every blue-gloss tattoo told the story of how the wearer had achieved it, but I didn't recognize any runes in ours. The only shape with any meaning was the three slash marks. How it had all begun.

Gabel lifted his blue gaze to mine, a smile lurking on his lips. "If you are thinking this means we can delay because no one at Beltane will realize it is a Mark, the answer is no."

I sat up, aggravated. "I—"

"You were going to suggest it."

"I was going to contemplate it," I shot back.

"No," he sat up. "You won't lie to the pack. I am Alpha here, and I will not lie to them."

"And it's my den and I want to be safe inside it while you're out waging war!" I hissed.

His anger banked, and withdrew, like the door on an old iron stove being slammed shut. He touched the scar at the base of my neck. "The silver cost you. I shall go hunting and bring you fresh prey."

"A winter-skinny rabbit isn't going to do anything to fill my stomach," I said, barbishly. Maybe Gabel was at peace with the end of the world, but I wasn't.

"I will take that as permission." Gabel captured me with one strong arm and pressed me back down into the blankets. "I shall feed you by hand, bite by bite."

He brushed my lips with his fingertips.

"I can feed myself, thanks," I said, then I bit the tip of one finger. Hard.

He grinned.

I released his fingertip and rolled away from him. "I can't stay. Dinner is in two hours. The pack will expect all of us."

A DANGEROUS TRINKET

Gabel wasn't at dinner. Flint sat in his place, his intricate blue-gloss tattoos getting quite a bit of attention, along with his polite, but brief answers to even casual conversation. Kiery and I tried our best to redirect the conversation away from Gabel's notable absence (because if SableFur knew I knew he was out hunting on *my* territory they'd blow a fuse) and casual conversation about the brewing war (Flint wasn't going to give away any details or clues) but failed spectacularly, because it was *all* the males wanted to discuss.

"Where did Gabel find you?" Bernhard finally asked, plowing right through the polite veil we'd tried to weave and obliterating any sense of propriety.

Kiery sighed and tossed down her fork. She looked longingly towards Ana—seated at a low table that night—and we both had the same thought: invite Ana up to the high table to make things awkward and weird with Flint. Because Flint, at that point, might be grateful.

"I found Gabel," Flint answered, weaving his fingers together in a single large fist and resting his chin upon it.

"*You* found Gabel," Bernhard echoed. The room got quiet. "So we have you to thank for him."

If Bernhard didn't shut up in exactly five seconds, I vowed to stab him with my fork so the next thing that came out of his mouth was *ieee!* And then send him away with Ana for doctoring.

"The Moon sent me to him," Flint said, shifting his inked shoulder slightly so that the muscles moved, and the tattoos slid across his skin. "You may thank Her."

"You didn't teach him much except how to be a monster," Bernhard spat. "Where is the IronMoon Alpha? Did you let your dog off his chain?"

"Bernhard, enough," I growled. "They came here under parlay."

"And we are just talking, Luna," Bernhard retorted.

"I am not your enemy," Flint said.

"You're an IronMoon, and you should have left that lupine brat to die in the forests and spared us all," Bernhard shot back, starting to get out of his chair.

"Sit. Down," I snarled. "They're here under parlay, and you're trying to start a fight. Knock it off."

Bernhard grumbled something, but put his rump back in his chair.

But at least that squashed Bernhard grousing, and if the other tables wanted to whisper to each other, they could do that. Flint wouldn't care, and his advice to me would be to let it happen anyway. Conversation drifted to Beltane preparations, which were completely innocuous and of no tactical concern to the IronMoon, and IronMoon wasn't having a celebration at all, for obvious reasons.

I wanted to talk to Flint in private, but he excused himself right after dinner and retreated to his rooms. I didn't dare follow him. I'd already chanced that part of the house once, and while I wasn't getting any sideways looks, I couldn't risk it.

All eyes were on me, every move and gesture, weighing just how well-disposed I was towards the IronMoon.

As far as they knew, Gabel was my ex, who had dumped me on the word of Oracles. Oracles who had now proven to be corrupt, in the service of an Alpha who had been worse than corrupt. Nobody would be wrong to think there was a chance we'd reconcile if Gabel groveled at my paws for forgiveness, especially if Gabel intended to pursue his blood-claim to the throne. War with the IronMoon was a terrifying prospect. Perhaps more terrifying than him being Alpha.

GABEL's howl came as I was brushing my teeth.

"Mmmph?" I asked, mouth full of froth. I stopped brushing.

The howl again: the howl of a male announcing he'd returned from a hunt, and the pack should come see.

"Oh, you ass," I muttered. "What have you done now."

If he was making such a fuss over a rabbit, I'd kill him. It better not be a rabbit. Gabel, the Moon's Dark Comet, didn't get bonus points for a *rabbit*.

I shrugged a robe over my naked shoulders, sashed it shut, and padded down the hallway towards the backdoor.

Now his song changed to one that made me blush: an out-of-favor male calling his mate to him, that he has brought her a gift.

The whole damn pack was going to be awake for this. Nothing like lupine soap operas to kick off a morning.

The cold morning chill ate through my thin robe instantly.

Gabel sat on the porch in wolf-form, the blue-gloss Mark absurdly bright against his leather-hide shoulder. His rat-tail thumped on the stones as he wagged it, and his ichor-yellow eyes glowed. Laid out before him was the carcass of a young buck, skillfully killed with a single tearing bite to the throat, the hide unmarred by so much as a scratch. He was filthy, and frost clung to the tips of his hairless ears, and muckballs clung to the long, coarse hairs that ran down the back of each leg.

Upon my setting foot on the frosty porch he twisted into his nightmarish war-form. With a yellow claw he sliced the buck's belly open. He shoved his claw inside, dislodging various internal organs and bowels, and removed the liver. He offered it to me in his claw, then set it down upon the stones before shifting to his human form.

Flint slipped around me. Without a word, he sashed the kilt he was carrying around Gabel's hips, and drew an additional length of fabric over his chest, draping the remainder over the Marked arm.

I licked my lips and fought the urge to go to him and kiss him, and plunge into the carcass and gorge myself.

My resolve wavered under the throbbing in my arm, and the pull of the hungry Bond. It was fresh, new, alive once again, and needed to heal—and it wanted Gabel. His touch, his caress, his lips, his body within mine—

I bit my lip against the crush, and the heat between my thighs. Gabel's prestige pulled hard.

As the sun's fingers crept through the trees Gabel seemed a half-bronze, half charred iron creature, with eyes like blue tourmaline.

"You presume to sing for me like you are only out of favor?" I demanded, managing to keep my tone somewhat steady around my dry throat. "You repudiated me, IronMoon."

He ignored the accusation. "You decline to partake, Luna?"

I struggled, biting my lip so hard I tasted blood, and it

wasn't that carcass I was hungry for. The breeze pulled my robe around my ankles, lifting the light fabric teasingly.

But I couldn't show I had a matching Mark on my arm. Not yet. My voice shook. "You cannot expect to win me back with a buck."

He grinned. His teeth gleamed in the fiery dawn light. "Still so demanding. Does this trinket of my esteem insult you?"

He called a solo-killed buck a trinket. Now he was just fishing for compliments. If he couldn't get me to eat the liver in front of the pack, he'd get me to say something nice about him.

"Your gift is… well received," I said, turning away before I did something really stupid, like lunge for that liver and gulp it down, because it looked like the most tasty thing I'd seen in months. As I turned, I saw that a number of SableFur had come down to see what the songs were about. No surprise.

Gabel's grin widened into something distinctly feral, and his teeth seemed made of fire, and fire and shadows played through his hair. "I would always see you well-pleased, Luna."

If I didn't get out of here quickly, I was going to do something stupid, and Gabel stood there waiting for me to do just that, one hand hooked at the waistline of his kilt, ready to tear it off and welcome spring right there in front of the entire pack.

I could not tell the pack to help themselves to the raw kill. Too much risk they'd refuse to partake. I turned and left, ignoring how Gabel's presence within me laughed at my hasty exit, and retreated to the kitchen where Cook and his wolves were already at work.

"Gabel went hunting," I told Cook. "He brought back a buck."

"Solo?" Cook asked, brows raising.

"He had a busy night. He brought it back to me, but I'm

not going to eat a whole buck. Can you do something with it that the pack will eat?"

Cook grinned. He barked an order and shouted for one of the assistants to get a knife. "Of course, Luna. I can make anything the IronMoon Alpha cares to hunt palatable. It's only a matter of knowing how to season it."

I HEADED down the hallway to Gabel's room. He grabbed me the instant I opened the door. Pushed me against the wall, kissed me hungrily, and tore at my scarf.

"Yes," I breathed. He grabbed my thighs and hefted me over his hips, his cock rigid and already between my thighs, my core wet and begging for him.

He growled, deep and savage, and bit my shoulder. Hard. I clawed at his shoulders, raking deep trenches into him.

He carried me to the bed and dropped me onto it. His hands—broad, the nails sharp and whispering like knives against my skin—pulled me onto all fours, his claws whispering through my robe until it fell into ribbons to the sheets. He drew his hand—not quite human, not quite lupine—down my spine and I arched like a cat, rocking back against him, where his shaft brushed my body.

His grip closed over my hips, and his body filled mine with a swift, sure thrust.

I cried out, then buried my face in the blankets as he strained over me, and I didn't care, I didn't *know*, there was just him, and the Bond writhing in pleasure along with us, and I sobbed into the blankets because this was so, so, so foolish...

He growled deep in his throat and I mewled in response. Sharp nails grasped my hips, and I buried my face in the blankets as my body clenched around his and pleasure rippled and crashed over me like a wave.

He shuddered a second later, his claws pricking through the skin at my hips and piercing my haze with a salty pleasure. I shifted backwards so my spine was against his chest, and he stroked my body, his rough tongue against my throat as we shuddered on the same waves together, bodies still joined.

Then, gently, he laid me down, his body slipping out of mine, and disappeared a moment. He came back with a damp towel that he drew over the welts bitten into my shoulders, the rake marks into my hips, then swept back up between my thighs. I squirmed and swatted at him. He chuckled, then dabbed some more at the thin red lines he'd put into my hips.

"We're even now," I told him, pushing his hand down over the red line. His shoulders were still striped and pocked from the previous day.

"I will never do this again," he vowed, dabbing at the lines.

"I don't recall complaining," I said. One didn't go to the bed of the Dark Comet not having a particular taste or set of expectations. I let him minister to me in silence for as long as I dared. He curled up around me, his body cupping mine. "I can't stay."

"I know. Nor can I."

"I will show you my warriors. Then you will get out."

A chuckle. "I have served my purpose?"

"You were never invited to begin with, and you're causing me enough trouble." I clutched his strong wrist with one hand. My soul howled with happiness at having him close again, but the truth was: he had just shown up, and he was causing problems. A lot of them.

"Isn't it better that they know I didn't kill Anita?"

"I don't think it makes much of a difference." I sighed. Then I remembered Kiery's warning about SableFur being forced to look into the void. Gabel had just chewed away another one of their defenses. "You have to be patient with them."

"At what cost?" he growled. "I will deal with Adrianna and come for you at Beltane."

I untangled myself from him. There was no point arguing. I bent low and kissed him lightly. "Presentation in a few hours. Be at your most civilized."

RECOGNIZE THE DARK

"Are you *sure* you want to do this?" Lucas asked for the millionth time.

"Yes," I said, adjusting my sleeve a bit over my Mark. With Gabel and Flint close at hand, I wasn't too concerned about my immediate safety. "Unless you think it is the worst idea I've had in a while."

"Not the *worst*," Lucas said.

What a vote of confidence. "Thanks. So how far am I off track with these wolves?"

"So far off they aren't even sure which way to run at this point," Lucas said. He lowered his voice. "You fucked him, didn't you."

No point in denying it. "Several times. Why? Was I too loud? Can you still smell it?"

Lucas closed his eyes like a long-suffering parent. "You couldn't keep your panties on?"

I sighed at him now. "Stop being squeamish. I know you and Kiery have a good time."

"I am not some deranged marauding Alpha intent on becoming King."

"Well, there's that key difference, yes."

The late morning was sunny, but not especially warm. He wore just a kilt—a clean one—for the presentation, his various half-healed injuries on display, bruises faded to greenish-purple, but his body unbent and strong and in his prime. Lucas turned his attention to the lawn, eyes narrowed slightly against the glare, and asked in a barbed tone, "Do you and Gabel disagree on how to accomplish things, or do you just go along with his whims?"

I suppressed a laugh. "You must not get very good information here."

"I don't know what to believe and what not to believe when it comes to him. You're playing dangerous games. The instant he shows up you get into his bed even though you know getting caught riding his dick is a bad idea. Tell me it's my Luna doing those things, and not Gabel manipulating you. I know since mating with Kiery there's been a change. The stories about the Bond being alive are true. How much of him changed you? How much of you changed him?"

"I don't know," I admitted. I'd refused to let Gabel leave the RedWater wolves to die alone. I'd refused to fight over Gardenia. I'd refused to play his sick games with Anders. I'd refused to let him bully me from training, or tolerate his jealousy over Hix.

But I'd also been the one to order Gardenia thrown into the basement. Not once, but twice. I'd ordered her death and left her to die. I'd accepted Gabel's gift of Marcus' blood and then promptly gone off to bed with him. I'd refused to intercede when begged for mercy. I hadn't let Hix out of the SableFur dungeon. I could have killed myself and taken Gabel, the Moon's Destroyer, with me and freed the world of whatever darkness he brought.

I *could* shift into wolf-form and ask Ana to inject me with that pink drug she talked about, and my death would take

Gabel with it. Or at least his sanity, and that would make him easy prey for Adrianna.

I chose a middle of the road answer for Lucas. "It's within my power to stop all this. At least on the surface."

If I killed myself and took Gabel with me, the world would return, somewhat, to normal. IronMoon would dissolve back into a mindless pack of cretins. Adrianna would come to power. SableFur and the rest of the packs would be happy. The Moon's Dark Comet and his Balance-Keeper destroyed.

I'd berated Anita for not being the one to stop the darkness when she'd had the chance. I didn't think I could cut my arms while in a warm tub, but I could tell Ana to inject me, drift to sleep, and never wake up.

"Do you think about that option?" Lucas asked.

"Yes."

"So you don't trust him."

"It's not about trust. I'm just trying to figure out what the Moon wants from all of us and then making sure She gets it."

"It seems like there's no way out of where we're going," Lucas said. "Kiery's dreams..."

The scythe-Moon has fallen, and the Sun has set.

"Lucas, have you ever wondered if wolves entering one of our dark ages recognized the dark age as it arrived?" I pondered out loud.

Lucas gave me a horrified look. "I've never thought about it, and I'd rather not."

The Bond between Gabel and I shifted, dark and seething. I ducked my chin and looked back over my shoulder. "Gabel."

"Gianna," he rumbled, emerging onto the patio, wearing just a kilt, feet bare, and blue Mark on display.

"I wish you would wear a shirt," I said shortly. Someone was eventually going to figure out or at least speculate that blue-gloss tattoo was a Mark, especially since his skin sported deep, red marks from where I'd raked my fingernails. Way to start the gossiping and murmuring.

He smirked. "Are you afraid I may get too many admirers dressed as I am?"

Lucas snorted.

I didn't even dignify Gabel's comment with a response, which had probably been his plan. "Show us SableFur's warriors, First Beta."

Gabel came to stand next to me. "He does have the look of a First Beta. Does he have the mettle?"

"Yes," I said. Lucas just hadn't been cut down to the bone and stripped of his illusions. But when pressed, Lucas was blood and steel. "He was the one who called Magnes out, and would have challenged him to the death if I hadn't intervened. Lucas might growl and snarl, but when it's time to bite down, he does."

"I am not sure he and I will get along."

"I am sure this is not a conversation to have right now."

Lucas shouted for the wolves to line up. He'd gathered about fifty warriors for this. A mixture of prestigious warriors from in and near the heart and then issued hasty invitations from wolves farther out to rush down for presentation. The wolves lined up in ten rows, shoulder to shoulder, barefoot, in kilts of black, blue, dark gray, hair short or tightly bound.

A number of other packmembers stood around the perimeter or watched from windows. Flint emerged from the house, and stood off Gabel's left side, hands crossed in front of himself, and observed the proceedings.

Inspections were ceremonial. Jermain from my birthpack had always done them as a way to let the warriors present themselves to the pack, and make the pack feel safe, and the warriors proud.

It was also a way to assert dominance, because it was an

optimum time for the Alpha or Luna to be attacked. It sometimes could be punitive and a way for the Alpha to catalog all
the specific weaknesses they saw. In my case, I was showing a
visiting (and hostile) Alpha my warriors, and how fine and
strong they were, and how loyal. It also gave me a chance to
expose the warriors—a mix of prestigious and not-so-much—
to Lord-Alpha Gabel, the Moon's Dark Comet.

Lucas spun around—heedless of the mud—and said,
"Luna! Your warriors greet you!"

They howled the Luna's song. Not as enthusiastically as the
IronMoon, but it wasn't a completely half-hearted chorus and
someone didn't start coughing or burping along.

"Be careful," Gabel rumbled.

I walked to the far left corner of the ranks.

"Do not *move*," Lucas growled at all of the warriors. "You
will stand quietly for your Luna's inspection and be pleased she
flatters you with two seconds of her attention."

I walked down the outside of the first row. Their scents
were a mix of wary respect to disgust. They clenched all over
like they'd been stung by a mosquito and wanted to rip my
head off, or to charge right at Gabel, who had walked halfway
the distance between the patio and the warriors, watching all
of us with a predator's cruel eye.

I walked up the third row, right into the middle of it, and
Lucas seemed very far away.

I stopped, right in the center of the bodies, the farthest
point from safety I could have been. The wolf to my right
reeked of hostility, and his body twitched with the nervous
jumping strength of a warrior ready for a fight.

I moved forward enough that he did not have to turn his
neck to see me, and we could meet eye to eye, and I could *dare*
him to do it. He wanted to kill me. He wanted to kill me so
desperately the warriors around us shifted in anticipation, elic-
iting another growl from Lucas.

Kill me. Do it. Gabel will die too. You can save everyone.

My lips twitched, and I fought the urge to bare my teeth at him. He didn't deserve my growl. My heart thudded, and the blood pulsed through the still-delicate flesh on my fingers, and my Mark squirmed like a smoldering serpent.

Kill me. Do it. You can free all of SableFur right now. Prove to me you aren't the soft creature Gabel says the SableFur are.

He turned his head *just* enough to adjust his gaze to see the mark in my eye.

"Do it, wolf," Gabel said from where he stood. "Use your claws or bow your head."

The wolf snarled at Gabel. "I do not answer to you, IronMoon!"

"She is standing there waiting for you to act, if you did not notice. You will have to be a little bolder if you want Luna-Oracle Gianna to take you seriously," Gabel said, a cruel smile on his lips.

Any remaining defiance evaporated and got replaced with something between sullen resignation and pure shame.

Coward. Wanted to bitch and moan, but when given a chance to be a hero, kept his claws behind his back and shoved up his ass.

I finished my inspection and returned to stand by Lucas. I pretended to survey the ranks once more. "Thank you, First Beta. You are well-represented."

He bowed deeply. "Thank you, Luna. Wolves! Your Luna has found you satisfactory. We shall improve on that!"

Howls of approval, mixed with half-hearted howls of *yay*.

Lucas dismissed them, then joined me for the walk back. "That almost went badly."

"He wasn't as brave as he thought," I said.

"How did you know he wouldn't attack?"

I laughed. "I didn't."

Lucas' eyes bugged out.

"I had to," I told him. "If a Luna can't stand eye to eye with one of her warriors, she will not be standing long."

DO NOT COME BACK

"Well done," Flint told me.

Gabel smiled, his eyes dark and smoldering, his scent ash and arousal. "You are so fierce. I am jealous he got to feel the lash of your claws."

Lucas coughed. "You've felt the lash of her claws enough recently."

Gabel rubbed his hand over the clawmarks raked into his bronzed shoulders. "What is *enough*, First Beta? Perhaps you could clarify that for me."

"It's time for you to go," I told Gabel.

"We should return to the front," Flint said.

Gabel tried to step towards me. Lucas shoved his arm between us and growled.

Gabel snarled at him.

Lucas snarled back. "*No.*"

"Get out of my way," Gabel hissed.

"I am *your* First Beta," Lucas whisper-hissed. "And I'm telling you not to be an idiot! No kisses goodbye. You've fucked her enough."

"If by enough you mean *twice*, which is hardly *enough*," Gabel retorted.

"It's enough for now," Flint said.

Lucas grabbed Gabel by the arm and gestured for him to precede him into the house. "After you, IronMoon."

Gabel permitted himself to be herded through the house and out the front door where Bernhard had deposited the two small bags Gabel and Flint had come with. Ana was also with him, as was Kiery.

His body was pocked with new bruises and scars and half-healed wounds, including the scratches I'd gifted him.

I wanted to hate him. I *did* hate him for showing up and dragging Anita in front of the pack and showing his blue-gloss Mark.

I also loved him so much my heart broke at the thought of him leaving once more.

"Oracle," Gabel greeted Kiery. "Ana."

Ana raised her teacup to him with one hand and flipped him the finger with the other.

"It's time for you to go," Lucas told Gabel. "We have been more than gracious."

Gabel paced closer. He didn't try to touch me. Our Marked arms brushed.

I grabbed him by the throat.

"My Luna," he rasped, the scent of desire and lust and pleasure blooming off him. "You do still love me."

"Listen to me, Gabel of IronMoon," I told him, squeezing hard on his windpipe, *so* hard, as hard as I could, snarling, anger lashing through the Bond, "You will be a proper instrument of divine wrath. You want pups. I do not need to nursemaid you as well. You will be *patient*."

"Understood," he wheezed.

"I hate you," I whispered to him. "I hate you *so* much, I hate when you are a petty, spoiled tyrant! I love Gabel of Iron-

Moon, the Moon's Dark Comet, the Destroyer. I hate Gabel the Bastard."

"How fortunate I am the Moon's Dark Comet."

"I will castrate Gabel the Bastard if I ever see him again," I said.

"I do not believe he will be back," Gabel rasped.

"Make *certain*," I shoved my thumb into his windpipe, "I never see that pathetic excuse for a male again. He offends me."

Gabel grinned. "You need not suffer any male who offends you."

I released him.

He dusted himself off. "What have I told you about that temper?"

"That it arouses you." I flicked a finger at the evidence under his kilt. Bernhard coughed and looked away. Lucas groaned and rolled his eyes. Ana and Kiery snickered at each other.

Flint headed off down the stairs to the drive, his small bag over his shoulders.

Gabel picked up his own bag and walked after the Master of Arms.

I watched until they disappeared.

GABEL: JUDGEMENT

Gabel shifted the bag over his shoulder. The road split here, and they'd moved off to a cluster of trees. To the north was the front, and to the east, the way back to IronMoon. "Going with me, or headed back to the heart, old man?"

Flint inclined his head towards Gabel. "East. I will stop to check with Second Beta Eroth on my way. Your forces are fragmented and your attentions divided. Losing Hix has diminished the pack more than you realize."

"I realize what has been lost," Gabel replied. He knew better than to ask Flint to get involved on the battlefield—the old wolf had made it clear he wasn't there to fight battles for him, or to save him from his mistakes. Flint taught him how to fight battles, and Flint pointed out his mistakes. "It was also his choice, and his life was well spent. No death I could have given him would equal the honor of the death he received in Gianna's service. I'm not going to grieve for him."

The weak sunlight glanced off Flint's blue-gloss tattoos, sending the ink twisting like a snake in shallow water. "You are closer to victory than you've ever been before. Closer to

achieving your goal. She will make you, according to many,
King-Alpha."

The goal was so, so close now. His father had overplayed,
and the Moon had all but handed him the crown to SableFur
through Gianna. A year ago he had expected a long, bitter
bloody war gnawing flesh off SableFur's bones, but now? Now
he had a birthright claim, and his mate sat on the throne.

"But you are also closer to defeat than you have ever been,"
Flint added. "Gianna senses how the future is on a knife's edge.
How it tilts and sways to the slightest breeze. You would do
well to heed her."

"I was respectful," Gabel said. "I was *perfectly* polite."

"You took risks," Flint said sharply. "You brought her prey.
You made it obvious to SableFur that you intend to have her
back. You forced her to dance between two points."

"She is mine, and I do intend to have her back, and my
birthright," Gabel said, just as sharply.

"Has it occurred to you that the Moon gave you the Mark
you have now so that wolves would not instantly know it was a
Mark?" Flint retorted. "Yes, time is short, risks must be taken,
but careful risks. You stormed into your mate's den uninvited.
She tolerated you."

"She did more than *tolerate* me."

"The Bond calls souls together." Flint dismissed it with an
abrupt gesture. "That is her den, not yours. Who cares if she
took a male she found attractive to her bed to pleasure her? It
does not make him her mate."

"And you always told me it was a stupid Alpha who had his
dalliances."

"I did not say it was *wise*, but it would be no more than
house gossip. It is her den, and if she wishes to bed males, that
is her business. It is not yours to show up to her den uninvited.
You took liberties. You declared your love for her. You brought
her prey. You *courted* her. You forced her to respond as your

consort, not a Luna speaking to an Alpha. She will have questions to answer now. And for what? Your impatience. Your belief you are *owed*. You have learned *nothing*."

Gabel clenched his teeth, annoyed. "She is my *mate*. How long would it be before SableFur saw the matching Mark on her arm and did some simple math?"

"How readily a mind in denial will ignore the ugly truth in favor of an appealing lie. Your father was destroyed by starlight wolves, but many wolves refuse to believe Adrianna had anything to do with it. They'd rather believe *you* killed the Oracles than consider Adrianna—who has every reason and opportunity—did it." Flint's tone hardened and impatience crept through his stoic calm. "You believe a clever story about redemption couldn't be told for your arms? That you two are yoked together by destiny, but nothing more save she choose it? Your mate is alone in her den, with few true allies, and you have left her to manage it *and* increased the danger and difficulty."

"What have I done?" Gabel demanded. "I brought proof of my innocence, I brought her a buck, *she* came to *my* room for pleasure."

"You dragged a corpse to *her* den. You were in *her* den and she came to your room to make use of you," Flint retorted, tone harsh. "You did not need to bring her the buck. You were just showing off."

Gabel scoffed. "She made it *very* clear why she'd come to me. Of course I brought my estranged mate a gift."

"And she would have *much* preferred you be at dinner showing off the table manners I spent many years convincing you have value. That is *exactly* the situation they would have been more valuable than a buck she could not possibly eat. Enough talk. We are both needed elsewhere, and I've known you long enough to know you need time to reflect on what I've said. Time will prove me out."

"You want to ignore the fact that she came to my room. Twice. Just like those SableFur want to ignore the truth."

Flint flicked jungle-green eyes in his direction. "I never ignore anything you say. I am telling you that you could have done more, and done better, and done *wiser*. She loves you, despite all your hideous flaws and the pain you've caused her. Do not confuse meeting the minimum standard with doing well. You set the bar *very* low in the beginning."

Gabel shifted the straps of his bags across his shoulders and twisted into wolf-form. Flint's scent, the scent of the trees and grass and road and humans rushed to him. Flint struck off towards the east, his scent *Flint*, but nothing else.

Flint never smelled of anything *but* Flint. Gabel slicked his ears against his skull and watched the old wolf walk down the road, thumb out. No clues about what Flint was really thinking. A closed book without any text on the cover.

And Flint, more often than not, did eventually prove to be correct. But not always.

Gabel headed out down the shoulder of the road. An hour later he was able to jump into the covered bed of a north-bound truck, then another, and another, hopscotching his way towards the rural north. Not the most direct route, but effective, and safe from getting bothered by SableFur.

This waiting game annoyed him. Gianna held him at arm's length, not trusting her ability to keep hold of SableFur if they knew about him. She should be more confident. She had looked every inch a queen inspecting her warriors, her dark hair shining in the weak sunlight, and the way she'd stared down that one overly ambitious warrior… he clicked his teeth with appreciation. So fierce. So reckless. Some of those warriors despised her, but none were brave enough to act against her. She didn't see it that way.

And he did not like Bernhard. The Second Beta did not smell right. He approved of Lucas. Bernhard? Bernhard was going to meet Eroth, and they would see who would be Second when it was over.

Gabel grinned to himself as he bounced down off the bed of the last truck and darted into the woods by the rural road. From here it'd be his own paws taking him back to his wolves.

The memories of moving through the woods alone gnawed at the back of his brain. The cold sense of violence and emptiness, the *nothing* of being alone out here. His senses sharpened and the familiar *clench* of an invisible hand squeezing him started. His legs lengthened from a jog to a run, carrying him swiftly across the semi-familiar terrain as the unspecific storm in the back of his mind, in a place far and long from here and a prey that had eluded him, drove him back to his pack.

The scent of death intruded on his run.

He slowed. Death and blood clouded his snout, and something familiar. Something that said *IronMoon*.

The scent led him to a battered, broken body laying in the shadow of an old tree.

One of his wolves. One of his scouts. Gabel sniffed his ears. The scout was still alive.

"*Alpha,*" the wolf keened softly. Blood drained from bite wounds on his belly and throat, and the bite wounds on his belly were deep, and a few swollen pink loops pushed through the holes. "*I... tried...*"

"*Tried what?*" Gabel asked, sniffing carefully. The scent and saliva of unfamiliar wolves on the scout. The scout was going to die, there was no saving him. A war-form had done this. Several war-forms.

The scout was too weak to answer.

Another memory passed through his brain, but this one of a damp forest and a she-wolf shouting at him what a terrible Alpha he was, and refusing to heed him. Her silvery-blue pelt overlaid with the one from a deeper memory of blood and ruin.

Gabel's jaw snapped outward, and he bit down on the dying scout's throat without hesitation. Blood bloomed against his senses. He couldn't wait with the scout for death, but he could do that much.

He bolted, running hard, and his ears rang with howls not his own: *retreat. Retreat!*

IronMoon howls. He knew that voice and that song.

And another song: victory, victory in a female's voice, howling the Luna's song of victory.

Adrianna.

The scent of blood and death and panic led him into carnage. Dead wolves. So many dead wolves.

A wolf slammed into him.

He snarled, body shifting into his war-form, and he grabbed the wolf-form with one claw and flung it against a tree. *Crack*, and a horrible *yelp!* He dropped the body like a rag. He charged, stabbing claws into bellies and ripping entrails out, then bit through another's skull.

The SableFur overran the field he was on. His wolves scattered through the forests, their songs and yips of fear and defeat echoing over the trees and sending birds fleeing. More wolves came over the hills and through the trees.

And one stepped onto a ridge, peering down at him. A large, silvery-black female with a Seer's distinctive sheen. She had a huge bald patch on her shoulder, her strong frame glorious and beautiful, and pure hatred burning in her piercing ice-blue eyes.

Adrianna.

She pulled her lips back over large, gleaming fangs, grinning at him. Then she threw her head back and sang the Luna's song for the glory of her warriors, and the weakness of her enemy.

"Kill them! Hunt them and kill them all!" she howled, her song tinged with madness and grief.

The horde of SableFur wolves crashed through the trees towards him. Gabel snarled to himself, dropping back into wolf-form.

Hai hai hai! The SableFur sang the song of war. *Hai hai hai!*

No choice but to retreat and regroup. Violence told him to stay and fight to the last bloody shred, but that'd play into the bitch's maw. She dared him to, luring him closer with her howl.

He whirled and broke free of his mind and pride. *"To me!"* he howled the unfamiliar cry, hatred and fury broiling every nerve and instinct. *"Your Alpha summons you!"*

Adrianna's howl sailed over his, "*Hunt! Kill! Hunt!*"

Gabel fled deep into the forest to find what was left of his army.

WITHOUT PITY

I skimmed through the long list of names Cook had given me. All these wolves would be at Beltane. Just rows of names that meant nothing. I wandered upstairs to my office to memorize the region names with the wolf names so I'd at least know what corner of SableFur everyone hailed from, not that I actually expected I'd remember anything.

"Should remember the local leader names," I muttered to myself. Francis, of course, was on the list. "I wonder if you'll show up, Francis."

Someone burst through the front door on the lower level. "Luna!"

Oh hell, what was on fire now?

A warrior I didn't recognize bounded up the stairs towards my office, with Lucas hot on his heels. The First Beta grabbed him and hauled him to a stop, nearly throwing him down the stairs in the process.

"What is it?" Lucas growled at the wolf.

"The IronMoon," the warrior panted, slumping forward on his knees. He was filthy and splattered and had come running from the Moon Herself it looked like.

"What about the IronMoon?" I asked. Gabel and Flint had left a few days earlier. There couldn't be *that* much commotion already. Although this was Gabel, so who knew.

He drew a huge breath. "They've been defeated."

I stiffened. *Defeated?* "What? Where? How? When?"

"Yesterday," the wolf said. "Yesterday evening. Adrianna's forces routed them."

I growled. This wolf wasn't giving me the right information. "To where? How many losses? Did the IronMoon *surrender?*"

"No, just a retreat…" He waved his hands, still gasping. "Halfway between their old position and Francis' position. Unknown casualties, but it sounded bloody."

Still useless information! That told me nothing about what was going on in the north! "Lucas, translate for me."

Lucas walked over to the map and pointed out where Gabel's forces had been routed against Adrianna. "Here. As best we can tell, while Gabel and Flint were here, a less-than-capable commander was in charge. Gabel made it back just in time to round up his forces and fall back to an unknown position. We believe he's fallen back to about here."

Lucas indicated a position significantly different. Gabel had previously had Adrianna's forces pressed west of Anita's cottage, and now Adrianna had pushed him back thirty miles east. Adrianna had a far easier route to the heart.

"He snatched total defeat from Adrianna, so I'm sure she's furious about it. I'm sure Gabel is bringing up more forces from his basecamp to reinforce his forward position, but Adrianna won't miss the next time she strikes."

Finally, a damned translation. Even if the news was devastating. "She waited until his back was turned to attack."

"It's what I'd do," Lucas said. "If I thought Gabel was the only competent battlefield commander? She must have had eyes on him for weeks. She has him pinned down now. She knows his weakness. IronMoon's a serpent, not a hydra."

"Hell," I cursed. Now Gabel was pinned down north of here until Adrianna was dead.

Lucas told the scout, "Send more scouts to the north to keep an eye on it. Luna, I'm sending some warriors to the north to make sure the hamlets up there aren't dragged into this. It seems a fair number of SableFur don't care who is the Luna as long as it doesn't affect them one way or the other."

Reluctantly, I nodded.

"What do you think Gabel will do?" Lucas asked.

Oh, that was *easy*. "Regroup and make her pay for it."

"Spring's here, we should expect this. The fighting will get more intense now that everything has thawed," Lucas said.

Gabel getting routed by Adrianna threw a wrinkle in the fragile, half-formed plans I had. IronMoon had wolves who could be trusted to front skirmishes and raiding parties. Splash-and-dash violence. Competent battlefield commanders up to dealing with SableFur were in short supply. Gabel had personally led every major offensive he'd been in since I'd known him, and I'd never heard of him doing otherwise.

Adrianna had the advantage, and she was going to press it. Gabel wouldn't be able to take his eye off her for a second, or he risked losing everything, including his head, as Aaron would say. And with the spies in SableFur's heart Adrianna would know within hours if Gabel wasn't in command.

Lucas said, "We need to make some alternate plans for Beltane. If I was Adrianna, I'd attack knowing the entire pack was distracted, especially if half the guests were loyal to me."

SOMEONE KNOCKED on the door to my office. Lucas snapped, "What?"

How did anyone get anything done? I was constantly interrupted.

"Alpha Aaron is here to see Luna Gianna," the wolf said in a small voice.

"What is that wolf doing here?" Lucas demanded. He twisted around to face me. "Did you summon him here?"

"Of course not."

"He's like a damn cat just showing up whenever it pleases him. Tell him to get lost," Lucas said.

"No," I snapped. I couldn't afford to piss Aaron off and the damn wolf knew it.

"You don't have to humor him just showing up," Lucas said indignantly. "You're the Luna of SableFur. He can't just march in here whenever he wants to."

I gestured to the wolf at the door to close it. Once closed, I told Lucas, "We'll finish this conversation in the morning. It's getting late, and if Aaron's here, I should see him."

"Why?"

"It's complicated."

"It's also not a good idea."

"Your mate was the one who told me I needed to stop catering to *my* mate's jealousy."

"This isn't jealousy, it's fucking rude."

"There's some Oracle business mixed up in this. Aaron has a part to play," I said.

"You mean that dream Kiery had about him with the rune on his arm?"

"*Instrument.* He's playing a part in this, Lucas. He's been in my visions and dreams since the first time I scryed for Gabel. Go on, it's late and Kiery hasn't seen you today."

Lucas grumbled about this being a bad idea and Aaron being a rude, entitled asshole, but he got up and went to fetch the IceMaw Alpha.

The wolf was alone, and dressed once again in a kilt, this

time with a small leather bag strung around his hips. Combat
kit. As if I needed more reminders that SableFur was about to
catch on fire.

He walked into my office and took up a place right in front
of my desk. Then he sniffed the air, and after a too-long
moment, asked, "Is it true?"

He could be asking for confirmation on so many things.
"You'll have to be more specific."

Aaron said, "Gabel was here a few days ago. I hear he has
a blue-gloss tattoo where his Mark once was."

My heart started to thump. I managed to stay composed,
but Aaron could smell the shift in my scent. "You heard
correctly."

"And he brought you a kill. A buck."

"The pack ate it."

"I can still smell your lure-scent," he said. "It's so thick in
this room I can smell nothing else except it. But I'm told you
have a Mark. You have a matching Mark to Gabel's. Blue-
gloss."

"Who told you that?" I asked sharply.

"Is it true?"

I stood and pulled my sweater over my head. My blue-gloss
Mark laid bare against my upper arm, limned in ice blue.

Aaron stared at it, face frozen and body stiff.

I had never promised Aaron anything, but my heart still
broke for him. I didn't have an answer for why the Moon
tortured him. "Are you sure it's my lure-scent you smell? It's
impossible."

Aaron stared at me, shifting like a chunk of cold, frozen
earth. "You don't have to apologize, Gianna. You told me from
the beginning the nature of things. I'm the one who led myself
to believe there was hope it would not come to this."

My ribcage hummed like a tuning fork, my heart and even
the Bond twisted, and my Mark burned like a hot bruise, and

my instincts howled at how wrong all of this was. It wasn't right. I moved my tongue to try to form some words that weren't a bunch of useless platitudes, and ended up with, "I don't believe the Moon is punishing you. You did exactly what you were supposed to do. The Moon sent Gabel *because* there aren't wolves like you!"

A bitter smile. "You flatter me. But perhaps I *was* in the wrong about everything I've done."

He shrugged, and his left shoulder made a terrible cricking sound. Pain flickered over his face. He said, "In my own mind, I am just a wolf. I have no ambition beyond staying Alpha, and making certain my pack never kneels to your mate, or anyone else. Unfortunately, that will ultimately place you and I at odds."

"So it would seem," I agreed.

"I didn't come here to offer you my help, or an allegiance. I came here to see if it was true you're Gabel's mate. I see it's true. In the morning we will meet again under terrible circumstances."

"Are you going to ally yourself with Adrianna?"

"I am not inclined to tell you anything of my plans, Luna."

"I'll take that as a declaration of hostilities."

"I'd prefer to keep the hostilities to a minimum. Take it as a declaration of I'll do what must be done. I'll call no wolf King. That should tell you all you need to know about my plans."

Aaron deserved so much better than this. "For what it's worth, Aaron, the Moon isn't punishing you. Kiery and I have both seen a Mark carved into your arm. It is an ancient rune meaning *instrument*. The Moon is using you."

He stood quite close. Too close. I refused to back up a step. He bent closer, and said, scent a confusing swirl of violence and grief and resolve, "Thank you."

"For what?"

"Not pitying me," he said.

I laughed. "If there's one thing you don't need, it's pity."

"Then I will definitely need forgiveness."

Aaron moved faster than I could blink. A split second later and he was behind me, my neck in the crook of his elbow, crushing my windpipe. I clawed, couldn't scream, gasp, anything. Within seconds my brain swam red, choking, dying, and a searing pain stabbed into my left thigh.

I knew nothing else.

BOG, RIVER, THICKET : REDUX

I woke up in a bedroom the color of dawn fog, where the brightest color was the white of the linens and shaggy rug, and the brilliant green expanse of lawn unfurled beyond its massive windows.

Where the fuck *was* I?

The angle of the sun told me I was far from where I'd started. I was in the south.

"Aaron," I snarled. He'd brought me to IceMaw!

How had he managed that? Had he just waltzed out of SableFur with me slung over his shoulder?

I threw off my blankets. I had on a *nightdress*. Who the hell had changed my clothes? Who had seen my Mark? For fuck's sake. I tore through the room looking for anything I recognized, but there was nothing. Clothes, sure. Towels, toiletries, everything beautiful and tasteful, but nothing of *mine*.

I grabbed some clothes and yanked open the door, half-expecting to see some new Aaron-assigned goons. Nope. Just a vacant hallway of pale paneled wood and more pale paint colors opening up onto a massive central hub that seemed filled with sunlight.

The house, though, was not silent. It buzzed with the movement of bodies, and even this empty hallway carried many scents.

Cautiously, I headed down the hallway, which presented me with a staircase down to a bottom floor, and more hallways. Aaron's scent was here, mingled with the others, none of which I knew. I descended the stairs and followed the noise, which led me out the back of the house and to a wolf working in some flowerbeds. It was warmer here than in SableFur.

The back of the house opened up onto a huge spread of greenery dotted with a large, still lake, and edged with forest far in the distance. Hanging low over the treeline was a line of clouds. It'd be overcast by nightfall. The ground sloped away to the left, dipping down and around. I glanced up to the top of the house. It was a large mansion sort of affair (no surprise) with small towers built onto each corner like crows' nests on the masts of old tall ships. Each of the four perches had a warrior on it, and the position probably afforded them an excellent line of sight for many miles.

No where to run. The sentries would spot my pale wolf-form crossing the sea of bright, groomed green grass instantly. No doubt Aaron had many more sentries and scouts on the ground if he was so paranoid he had four perched on his roof like furry gargoyles.

"Luna Gianna. Good morning!" The gardener seemed startled to see me, but only in the *I didn't see you there* way, not the *oh shit, what are you doing here* way. I hadn't been shackled to my bed or gnawed my way around a barred door, but his almost non-reaction bewildered me. He didn't seem *shocked*, just surprised I'd even looked at him.

"Where is Alpha Aaron?" I demanded.

He flushed and smelled of awkward embarrassment. Again, not the reaction of a wolf talking to a prisoner, just a guest who shouldn't be lost. The wolf pointed down a well-worn path that followed the dip of the earth on the left. "Training, Luna. I can—"

"I will find him myself, thank you," I said, setting off down the path with bare feet.

The path led me down and around the hillside's rolling slope. The manicured green grass extended like a carpet, with multiple groomed paths leading in various directions, and clusters of flowers and obvious landscaping and features tastefully arranged everywhere. Far different from the wild encroachment of IronMoon, or the rustic shape of SableFur. The treeline had been cut back very far to create a vast groomed perimeter around the main house.

"Nobody gets in or out under cover," I muttered to myself. Shadowless had been the same way: the main house plunked down in a large space with no brush or natural cover.

It wasn't of interest to me except it made my chance of escape just about zero. Not that they were very good to begin with. Aaron's Hunters would have found me within a day. Still, this was all *very* groomed. SableFur and IronMoon had been far from human civilization and even busy roads. Where was IceMaw's heart? Was a main road nearby?

Just when I got confused as to which path to take I heard the sound of training: bodies impacting, shouts, growls, snarls. They were downwind of me. Even if Aaron wasn't with the warriors, they'd point me in his general direction.

"Wait," I said, stopping dead in the center of the sand path. Ahead of me in the distance was the treeline, behind me, the house, to my right, the front of a spring storm sat on the horizon, drifting lazily towards us, and on the left, Aaron.

If I followed this path—which forked in three directions— to the trees, would I find a bog, a river, and a thicket?

I twisted around, fully expecting to see an old female warrior with a damaged eye shouting at me about getting below with everyone else.

Coincidence? Maybe.

The end of the path would have to wait. I wasn't about to turn into one of those Oracles who started seeing her dreams reflected in every waking moment. I had enough of those problems, I didn't need to borrow more just because it happened to rain in spring.

The IceMaw training rings were similar to IronMoon, save there was no Flint supervising. There was a warrior dressed in a kilt shouting encouragement and corrections to the two war-forms grappling in the sand ring. I paid it only a little attention because I spied who I was really there for: Aaron. Dressed in a kilt, shining with sweat, his hair soaked with it, and sand stuck to various parts of his body, and a few trickles of blood and rising bruises.

"Luna Gianna," Aaron greeted me, raising his voice just enough it would carry to me as I approached, and instantly the warriors in the sand ring froze, and in unison they swept low into half-bows.

"Alpha Aaron," I returned in kind, trying not to sound too pissed off at him.

"I imagine you have an interest in warriors and war." Aaron gestured to his warriors.

They all gathered themselves with pride, and all were a good-looking, no-apologies bunch. A few gave me feral grins, pretty damn pleased with themselves and having their prowess on display for a Luna.

This was just weird. Why the fuck were they so damn happy to see me? What lies had Aaron told them?

"A necessary curiosity." I glanced at the warriors again, then back at Aaron, who had a smug look in his eyes that made me want to bite his throat. He was going to force me to compli-ment his warriors. Well, fine, then. Credit where credit was due, and if even one IronMoon died at their claws, devaluing an IceMaw devalued an IronMoon. It didn't make for good story-telling if the story was *and then our pathetic opponent was easily bested, two of ours died, and we went home. The end.*

"A fine assortment," I said. "Are they all yours?"

Aaron chuckled. "All IceMaw, although some of my allies come through from time to time."

His southern allies. "Shall I call you Lord-Alpha then?"

Annoyance flickered on his face, but his warriors grinned approval and made little noises of excitement and thrill. Aaron's flicker turned into a mild scowl, and I smirked at him.

A little too close to Gabel. He hated it.

Well, that's what he got for abducting me.

He didn't reject the title. I wondered what his southern allies would think about that once it got back to them. Aaron nodded to his warriors. "I'll return later."

Without a word he gestured for me to precede him back up the path. It would have been a nice garden stroll if not for the fact it was with my abductor.

"A *nightdress*?" I asked darkly, just to make conversation that wasn't *what the fuck are you doing?* It'd been a hideous nightdress too, complete with ruffle laced collar.

"I needed to keep your arm covered."

And probably put me in the least sexy thing he could have thought of. There was a potent visual for him: me in a night-dress a granny wouldn't have wanted to wear. "So you *haven't* announced to IceMaw what I am."

"No. Do not worry, I did not take any liberties with your body."

"Your restraint is commendable," I said dryly. "How did you explain this to the wolves who were with you?"

"I took my two most trusted retainers with me. They do not know about your arm. They do know I brought you here without your consent," Aaron said, hands clasped behind his back, walking with a very slight limp.

"And that you're up to no good."

"That is somewhat implied by the circumstances of your arrival."

"So not even your First Beta knows."

"I did not say that. My most trusted wolves know about your arm. My *pack* does not."

"So why don't your retainers know?"

"I am limiting how many wolves I burden with certain knowledge," Aaron said like it was nothing. "It's not an issue of trust. It is an issue of burdening wolves with keeping secrets."

How noble. "So how did you get me out of SableFur?"

"An issue of trust on your side," Aaron said with a feral grin.

"Who sold me to you?" I demanded.

"Bernhard."

"*Bernhard?*" I exclaimed.

Aaron shrugged, and I wanted to smack that toothy grin of his off his face, but not before I dumped him in a vat of lye to scrub that smug stench off him.

So *Bernhard* had been his spy. Couldn't say I was completely surprised—which sickened me—and it explained how Aaron had gotten me out of SableFur with minimal fuss. "How long have you had Bernhard in your pocket?"

"He's never been in my pocket," Aaron corrected. "I recruited Bernhard about a year ago, when I saw Gabel's threat growing and SableFur unwilling to stop him. Bernhard and Lucas were similarly disgusted. Lucas is too principled to think of whispering anything to anyone, but Bernhard grasped that I was the one willing to do something, so he'd pass me Gabel-related information. He held out for some time, weighing if he should tell me about your Mark or not. Gabel showing up was too much for him to endure. Nothing like getting a look at the future to know you want no part in it, hmm, Oracle?"

"So he'd rather Adrianna? The coward."

"He'd rather neither of you. If you ask me, I think Bernhard thinks he's Alpha material. He's not, but that's not my problem."

"What is with Second Betas being slime," I said, disgusted. "First Romero, now Bernhard."

"Common problem with Seconds," Aaron said sagely. "Always keep an eye on a Second that isn't happy in his position. A First is never happy with his Alpha."

I laughed humorlessly.

We returned to the house. He guided me through the snakework of hallways. The entire house, as far as I could tell, was the same pale, spartan style of my bedroom. Especially his office, which was large, and had open floor-to-ceiling windows all around it, and almost nothing in it except a single woven rug and desk and chair. He didn't even have a map. A white porch wrapped around the entire office's exterior, accessible by a sliding door to his right decorated with a single white silk cord tied with engraved brass bells.

At first I was impressed by the glorious view, then it dawned on me this wasn't something he'd hired a designer to come up with.

This was pure paranoia.

There wasn't anything here that could be shattered and used as a weapon except the desk and chair. No map spies could glimpse. The glass gave him an unobstructed view, access to three sides of the house from the porch, and bells to jangle if anyone tried to come in from the outside.

Gabel's office had been books, old weapons, armor, furniture, and massive windows on one side, yes, but not really useful as a sentry outpost.

IceMaw's ascetic was not *simple*, it was *unencumbered*.

Gabel didn't like windows in our bedroom. They worried him. Too many points of entry. Aaron had the exact opposite approach.

"Not what you expected?" Aaron asked.

I hadn't expected anything because I didn't care. "I've played along with your game long enough."

"I informed your precious SableFur that you decided to accept my invitation to IceMaw to discuss politics of a more personal nature," Aaron said, a smile lurking on his lips. "That's going to give any revolution a pause, and the handful of SableFur who know the truth about your personal situation aren't going to say a single thing to counter me. Gabel will howl about his mate, and he will sound like a madman, and I know you will keep your arm quite covered."

A more *personal nature*. I curled my lip. "And you don't think Gabel is going to come looking for me."

Aaron chuckled. "No, he won't. He's trapped where he is."

"I don't know what lousy spies you're using, but Gabel is not trapped."

"But he *is*." Aaron's handsome face shifted into a bright, much too sane grin.

"How?" I asked. If anyone could trap Gabel, it would be Aaron.

"He ceded all the land south of Gleaming Fang to me to enact our little farce for Magnes," Aaron said pleasantly. "He *could* leave SableFur, and give up all the ground he's gained against Adrianna, and then come for me around the mountains via the southern route. The instant his back is turned, Adrianna burns her way south and takes back the heart."

Aaron walked over to one of the walls, slid a door to the side, and revealed a small sink and wetbar. He splashed water on his hands, and over his shoulders. It cut paths through the grime on his body. "Gabel will stay in SableFur and pursue the war. He knows I won't harm you, and the price of repossessing you is more than he cares to pay. Once more *you* will pay the price for his ambitions."

I snarled at him. "Monster."

"How am I any different from him in this moment, save I didn't brutalize your soul and degrade you? Or are you going to tell me *it just is*?" Aaron drew a damp towel behind his neck and sighed, shifting slightly to favor the pain in his spine, fully aware of the monster he was.

Gabel had been like a wild animal: insane, arrogant, careless, cavalier, cocky, revolting. Coarse and grown blunt and dull from years of hanging out with the likes of Romero and grown slovenly on easy victories.

Aaron was sharp, honed to a cruel edge.

He'd played all of us. He'd even preyed on Gabel in Gabel's weakest, most broken moments when his mind was twisted from grief. He'd betrayed my trust and played me for an idiot.

Aaron left the clump of towel on the marble bar. "This is about a crown no one should wear. Not Gabel, not Adrianna, and not even you. The reigns of the King-Alphas always rose from death and burning, and they always ended in death and burning."

I said nothing.

"You don't want that crown either," Aaron said.

"Don't you dare act like you're doing me a favor," I snapped.

"Merely pointing out the obvious. You are my guest here in IceMaw, a visiting Luna. You can behave that way, or you can let them know the truth."

Mild words said in a mild tone, but there was an air of something unsaid in his words, a pause that implied he wanted to say more, but didn't. "How long are you keeping me here?"

An arrogant shrug. "Uncertain. I need to observe how things up north go. I don't suggest you run. You won't get far, and it'd be very embarrassing when someone finds you. Gabel does know where you are. I've already informed him myself."

This Alpha's arrogance never failed to astonish. "And how furious was he?"

Aaron laughed. "Exceedingly. I assured him I'd be a perfect host to the Luna of SableFur-IronMoon. He did tell me that you were his future Queen, and the last thing I would ever do with my life would be to kiss your toes before he ripped my broken spine out of my bent body."

"Sounds right," I said.

Aaron swept low, his face terrifyingly close to me, and his scent of power and prestige sinking into my nose and even against my skin. He inhaled my scent, then said in a low, rough tone, "So I told him I'd rip out your spine before I ever let him set a crown upon your head."

Charming.

Aaron pulled back, straightened, and one of his joints popped audibly. "I hope it doesn't come to that. You're the only hope I have for the future."

EVIL OVERLORD LOVE PALACE

A aron hadn't taken me to IceMaw's heart. IceMaw was large enough (and old enough, as far as packs went) that I was at a secondary holding several hours further south. The heart itself housed a number of IceMaw, but Aaron's seat of power was in this place.

"Come," he said, "my senior members are ready to greet you formally."

"What?" I asked. I did not want to get presented to the pack. That idea could fuck off.

"Since you weren't available for it last night," he said.

"Oh, since you mean how you *abducted* me and carried me in while I was sedated?" I asked darkly.

A smile, and he went to the door to hold it open. "The hour *was* late. After you, Luna."

Fuck, was I going to have to keep up this farce that I was here for "personal" negotiations?

Same game Gabel had played. Different circumstances. But the same game. This time with an opponent who had done it for a very specific reason, and not a rash impulse. Aaron had come into this fully prepared, and like Adrianna, he had nothing left to lose.

"So why do you rule from here?" I asked as we walked down the pale, paneled hallway.

"Bad memories. IceMaw's heart has been there for a hundred years, but I refuse to rule from it. It is just a place and I am not sentimental."

If he had been sentimental, he wouldn't have been able to kill his family. "Spring is coming. Beltane. Even if I chose to celebrate it down here with you, my Mark will still be on display with yours conspicuously absent."

"Who is to say what any given wolf sees on an Oracle's pelt in the light of fire and Moon?" Aaron gestured airily.

I suppressed a smirk. He didn't know what to do come Beltane. He was on as much a timetable as the rest of us. I'd play along with being Aaron's prisoner-guest until I figured out how to get out of here.

"Honestly, Aaron, I never thought *you'd* deal in abduction," I said, mildly disappointed.

"I deal in familicide. What makes you think abduction isn't within my capacity?"

I inwardly flinched. Aaron's scars were still on display, although his limp had disappeared from his gait. "Making off with a female seems base."

He smirked. "Is that what you told Gabel? Or are you saying you expected more from *me*?"

I pressed my jaw closed as my cheeks burned with mortified anger.

Fifteen wolves had appeared on the stone terrace at the back of the house, lined up shoulder to shoulder. It was a formal greeting that should have happened the previous evening, but obviously hadn't. I swallowed my nerves and unhappiness. Only a few of these wolves knew the truth about why I was here.

Aaron presented me with all the grave, easy grandeur of an Alpha who'd forgotten how to be anything but an Alpha. "Luna Gianna, my IceMaw. Enjoy my pack's hospitality. We pride ourselves on being gracious hosts."

Sure. Out here in Aaron's little evil overlord love palace. And to think I'd actually liked this Alpha, respected him, felt sorry for him, had him in my private room, and endured rumors of carrying on with him.

The problem was I *did* like Aaron, and I *was* impressed by him, and the prestige rolling off his scent so strong it got through my Mark. He was Gabel's worthy opponent. Right now, he was winning.

After the introductions the wolves excused themselves, leaving us alone on the patio. I was supposed to compliment Aaron on his wolves, but I just said, "I noticed you like things spartan. Fewer pillows and drawers to hide a knife?"

"Exactly."

"How long do you really think you can keep me here before this falls apart in your hands?"

"I'm not sure. Gabel Marked you to see how long he could resist the Bond and have a toy."

"And he didn't last six months," I snapped.

"I don't need six months," Aaron said with a grin. "I cannot let Adrianna or Gabel triumph. Now they will both be fighting over the heart of SableFur. They will destroy each other. I am merely holding you out of their grasp."

Like a piece of meat used to taunt two dogs. I raised my chin. "And what happens then?"

"It depends which way Gabel's tower to the Moon falls," Aaron said, unmoved. "And how splintered SableFur is by the time it's over."

"And you are just going to return me to Gabel," I said.

"I am not returning you to Gabel," Aaron said. "And Gabel isn't coming for you. That wolf will not give up his chance at the SableFur throne to rescue you. He knows I won't kill you. Him, yes. You? No."

I grit my teeth. Gabel wasn't going to come for me. He was the only thing holding Adrianna at bay. Aaron was right about that. I was on my own to deal with this particular monster.

"I can promise you I will not kill you," Aaron said. "You're still an Oracle. The second to the last of your kind. Perhaps if Gabel is gone, you and I will have something to discuss. After enough time has passed your hatred for me banks to a slow simmer."

"You're *just* as crazy as Gabel."

"Am I?" Aaron paced around me, coming up to me like he had before, his prestige and strength saturating my senses.

Yes, yes, he was. And that's how I was going to play this: like he was Gabel. He just wanted the *opposite* of what Gabel wanted. And I was going to let him think whatever he wanted to think. I also wasn't going to stand there and lie and say he wasn't magnificent in his own way, that he wasn't a worthy adversary, and that if we'd met under other circumstances, maybe it wouldn't be *his* Mark on my arm, and me talking to Gabel right now.

I met his gaze, feeling like I was staring into the void beyond the Moon. Gabel had wanted me to fight to amuse him, Aaron wanted me to fight to trap me. Both were prepared in their own way for resistance.

"You will eat dinner with the pack," he said. "Then I have a question that requires an Oracle to answer."

I ground my teeth. I couldn't refuse to help him. I *still* was an Oracle. "I have no tools, IceMaw. They were destroyed."

"Yes, I know."

"So *you* told the SableFur stoneworkers to shatter my stones?" I fought the urge to lunge at him and claw out his eyes.

"No, of course not. A pathetic, small-minded act of disobedience."

I eyed him. "What is your question? Presuming you can supply me with the appropriate tools."

"Why is the Moon punishing me?"

I *almost* laughed, because aside from him abducting me, Aaron seemed to have lived a flawless life full of sacrifice, nobility, and heroism. Even abducting me had been in service to that: prevent Gabel and Adrianna from putting on a crown I didn't, if I was honest, want *either* of them to have. I didn't want the time of the King-Alphas to return either, and I didn't want to be Queen.

"Dinner." Aaron half-bowed, the twisted scars on his spine moving and shifting like they had a life of their own.

GIFTS OF DESTRUCTION & TIME

The IceMaw ate in a large room that Aaron told me had once been an indoor tennis court. Dinner was very loud, and very busy, and chaotic as pack members arrived from the surrounding area. Any could attend, and many lived so close they simply walked over.

Aaron came to get me personally.

"I could have fetched myself," I told him.

"You will walk in with me. It is rare to host a guest Luna, and your pack would be incensed if I didn't show you every politeness."

"So when am I getting jabbed in the ass again?" I asked dryly, arranging my cardigan over my shoulders.

He didn't deign to answer that and gestured for me to walk with him down the hallway. "I will walk with you so you don't get lost or waylaid by my family."

"I thought you killed your family," I said.

"Not all of them. Not yet, anyway. I'm not on the best of social terms with any of them. Revolting and killing your own kin to become Alpha is socially awkward."

I shouldn't have laughed, but I did. "Yes, I guess that makes holidays uncomfortable."

He paused. "Most she-wolves are not comfortable hearing the truth."

I had seen the truth of things. "Most she-wolves haven't been in the belly of the Moon, or been Bound to Her Comet. You killing your own family to free your pack from an unfair yoke is—well."

Aaron raised a brow and his lips curled back in a rancid grin, like we weren't supposed to laugh at some unspeakable but unavoidable truth. "I have a reputation as a monster."

"Those fools have no idea what a monster is."

"You may be surprised at how many females are put off by an Alpha who made himself Alpha. Add into that the particulars of who I had to kill to do it and it becomes more unsavory. Lack of an appealing scent not withstanding." He said this as he walked, his tone wry, and with absolutely no inflection to suggest I was the solution to this. "It's pleasant to talk to someone who understands."

"A conversation would not have required abducting me," I said.

"Many wolves had their political fortunes change that day," Aaron said. "So like I said, I don't want you to get pulled by the current, because they would try to bring you to their side, Destroyer-of-Alphas."

"Should I be worried this pack is going to implode?"

He chuckled. "They wish."

The tables in the dining room were not large, only able to seat about six comfortably, which made for easy conversation in the otherwise immense room, and also made it so that really, there was no room for Aaron's family. There was his First Beta, Carlos, and his mate, Nandia, the Second Beta Mysard, and one of Aaron's most senior advisors, Jarjis. The seat to Aaron's left had always been symbolically empty, the seat saved for his future Luna, and that was where I sat.

There were also representatives from the southern packs that were forged under the IceMaw banner, and Aaron bid each of them good evening before rejoining our table.

The entire room noticed where I sat, and the din paused like the dip of the ocean before rising again.

I found myself watching Carlos, expecting him to say something about fine pups, then my heart hurt for Hix.

"He is a bit ugly, but he does the job well," Aaron told me, pointing his butter knife in Carlos' direction.

"A *bit* ugly?" Mysard said in jest.

"Pretty warriors don't work hard enough," Carlos said.

"Always serious," Mysard told the table.

"What is happening around us is serious. We can joke later," Carlos said.

Typical First Beta.

Everyone at the table knew Aaron had abducted me and I wasn't ever going to be his Luna, but they acted like I was a standard-issue guest. Probably for the benefit of the rest of the pack, who didn't have a clue, and kept casting me looks that ranged from annoyed to hopeful.

It was bright, cheerful, and there were children who ran around the perimeter of the tables once they had finished, and it was just… what I had grown up with. Only much larger.

"Cousin!" a male voice shouted, as one of the men stood up from his table.

Aaron's face drew into an annoyed pinch, then he raised his gaze to the wolf who had shouted, as the room's cheerful din faded.

"Cousin!" the young man shouted again. "You have not introduced your guest! Is it that she needs no introduction?"

"My uncle's son," Aaron told me as he stood. He picked up his own glass, and the entire room now quieted, even the pups sat down, as pups are trained to do when the Alpha speaks. He gestured to his cousin. "Byron, you make an excellent point. It slipped my mind that not all of IceMaw would know her by sight, although many of you know her by reputation."

"The former Luna of IronMoon and former Luna of SableFur," Byron said, "Yes, quite a reputation, cousin."

His ugly tone earned quite a few disapproving looks, and a few contemplative ones.

Aaron gestured grandly with his cup, taking in the whole room and directing the combined attention on the young man. "You are misinformed, cousin. She *is* the Luna of SableFur and has a reputation as a destroyer of troublesome Alphas. I am certain, however, she will not turn her wrath on me. Your concern for my safety is not necessary. Enjoy your meal and worry not."

Carlos snerked.

Aaron reached out with his other hand, clasped mine, and pulled me to my feet. I shuddered all over at his touch and fought the urge to snatch my hand out of his grip.

"Luna Gianna," Aaron gestured to his pack, "the IceMaw. IceMaw, the Luna Gianna of SableFur, who made herself Luna of that old and noble pack by right of conquest. She is here to discuss the matter of Adrianna and Gabel. Matters she and I have a communal interest in. Both want her throne, and should they achieve it, they will crown themselves with bones. No one here wishes to see that happen. Bid her welcome."

The song of greeting to a high-ranking female only wounded raw nerves.

I pulled my hand out of Aaron's grip and sat down just as the song ended.

Someone grabbed Byron and shoved his skinny ass back into his seat.

Aaron said, "Ignore him. He was twelve when I killed his father, and by extension his mother. He and his three sibs were just children, they couldn't understand. Those were their parents, and I dismantled their lives and future that day."

"That is reason enough to despise you," I said darkly.

"I should have done more and taken greater responsibility for the pups, but I was young, and occupied, and by the time I could appreciate what I had done to them, it was too late. One day I hope that they understand why I did what I did."

"They won't, and even if they did, it won't make it easier on them," I said. "They will never forgive you."

"Is that why you had Gabel kill your own father?"

I froze at his casual inquiry. Aaron did know the truth of that: that Gabel and I had had a way to communicate that the SableFur had not known about nor been able to intercept. "I did what I had to do for the greater good."

"Exactly. You and I understand each other far better than you care to admit."

After dinner, once it grew dark, Aaron took me outside. The massive stonework terrace off the back opened up onto rolling hills just turning green from spring. The lake glimmered in the half-moon's light, and the air was damp and cool.

In the moonlight Aaron's dark hair seemed tipped with glimmering bright white-blue, and the light seemed to cling to his skin.

I quivered, though, in the cool spring quiet, and the beautiful pond, and the greenery, and the dew clinging to the grass under our bare feet, and the silent house looming behind us.

It brought back different sorts of memories. It was a different place, and time, with a different man, but it was still the same, just turned around. Aaron paused, sensing my hesitation, and waited, close enough to me I could have touched him, but unreadable and removed.

He took me down the path I'd been on that day, but where the path forked, we headed straight towards the treeline. The path ended at a cluster of small utility sheds.

Okay, not a bog, river, nor thicket.

The sheds were not locked. He led me into the centermost one. The scent of pungent, deep earth hit me, and cold. In the darkness he reached for a flashlight, and the interior of the shed illuminated to reveal a single storm door under our feet.

He unlatched it and heaved the wood up to reveal stairs bending into darkness. The scent of earth hit me hard.

Hix.

The scent of earth was damp, lichen, not unlike the SableFur dungeon. Hix had died there, thrown away like garbage until Adrianna wanted to punish me.

The damned basement from IronMoon, all bleach and darkness, and stairs disappearing into shadows.

The grotto bending into moist darkness.

Bog. River. Thicket.

The first step creaked gently under Aaron's weight.

Nothing waited for me down in the cellar. It was a different place and time, and it wouldn't be the same, even if it was.

I gathered myself and walked into the darkness with him.

The cellar itself was a small subterranean structure about ten feet underground, carved out of the earth and braced with a frame of wood. It was just a dirt box, complete with roots reaching out from the dirt into the air of the room. Along the walls were a few small, crude shelves holding random items. My eyes went right to the velvet-wrapped lumps sitting on one wooden shelf.

Aaron gestured for me to go to them. "You need tools. See if any of these suit you. They are prepared and can be cut within the week."

I reached out to the first one, fingers closing over the rough, sharp edges of the chunk through the velvet. Obsidian. I sensed it under my fingers before I unwrapped the velvet. The stone's surface was still and cool. It had been dormant a long time.

But it was not for me.

I put it back on the shelf, then reached for its neighbor, a rounder stone, a little smaller. And the next, and the next. None for me. The fifth, however, was very different. Not obsidian at all, I sensed that much even through its velvet wrap. Smaller, smooth on one side, and warted on the other.

I unwrapped it. A polished, brilliant surface as intense as any mirror shone back at me. The surface was slightly concave, somewhere between a bent mirror and a bowl. I turned it over, and the back was nothing but large rust-red warts. "What is this?"

"A slice of a meteorite," Aaron answered. "I got it in a trade a few years ago and didn't know what else to do with it, so I put it down here. It's not a stone. It's almost entirely iron and nickel. Commonly called meteoric iron."

In the light the polished side was smooth, but not flawless like a mirror: it was etched with long, crystalline patterns arranged roughly in chevrons and triangles.

Any reflective, mirror-surface could do for scrying, but was there any danger to using an almost entirely metal mirror, especially one not from my world? "It sounds dangerous."

"I wouldn't have wanted it to hit me on the head." Aaron chuckled.

None of the obsidian chunks spoke to me. There were some other chunks: agate, quartz, jasper, but none for me. I kept sorting through them, hoping to find *something* normal and familiar. One of the chunks had a strange residual heat that reminded me of obsidian, the same sort of residual heat like the sensation of walking by hot peppers being cooked, and it was *old*. It was *so* old and so alert, and it moved against my senses.

I peeled back the velvet and a dull, ugly stone met my eyes. Not obsidian. It was black, but it looked like mushy coal. "What is *this*?"

"It's a tektite."

"What's a tektite?"

"Asteroid glass," Aaron said. "Formed from the heat and shockwave of an impact. The rock and sand gets flung up into the air, melted, then crashes back to Earth."

"I've never heard of anything like them."

"Ones that size are valuable and expensive, made from an utterly massive impact. Usually they're pebble sized. I got them in a trade." Aaron sighed a bit to say he had been gracious taking the objects in lieu of something only a handful of collectors might be interested in having.

"This is not a pebble." It was easily large enough to be carved into an useable bowl, and the excess into runestones.

"If you can use it, it's yours."

"I don't know if I should. It is…" I stroked it, and the surface was cool, but it *seethed*, and why not? Its birth had been violent. Obsidian was warmed, melted, consumed, reformed. This had been formed by a cosmic breaking-and-entering. Nobody liked a rude smack in the face. I stroked it again, sympathetic to what it had endured.

It had been waiting in the dark for eons. It was ready. Only another Oracle would understand the way our stones and glass felt, and how they'd shift and move. They were vessels that kept us safe in the Tides, and any seafarer would tell you how fondly they spoke of the vessels that had always kept them safe.

"Do any suit you?" Aaron asked.

I wanted to say that one of the obsidian chunks did, or even agate, or jasper, or none of them. I swallowed a painful lump that had formed in my throat. These items had been placed in Aaron's path years before I'd gotten here. They'd been waiting.

For me.

I clutched the tektite like I'd once clutched my obsidian.

Bog, river, thicket. In the end neither choice mattered: we'd always end up on the other side.

Without a word, Aaron took the tektite bundle from me, and then plucked the meteorite off the shelf. He carried them both upstairs.

In the deep, starlight darkness, I said, quietly, "Thank you."

"Of course." He inclined his head in my direction. "I will send them to the stonecutter in SkyFur, and the meteorite can be fashioned here into a curved mirror."

SkyFur was a little pack to the south that had sworn allegiance to IceMaw some time earlier. "I don't need the meteorite refashioned. It's a flat plane, I can use it—"

"No." He cut me off. "It won't take long to have its face reshaped into a bowl. Then you will answer my question."

"There is not much time before Beltane," I said.

"They will have this done within the week," Aaron said.

"As you say, Alpha." I seethed with anger at the same time my heart ached for what the tektite was going to show me, and what using a mirror from another world might do.

The scythe-Moon has fallen, and the Sun has set.

EROSION

"How do you expect me to stay in control of SableFur locked up and silenced here in IceMaw?" I asked Aaron two days later, aggravated that he magically expected Lucas and Kiery and Bernhard to keep a lid on SableFur in my total silence. "There's a difference between my *absence*, and my silence."

"You are certainly welcome to contact the SableFur." Aaron pulled out his phone and tossed it to me. "Have a seat."

"Ah, I see. As long as you're listening in," I said dryly.

"You'll find my contact list exhaustive." Aaron grinned. "Wouldn't want you using it against me."

I debated throwing his phone back at him, but Aaron had been playing the part of gallant, vaguely love-sick host to the hilt, and IceMaw watched every, single, stinking move. Aaron didn't keep it a secret he smelled my lure-scent, or what I smelled of: the night-blooming cereus.

"Don't you have some dalliance you can shove in my face or pester?" I asked Aaron, annoyed.

"Like I told you, she-wolves are generally averse to males like me." Aaron's masochistic grin didn't falter, and his careless tone had a distinctive flavor of self-loathing to it. "You are the first who seems to understand that which is necessary versus that which is pleasant."

"I'm taken," I reminded him.

"For now." He shrugged.

"So you'd take another Alpha's scraps," I said.

"Scraps? Gianna, I told you, Gabel has no idea what he has and even less idea how to keep it. That makes you *anything* but scraps."

"Fine. But can't you find some IceMaw female to play with while I deal with this?"

"Alphas don't have dalliances. Smart ones, that is," Aaron said, echoing what Gabel had said to me a year earlier. "I haven't had anyone in my bed for at least a few years. Mercifully, without the lure-scent, it's been a trial of loneliness more than a trial of restraint."

In another time and place I'd have been all over Aaron. If we'd met before Anders' party, which hadn't even been a year ago, I'd have begged him to Mark my arm and gamble with my soul just to be free of Gabel. The guilty thought about what could have been chewed on my side, and although I kept reminding myself I should be angry at him, pity and vague sadness kept diluting it.

He's manipulating you, Gianna. The same as Gabel did.

I needed to get my new bowls and take his question to the Moon before I decided how to play this. The Moon had already given me my first clue: the Mark burned into my arm, and the Bond slumbering in my heart.

I skimmed through his contacts. Tons of names. *Magnes* being one of them. And Gabel. I scrolled until I got to the one I wanted. Lucas. I hit *call.*

"I know you're behind this, rodent," Lucas growled.

"Behind what, Lucas?" I asked, amused by his ferocity. Aaron cocked his head to listen. I flicked him my middle finger.

"Luna!" Lucas exclaimed. Abrupt shuffling, doors opening, closing, then a door slamming shut. "Where are you? We'll come get you."

"Play along with Aaron's plan for now, Lucas," I said, suppressing a sigh.

"He abducted you! He was *trusted,* and he abused it!" Lucas shouted.

"Keep it down if you don't want all the pack to hear you," I snapped. "I'm fine. Tell me what has been happening in SableFur."

Lucas, aggravated, relayed that the pack had accepted the story of my going to IceMaw for "negotiations" with bewilderment, although they expected (and needed) me to return quickly. Everyone now assumed I was humoring Aaron's attempt to court me and there'd be a Beltane announcement of a personal, formal alliance between IceMaw and SableFur.

The SableFur were distracted by Gabel's response to his defeat at Adrianna's hands: tearing through the north into her forces, chewing into the hamlets at the border of her most obvious influence and forcing them to either submit to him in my name, or die for Adrianna. Most of them had chosen loyalty to me instead of death. Chaos continued to reign up and down through the small towns of the north as fights broke out at bars, pool halls, bowling alleys and the like, as wolves willing to bleed for me beat up wolves who claimed to want to bleed for Adrianna.

"No one knows what to think anymore," Lucas said, his voice thick with bitter amusement. "Especially those of us who know what's really going to happen."

I wasn't even sure if I should be wounded or relieved that Gabel hadn't turned to the south to come get me from Aaron. "Tell them I'm an Oracle and know nothing about Beltane celebrations, so the wolves in charge of the party are on the job."

"Luna, you *need* to return to SableFur quickly. Gabel's Mark has been seen, and there are rumors swirling that it's *not* a tattoo, but a Mark. You can't keep asking wolves to fight and die against their own Alpha in ignorance."

"I don't believe she's going to return to SableFur just yet," Aaron said. "It sounds dangerous, First Beta."

"I'll show you dangerous, IceMaw. I'll—"

I cut Lucas off. "Gabel's putting down a rebellion, and the IronMoon wolves are doing the dirty work for SableFur."

"That's one way to look at it." Lucas laughed hollowly.

The Mark on my arm thumped.

There was *that* option. Kill myself. Kill Gabel. Just stop the clock.

Or I could kill Aaron. He was within reach. *Could* I kill him, though? *Should* I kill him? He was also reasonably harmless. He didn't want to rule the world or hurt anyone. He just wanted his pack, and a Luna, and some pups and to leave the world better than how he found it.

"Is Aaron even going to return you to us, or should I start preparing for Beltane to be an inferno?" Lucas asked, tone brittle.

"Lucas, I'm sort of being held political prisoner by an Alpha who murdered his whole family. I'm lucky I'm not getting obsidian shards shoved under my toenails. If I try to walk out of here, I won't get far."

"I didn't murder my *whole* family," Aaron corrected.

Right. Not all of them. Just a fair number of them. I rolled my eyes.

"Then we're coming for you and—"

"Will you shut up and stop that nonsense? You do that, Adrianna will throw everything she has at the heart. Deal with things as best you can until I can convince Aaron I'm more trouble than I'm worth."

I hung up on Lucas and threw the phone back at Aaron.

He caught it in one hand. "The mighty SableFur, tearing themselves apart."

He came around his desk and caressed my cheek with one broad palm. I jerked away from his touch. "I have a mate, Aaron. Don't. There is no *us*. There is no you and I."

"Then why can I smell your lure-scent? Why does your soul still cry out for mine?"

"I don't know. Maybe you're lying. Maybe you're deluded."

"You know both of those things aren't true. Why can I still smell your scent if you are not meant to be mine?" He tried to touch me again. "My touch doesn't sicken you. It's supposed to, isn't it? You're supposed to feel discomfort if I touch you like this."

I held my chin out of range of his touch. "Stop."

"Maybe this blue-gloss Mark isn't a Mark at all. Maybe it's something else. Chains, perhaps. Gabel's leash."

"It's a Mark, because there's a Bond."

"Is there?" His fingertips touched my shoulder. In the warmer weather of the south he'd given me diaphanous, light fabrics to wear, and his touch easily reached my skin. I tightened with annoyance that he wouldn't get his damn paws off me and shuddered with fear as his touch sent a strange sensation through my skin. He whispered, "Are you sure?"

I held stock-still while his fingertips trailed higher to the small hairs by my ear, pulling the locks through his fingers very gently.

The Mark on my arm didn't throb or threaten me, it slept in its fitful way, aching for Gabel to be close, but strangely soothed by Aaron's presence.

He leaned closer, his breath against my neck as he spoke. "Are you sure, Balance-Keeper, there is only room in your soul for one of us?"

I refused to answer. His lips almost touched my skin, sending terrifying flitters across my nerves. I didn't want this. I

didn't want to feel this, be here, with him, like this. I ignored
the way my body bloomed under his warm breath, my nipples
hardening under my shirt, the warmth tingling between my
thighs.

"If you were his, you wouldn't smell like this," he
whispered.

"I am his," I said, turning my head and trying to ignore the
crush of filth and guilt.

"And you will never be mine? Never is a very long time.
You told him never as well, didn't you. You swore it. Within a
year you were his."

I whipped around and snarled at him.

He backed away, a smirk tugging on his compressed expression. "The lure-scent does not lie. Your soul might be his, but it
is also mine."

"It is *my* soul," I snapped. "And considering you want *this*
soul—which is full of holes and in a very tired body—to scry
for you, leave me alone. Don't talk to me until my bowls are
back from the cutters."

Aaron half-bowed, one arm across his body, except he kept
his eyes upraised and on mine. "As you wish, Luna."

BURNING GLASS & STARS

Two wrapped velvet parcels were on Aaron's desk. He stood with legs slightly spread, hands behind his back, and quite pleased with himself.

"Your bowls, Oracle," he said, choosing my most relevant title for this particular conversation.

Cautiously, I stepped into his paranoid aquarium of an office. No one else was there. So much for thinking I'd have at least two weeks without him nagging me or crawling all over me. And damn the wolf, he'd really kept his promise to not be anywhere near me while waiting for them. My meals had been brought to me, and no questions asked.

I gathered up the loose velvet. "Thank you, Alpha."

"My question. When will you be able to ask the Moon?"

"I can do it this evening." I should take time to attune myself to the bowls, but I'd need to trust my own power and experience.

I'd never heard of an Oracle *ever* having a tektite bowl, or a meteorite mirror. I hadn't even known those were things that were possible.

First time for everything.

These were the things that had spoken to me, they'd been placed into Aaron's path years ago—and the Moon had set all this into motion decades earlier.

Bog, river, thicket: the method of traversal didn't change what was on the other side.

I took my new bowls to my room. Aaron had supplied me with candles, salt, the usual implements of an Oracle's work. I drew the curtains, lit the candles, and unwrapped my bowls.

The meteorite's smooth surface had been expanded and polished outward into a slightly concave mirror shaped into a flared rectangle. Like a shallow serving dish. It had retained much of its warty underbelly. The pattern on the metal— called Thomson structures—was intact in the core of the mirror, but as the metal had been shaped outwards, they elongated and stretched, warping into a hypnotic pattern that instantly pulled at my Seer gifts.

The other parcel was the tektite. Contained in the bowl was a full set of tektite runestones. The tektite had been carved into a standard bowl, the exterior remaining lumpy and pocked, but the interior polished to a blinding shine.

Obsidian bowls were mostly opaque, and while they could be polished to a shine, they were *nothing* like this completely, utterly black bowl that had achieved a shine so intense it was like it had been glazed, and it was impossible for the eye to remain in one place.

The tektite runestones had been made from the remnants of the bowl's carving and had not been polished and were not uniform. They'd only been ground down enough to make them safe to hold and not inclined to crack. They were a mix of pumice-like texture and smooth, polished planes where the chisel had struck. Each one had a rune carved on the face, but the texture of the rough stone made each one look like the rune had been blasted into the charred surface.

There was a rune for *Comet*. A special request from Aaron, then.

I ran my thumb over it and placed it next to *Balance* in my palm.

Then I picked up the bowl. So ancient, so old, still imbued with a peculiar seething heat from the violence of its creation. When its world had been destroyed, and it had gone from being sand and earth into… this.

I hugged it against my breast. I could have crushed it, shattered it, broken it.

And I didn't.

I was going to use it.

~*~ The Vision In The Tektite Bowl ~*~

Back in the stone room lined with torches. Outside the sky had grown dark, and the wind blew the scent of ash and burning.

The necklace and haircombs that had previously sat on the stone table were gone. The door of blackness at the end of the hallway, though, remained.

I walked through it.

More darkness. I reached out. Felt rough, pimpled stone with sharp edges. Listened: heard water.

The grotto. I was in the grotto, but without the RedWater wolves to light the way this time. I felt along the rock towards the sound of water lapping the edges of the little island.

Emerged into the usual dusk-like darkness, walked around the path up to where the altar usually appeared.

It was there. Smeared with blood. Blood welled from each of its corners and flowed downward into the ocean where Aaron stood.

His back bled, with silver claws embedded into the vertebrae. His arm was flayed to the bone, skin hanging uselessly from the upper half, and the white-cream bone exposed to the air, burning with the mark for instrument. He stared to the west: where the storm came, closer now, and the Moon had set, the edge of the crescent just touching the horizon line.

In his hand he held the bone crown, and the unfinished obsidian/quartz/tourmaline necklace. The crown bled, and mingled with his blood, all of it flowing to the ocean.

The stone under our feet was pimply and raw.

It wasn't stone: it was blood. The entire island was—and had been— a massive scab.

I clapped my hands over my mouth to hold in my screams.

Aaron's attention shifted to me.

I gasped again. He shouldn't see me.

Then he looked to the storm. The ocean lapped the island with waves of increasing size.

"The scythe-Moon has set," I said.

"Yes," he agreed, his voice grim and far away.

"You can go into the grotto and be safe," I said.

"For when this floods?" he asked.

"There's a way out through it."

"That was the way we all came," he said, still watching the storm.

"Then how did we leave here originally?" I asked.

"Before the Tides were not so high. Now this is all that remains."

That made no sense, but this was a vision, so how much sense was it supposed to make? I reached down to take the crown and necklace for a closer look. With a sad look, he released them to me.

The crown bled, the stain spreading across my hand, wrapping my wrist in liquid threads, dripping off my elbows onto the island. Still a crown for a Queen's head. Of bones, blood, death.

"The storm is here," Aaron said, stepping to the very edge of the island.

Gabel came across the ocean. Behind him, as he walked, the ocean solidified into black stone, ash drifted around him instead of rain and mist, and smoke twisted off his veins and sinew. A crown of burning glass and gore sat on his brow. And he grinned, barring yellow fangs in a human mouth.

"*The scythe-Moon has fallen,*" *Gabel said, his voice carrying with the wind,* "*and the Sun has set.*"

Aaron drew himself up, despite his ruined spine and arm. "*He will destroy everything he touches. Even you, Gianna, and even himself.*"

"*No,*" *I said.* "*No, Aaron, listen to me!*"

"*I can't let him win,*" *Aaron said. He stepped off the island. As he did so, the island cracked and shifted, and began to sink, slowly.* "*I will do anything to stop him. I will do what I must.*"

Water rushed around my ankles.

"*Gabel!*" *I shouted as the island sank swifter and swifter, and the two males moved towards each other on a bridge of crusted blood and fangs and bones. I sank into the darkness with the bones and blood and swirling fangs, and darkness moved over the world, and smoldering glass and stars fell from the sky. Their heat and burning illuminated the water that choked me… and set it to boiling.*

I grabbed onto something, anything, *as the dark, fiery Tides boiled and tossed me in the churn of burning glass and stars.*

The Moon watched as Her Tides consumed me.

I sank.

And sank.

And sank.

And sank.

NO. NO. NO.

I yearned towards the burning, and away from the darkness under me. I reached towards it, trying to swim back to the top.

Something grabbed my left arm, hard, tight, sank into my Mark like Gabel's claws had slid into my skin that first day, and dragged me down.

"*WE REALLY MUST STOP MEETING like this. We have wars to manage.*"

I blinked. Opened my eyes. Saw oily fur and leathery hide and inhaled the scent of ash and burning and Gabel.

And sand, and heat.

I flexed my muscles. I was in wolf-form.

"Gabel?" I twisted my head around.

He pulled his lips back over his massive, yellow fangs in a lupine grin. Spittle dripped from his lips onto the sand below, setting it to sizzle and melt into tiny pieces of glass. "I told you if you were ever lost on the Tides I would come find you. I would spend eternity looking for you."

I twisted to my feet, staggering on four uncertain paws, and took in the desolate, hellish landscape. Nothing but a desert with some prickly-looking scrub plants that seemed like a knot of thorns and barbs. The sky was a dusty yellow, the sun blazing hot but obscured behind dust.

I turned around, and whispered, "Please tell me you didn't actually spend eternity doing it."

Because if this was the world, and this had ceased to be a vision…

A panted laugh, and he stepped alongside me, giving me a strong, bony shoulder to lean against. He licked my Mark. His scalding saliva did not hurt. Just a mild, antiseptic sting that cooled in the blazing heat.

I pressed my forehead into his shoulder. Was this really Gabel? The Bond told me it was Gabel, and we were in this hellish place together.

Whatever this place was. Another pocket realm, like the grove? Where had the tektite brought me?

He nibbled my ruff, and my ear. "This way, I think."

Bewildered, I followed him.

The hot, miserable breeze swept the tiny grains of sand about the air, but after an unknown time, we came to a glass path, brushed with the slightly gleaming sand. It burned my paw pads, and I whimpered. Gabel was unaffected, his massive claws crunching the glass instead.

He crouched down. "Crawl on. I will carry you."

"You are not that big, and I am not that small."

"Don't be bashful. You've ridden me before and quite liked it." He clicked his teeth, and the scent of lust mingled with burning.

Yes. Definitely Gabel. I contemplated the best way to do this. I settled on crawling over his shoulders, then squirming my backside over his hips. I gripped his oily, leather scruff in my teeth. He chuckled.

"Don't get turned on," I grumbled.

"Too late."

"Gabel. We're pretty much trapped."

"Together. We are together." He shoved himself to his feet. I clapped my paws against his big shoulders and squirmed back into place, draped over him like a wolf-shaped rug. "It's not so bad."

Compared to the basement? Sure. This wasn't that bad. I reached out with my snout and bit one of his ears. "If we stay here, we will never have sex ever again. Sand will get everywhere. No sex. No pups."

"Hmm." He tilted his head forward so my teeth raked at his earflap more than necessary. "Yes, that is disturbing."

The burning glass road went straight through the ruined landscape. I tucked my snout between my foreleg and Gabel's side and closed my eyes to shield myself from the blistering sand-laden breeze.

"Gianna," he said.

I raised my snout and looked between his ears. We'd come to a giant crater made entirely of glass. Like a massive bowl sunk into sandy Tides. The surface reflected all the miserable light like a mirror.

Gabel walked right up to the edge.

"That is the way back," I said.

"How do you know?"

Because it was my tektite bowl (sort of) and we had to get back into the bowl. I bit his ear again.

Carefully, Gabel placed one paw over the edge. His claws scraped the glass but did not crack it.

His front paws slid. He shouted as I tumbled down the burning surface, but he was falling, over and over with me.

G abel leaned against the back of the small abandoned shed. His wolves moved around in the clearing and forests not far away, sorting through the muck and a few of them piling the bodies of the SableFur rebels that had decided they preferred Adrianna to Gianna.

Their mistake.

But he had other concerns.

Aaron had Gianna. This was not news. He had chosen to tolerate the situation—Lucas had said Gianna didn't want to be rescued. They all knew the price of rescuing her from Aaron would cost everything and play right into Adrianna's hands.

The old SableFur matriarch was a fiercer, more cunning opponent than the IronMoon Alpha had expected. Her warriors weren't especially durable, but she was clever in how she used them, and where she put pressure on his own forces.

A second worthy opponent. A challenging opponent. Adrianna had greater numbers than he did, and she was not squeamish about sacrificing them, or treating her warriors as expendable.

But losing a day to a vision to save Gianna—the tourmaline had called him, and drawn him into a world of sand and heat, and a confusing jumble of sensations and pain he did not understand save his mate had needed him. Aaron was pressing her Oracle gifts.

He had resisted the tourmaline's call until he'd remembered his promise: *I will always find you.*

He'd made the promise. He had to keep it.

It was time to have a conversation with the IceMaw. Adrianna had chewed another hole in his flank in his absence. He could not afford to keep being distracted by the IceMaw pressing Gianna's gifts. Unless that was the IceMaw's intention.

Aaron picked up his phone. "Gabel."

"You have my mate," Gabel said without prelude.

"She is a guest here in IceMaw."

"You abducted her," Gabel growled. "That is not a *guest.*"

A pause that wasn't Aaron weighing his response, just Aaron weighing if he wanted to respond at all. Gabel waited. He needed to be patient. Aaron had the advantage: Aaron had Gianna. Every movement of their paws shifted the weight of the power between them.

Gianna did not realize it—or want to—but Aaron *would* kill her. Aaron wanted her for himself, and when he accepted he'd never have her, he'd turn her to some other purpose.

Aaron finally deigned to speak. "I told you the first time we met you had no idea what you had, and even less idea how to keep it. The fact she is with me now is proof. You are the Destroyer. You don't need a mate. Everything you touch turns to dust and bones. You can tell yourself you love her, treasure her, but all she is to you is a possession."

"That is not true," Gabel said, keeping his tone steady even as he wanted to squeeze Aaron's head until the brains burst out the top. "She is my mate, my Luna, and the mother of my future."

"You push her into danger with your games and ambition. You'll do the same thing to your pups. She didn't invite you to SableFur. You showed up, paraded your Mark around, and brought her prey. The SableFur are more confused than before, and Adrianna took advantage while you were arrogant and careless."

Gabel suppressed a snarl. "Beltane is coming. Are you going to try to keep her then, IceMaw?"

"Are you incapable of comprehending what you're truly against? Is it because you are a lupine and think being an Alpha is as easy as swinging your prestige around? Gianna constantly pays the price for your serious limitations. I told you I would never have given her to the Oracles. I would never have repudiated her. But you've constantly traded her safety and happiness and your own damn vows against *your* goals and what *you* want."

Gabel cricked his neck. *Limitations.*

This was his fault.

He turned the sensation of guilt over. He'd made many mistakes, and done things he realized were weak, small, the wrong thing. "What of our vows did I violate?"

"You promised to keep her safe," Aaron said. "What are those vows? *Will you protect our den, our pack, our pups with every drop of blood and fiber within you? Will you cherish me and love me so that I know no other male will ever be worthy of my glance?*"

"I remember the vows." He remembered every detail of that night.

"And you've failed in every single one. You didn't protect the den. You didn't love her enough to make her wholly yours. She has your Mark, and I still smell her lure-scent. Even now it fills any room she enters. You howl about building a tower to the Moon and how the Moon betrayed you, but you didn't fulfill your vows. You didn't defend her with *every drop of blood and fiber*. You threw her away, and you *think* the Moon returned her to you, but did She? You have blue-gloss on your arms, not a Mark."

The IceMaw was goading him, and it was working, because the IceMaw had a barb of truth. Gianna had never made any vow to cherish and love him—she'd vowed to bring him pups, to rule wisely at his side, and temper him. *He* had made the vows to defend her and cherish her. Gianna had told him the Moon demanded he surrender her to the Oracles, but perhaps Gianna had been wrong: perhaps the true path should have been defiance.

Had it all been a test, and he had not realized it? And he'd failed, and like Flint, was bound to Her service by the blue-gloss, and since Gianna was his mate, he'd trapped her with him? As Flint's mate howled her grief at their separation?

Aaron said, voice like thick silk, "She does not flinch when I touch her. She tells me to stop, but I sense her skin accept my caress in those stolen moments."

The statement twisted into his kidneys. He followed the sequence of events back, and he saw himself at the breaking points. Those moments when he could have—and perhaps should have—chosen differently.

Had she ruled wisely at his side? Yes, for as long as he'd had her.

Had she tempered him? She had tried to.

The female also was the one who decided where the den was. He'd always known that. He had not been paying attention. She'd called herself the SableFur Luna and said she could not leave SableFur. Clearly, SableFur had become her den. Noxious and intolerable, but ultimately, her right, and his obligation was to defend it. He wasn't defending it. He was pursuing Adrianna for his own purposes—but Gianna wanted the same thing.

So had he chosen wrongly?

Now Aaron had promised—and delivered—everything he may have failed to provide.

Limitations. He'd run afoul of his own limitations.

He would have to find a way around them.

But first, he would have to earn her forgiveness.

He turned the idea of *forgiveness* around in his head. Unfamiliar. He'd never felt the need to be forgiven before, or the shame that spawned it. It sat like a blister inside him. He'd been embarrassed by his actions, or chastised himself for foolishness, but he had never quite felt this deep, intense shame.

He'd told Gianna in the beginning there was no challenge if there was no risk of loss.

And the prospect of this challenge, for the first time, did not delight him. It worried him. He'd fallen prey to his own defects and limitations, so confident he was the master of them, and now he was about to lose the only thing in his life that truly meant anything.

Gianna had warned him *and I will be at your side as it crumbles.*

His lips tugged in a feral grin. She hadn't been speaking as an Oracle, but as a future Queen, far wiser than him in such matters.

But if he turned and left Adrianna unattended, Adrianna would overrun the den. For now, Gianna was safe with Aaron, she'd have to manage on her own, and he'd have to earn her forgiveness.

"What are you going to do with her?" Gabel asked.

"That depends on if you kill Adrianna or Adrianna kills you," Aaron said.

"Lucas cannot run SableFur forever without her," Gabel said, mind turning slowly on this new information, unsettled and restless.

"And I cannot let you become King," Aaron said.

Aaron hung up.

Gabel weighed the phone in his palm, brushed his thumb over the screen, weighed his choices. None of them pleased him.

He was as bound to the path he'd set himself on as the blue-gloss inked into his arm.

THE SCYTHE-MOON

My whole body hurt like I'd fallen down a mountain.

Maybe because I had.

I opened my eyes. Still dark.

But back in IceMaw.

I was passed out on the floor, and now eye-level with the tektite bowl, which shone with an eerie, too-bright but too-dark light in the faint starlight coming through the windows.

Groggy, I wrestled myself up. My eyes felt full of sand and heat, while my skull full of too much water and too little brain.

What day was it? How long had I been gone? Had it really been Gabel?

My left arm hurt. I grimaced, moving like I was a million years old, and touched it. My fingers sank into sore and broken spots.

I stumbled to my feet and to my bathroom for a better look.

My arm had the distinctive outline of a massive canine bite, but it was healed, all that was left was a nasty bruise that would fade.

Gabel had dragged me out of the boiling Tides.

I stumbled back into the bedroom and collapsed onto the bed.

I'D BEEN GONE ONLY two days, but I'd slept for two more.

"Oracle," Aaron addressed me as he served me some plain toast.

"Alpha," I replied, trying not to sound as drained as I felt. Beltane was dangerously close. Already the preparations for IceMaw's own celebration were evident in the back meadows. The entire pond had been ringed with stacks of logs for bonfires. "I have your answer."

"Excellent. We will discuss it after breakfast." Aaron had his attention on one of the lower tables, where there seemed to be something of a scuffle or general discontent going on.

The toast helped, along with a couple of cups of strong coffee. A number of messengers came to murmur in Aaron's ear during the course of the meal, or pass him short notes scrawled in the language of Hunters.

After breakfast he bid me follow him up to his private rooms.

"I'd rather not be in here," I told him.

"I prefer to hear these things in private," he replied.

"Your office is not private?"

"Not like my rooms."

I grit my teeth and permitted him to guide me into his private suite. I still flinched when he closed the door. At least his rooms had windows, even if they were just as spartan as his office: all whites, pale grays, panels of wood. The brightest color was the golden oak floor. There weren't even any paintings on the walls.

I sat on a low bench, one of the few items of furniture in

the room. As long as all his clothes stayed on and I got this over with, it'd be fine. I ignored the scent of want and desire that always clung to him, and the smugness that he'd gotten me this close to his bed.

The Mark on my arm slumbered in his presence.

Aaron sat on the edge of the bed. "My question, my answer. Why is the Moon punishing me?"

"Before we begin, Lord-Alpha, I should inform you I do not believe what I saw was purely intended for you," I said, choosing the title to needle him, and enjoying the way he flickered with annoyance. "I believe it was as much for me, and possibly for Gabel."

"I do not intend to share anything with Gabel."

"The Moon does not care what you want," I retorted. "She doesn't care what *any* of us want."

Aaron's handsome features pinched with annoyance. "Why do you think the vision was for anyone but me?"

"The vision started off in the same place my first vision for Gabel started," I said, walking a very fine line, but that vision had been as much for me as for Gabel. "And from there, it moved to places I have been in *my* visions, and the visions of other Oracles. There is a shared vision between several of us. That is why I am warning you what I saw is not purely yours and yours alone."

Aaron crossed one knee over the other, not hiding his annoyance, and his scent became salty and sharp. "Tell me, then, Oracle, what you saw on all our behalfs."

I told him about the ziggurat, the jungle, the stone altar that had previously had unfinished jewelry, the grotto that opened up onto the island at the edge of the Tides, and how I'd seen him, flayed and scalded, having taken the bone crown and unfinished necklace, then gone to meet Gabel while I sank into the abyss and the world rained burning glass into the

Tides. I left out how Gabel had pulled me out of (under?) the
Tides into the upside-down wasteland.

He absorbed it in silence.

"Your arm still had the rune *instrument* on it. Elder Oracle
Kiery has seen it too, and I've seen it on you several times.
There should be other rune that give context to what *instrument*
means, but we've never been able to see what they are, if any.
In her vision you also set out across the Tides to meet the
storm, while in my visions you do the same thing and also tell
me you would do anything necessary to stop Gabel. In a dream
I had, you told Gabel more of the same."

"Gabel," Aaron clarified, eyes very bright. "Wearing a
crown of glass and gore with the storm at his back."

"Kiery didn't see that, but I did."

"And all this means what? In the grand scheme of things."

The answer chilled me. "That the future is unchanged, and
things are unfolding along the same path, and we are still on
the same course we were."

Aaron surged to his feet. "You mean I've been a good little
instrument and done exactly what the Moon needed me
to do."

Wary, I said, "What She *anticipated* you'd do. You and
everyone else."

Aaron snorted. "For what? What does She want from me?"

"I don't know."

"So this path I am on: it ends with Gabel and I in conflict,
and you are killed."

"I didn't die in the vision. Close, but not quite. And it
ended with me holding the bleeding crown and unfinished
necklace."

"The necklace I stole from the temple room," Aaron said.
"And the crown I took off the altar."

I shrugged, not looking at him. "If you believe you stole the
necklace and crown, that's for you to say."

Aaron sighed, angrily.

I looked at my scarred hands. "I've seen Gabel many times in my visions and dreams. I've never seen him wearing any mark of station or rank. This is the first time I've ever seen him with a crown."

"So whatever path we are on, we are making him King," Aaron said, disturbed. "Even though everything I'm doing is to *prevent* that, you're saying I can't stop him."

"The future isn't set in stone," I said, insides coiling nervously as he paced in front of me. Everything seemed to point to an inevitable conclusion, and it didn't matter which way we'd gone. *Bog, river, thicket*, still the same place.

Arron frowned and looked beyond my shoulder out the window for long minutes.

I intruded on his pensive silence. "You did tell me you'd pay any price to ensure Gabel never wears a crown. Is it so surprising your actions to stop him may result in my death?"

He tore his gaze back to me. "I don't want you to die, Gianna. You are the only hope for a future I have."

He kept saying that, and he was wrong. There was no future for him and I. "You cannot kill Gabel and expect I will ever love you."

"Are you sure of that?"

I hated how he flung that in front of me. I no longer knew what rules my heart or world played by anymore. I'd sworn I'd never fall in love with Gabel after what he'd done to me. And part of me still despised Gabel for how things had begun, and I was frightened of what he was, and what he *could* be, but I loved him.

I couldn't be sure if Aaron killed Gabel and saved the world from the Dark Comet, and shattered my soul doing it, that somehow the IceMaw Alpha, Her Instrument, wouldn't sweep up the pieces and somehow put me together.

I had a hole in my soul, a mark in my eye, and a strange

Mark on my arm. One of my new bowls wasn't even from this world, and the other had been created from a celestial impact exactly like the one Gabel was about to create.

What happens to Comets once they serve their grim purpose?

"Is that your end game, Aaron?" I asked softly. "Kill Gabel, hope I forgive you in a few years, and I give you the crown of SableFur?"

Aaron's cold expression didn't change. "I don't care about SableFur, or a crown. Gabel destroys everything he touches. That *is what he is*, and I am not going to try to reason with it or excuse it. I am Alpha. I am sworn to defend my pack. I can't let him destroy them. I can't let him destroy you. You are the only hope I have. Without you there is no future."

Aaron looked down at his own hands. He traced the thick scar twisting along one of them with the opposite thumb, pressing hard into the old injury.

The planets are in motion. They will continue their dance without you.

We all had the same conversations over and over, the same arguments, made the same statements, I even had the same visions and dreams over and over. Slight variations, sure, but *nothing had changed.*

The only thing that had changed was the first jungle vision, where I'd seen Gabel arguing with Romero. The Moon had led me to the truth about Gabel, the truth about Magnes, and now Aaron, but for everything I'd learned and all I'd tried to do, we seemed destined for the same end result. Why show me anything if I couldn't change any of it?

Oracles couldn't scry for themselves. We couldn't petition the Moon with questions on our own behalf. Every question I'd taken to the Moon for a petitioner in the past year had had something for *me* in it. The first jungle vision I'd been stunned to see myself, with the runes that kept appearing over and over, with a necklace of fangs around my neck.

Every vision had had something for me in it—reflected in the questions of others. The Moon whispering to me what the Balance-Keeper was.

She'd shown me Aaron, Gabel, Magnes, Gabel's mother, Flint, Hix: everyone's part in this.

And She'd shown me mine. She showed it to me every time I looked in the mirror.

"Gianna?" Aaron asked as I straightened.

"Excuse me, Lord-Alpha." I uncrossed my legs and stood. "I am very tired."

I returned to my rooms and headed towards the bathroom mirror. The white mark in my eye, a slender white crescent, the tips touching my pupil, while the dip of the Moon just barely grazed the perimeter of my hazel iris.

In my dreams and visions the scythe-Moon *just* touched the horizon, but it hadn't set. It hadn't fallen on the world.

I touched my reflection and almost laughed. "I'm a moron."

The scythe-Moon hung in *my* eye.

STORMFRONT

Bog, river, thicket, it was always going to end this way. My place wasn't here sitting around eating Aaron's food and taking his tektites.

He also wasn't going to let me just walk out of here back to SableFur. Or IronMoon. Or down to the corner for some milk and eggs.

A knock on my door. One of the she-wolves poked her head around it. "Luna, Alpha Aaron has requested you join him for court."

"Court?" I asked blankly, grabbing a blanket to hold over my upper body.

"Yes, Luna." She kept her eyes adverted to the side.

"Tell the Lord-Alpha I will not be attending court," I said shortly.

"I—don't believe it was actually a request, Luna," she said awkwardly.

"Then tell him I'm not going to come sit next to him while he parades me in front of his pack like a rare bird in a gilded cage," I snapped. It was one thing to be dragged here under the pretense of *personal negotiations*, while he danced around and tried to court me, but I was *not* sitting next to him while he engaged in the old tradition when the Alpha was available to hear disputes, settle arguments, or hear requests.

I was *not* Aaron's Luna, and he didn't get to parade me around and put me in chairs like some propped up dolly while he counted on my good sense to shield him from public mortification. I'd gotten sick of those games with Gabel. Aaron needed a new script.

The she-wolf retreated. I got up and got dressed anyway, just to make sure my arm was covered. As I finished putting up my hair, another wolf entered my room.

"Play hard-to-get all you like, Gianna," Aaron said. "It won't end the way you think."

"What are you going to do, Aaron? Drag me down there by my hair?" I asked sweetly.

"I am not in the mood for this nonsense."

"I am not going to go sit in your court and sing for you like a caged bird!"

"You don't have to make a sound," Aaron said reasonably. "Your presence is all that is required."

"You are no better or different than Gabel. You want to think you are, but you aren't."

"Then I don't see what the difficultly is in accommodating me." He smiled.

Aaron might not kill me, but he could throw me in some pit or dungeon. As entertaining as forcing him to do that sounded, dying on that hill was stupid. I got cold, even as my brain remembered the boiling heat of the burning Tides.

Wait, in the vision, had Gabel and Aaron fought over *me*, and not the crown? And I'd become a casualty?

"Oh," I whispered. "Oh. I—I understand now. But I don't."

"Understand what?" Aaron asked.

I shook my head. "Nothing. Nothing."

A wave of weakness slammed into me along with the realization.

"Hey," I said, then I realized he'd been supporting me from cracking my skull as I fainted. The tektite had taken a lot out of me.

"It would not be good for you to be found dead in your own quarters after I had been in here," Aaron said. "They will automatically assume I killed you."

"Can't have that, can we?" I tried to extract myself from his grip.

"I told you, you are the only hope I have for the future. Come along."

"Tell me what's going on to the north. I know your Hunters have been bringing you information."

"Things are going badly, of course. Adrianna's forces are trying to push to the heart, but Gabel is using all his wiles to prevent it. Considerable losses on both sides, while Lucas is forced to watch, refusing to send warriors out to fight on Iron-Moon's side. He says it is a squabble between a bunch of rebels and a conqueror, so it has nothing to do with SableFur proper."

"Don't sound so fucking smug," I snarled. "You have to let me go back."

"And do what? You can't do anything except let it play out. Do you *really* think you can send your warriors out to fight on Gabel's side?"

"I know I can't let Adrianna win."

"It does not matter if Adrianna wins or not."

"She will come for IceMaw next, you dolt! Kiery's seen it!"

Aaron sighed impatiently. "Yes, I know all about Kiery's dreams. At least the ones she shared within earshot of Bernhard. You are not considering the practical matter of conquest now that you're no longer the goal, and you *never were*."

"Explain it to me," I said, pissed off.

"If Adrianna wins, she'll have to purge all the wolves in the heart who bowed to you, and replace them with less capable but more loyal wolves," Aaron said. "She will have to rebuild SableFur's heart."

I worked my jaw. He had a point there. There was the reason it was called *the heart*. Adrianna would have to do a transplant.

Aaron continued, "If Gabel wins, SableFur will fracture into a dozen or more pieces. Or they kill each other, and SableFur shatters into pieces. Either way, Gianna, either of them will be so occupied with their new toy that they will not have time for IceMaw. And that is when we will move in for the kill and remove the threat of SableFur and IronMoon permanently."

Aaron smiled and tried to touch my cheek.

I jerked away and growled. I despised how he'd figured all this out, moved all the pieces, and sure as the Moon Herself knowing the motivations of our hearts, set everything on its course. That damned doomed dance of planets.

"You were the point on which all this turned," Aaron said. "Without you, SableFur and IronMoon will die. If not at their own hands, at mine. I will break up SableFur and what is left of IronMoon into such small pieces that they will be scattered to the wind, never to be rebuilt into anything greater than a small pack. And in time, the wolves will be grateful, and the Moon?"

He smiled at me, gentle, affectionate, and a little deranged.

I swallowed. Hard. Because a year ago I'd have thrown myself at his plan. "A year ago you were everything I prayed for."

"I apologize for being late. Now, we must go. Your title as Luna of SableFur and IronMoon are worth nothing, but I don't believe you want the wolves of IceMaw to believe—quite yet—I am warming your bed."

"How about you file that under things that will never happen?"

Aaron just smiled.

A line of IceMaw waited on the terrace for us, with a single table covered in papers in the sunlight, and two chairs. One of Aaron's warriors stood guard over it.

Aaron gestured to me to sit in the chair next to him. I balked, because my place as a guest would have been off to the side, not sitting with him presumably hearing every small detail of lives and affairs that did not concern the Luna of SableFur.

"An Oracle's council would be most welcome," Aaron said with a winning smile I didn't trust.

He'd lured me into his private rooms, compelled me to sit in the Luna's seat, and now where I was, at his side during court, when I had absolutely *no* business being there.

But here I was: participating.

I was on a remote hilltop deep in IceMaw territory, hours away from SableFur or IronMoon, while Adrianna's toadies murdered Oracles and every vision and dream I had showed me everything ended the same way, and anything any of us did didn't matter.

Aaron had also made it very clear that if I made a scene, he'd downgrade my guest status to "prisoner."

I remained quiet while Aaron heard the first two cases. Nothing of any great interest, the usual arguments about property and debts being owed, and it was shameful because it had gotten as far as the Alpha to sort out, so nobody was having a good time. The beautiful spring day began to get a little cloudy. I commented, "Rain is coming in."

That's how desperate I was: conversation about weather.

"It usually rains in the evening this time of year," he said, making some notes.

I looked at the pond. Some wolves were setting up huge piles of sticks to use as bonfires. I was out of time.

The next wolf sat down in front of us.

Aaron shifted, his scent amused and hard-edged at the same time. He leaned over and whispered, "I can smell how anxious you are. Be careful what rope you chew through. It may be holding you above a pit."

I moved to shove him, he ducked back too quickly, leaving me only able to blush in fury and mortification at the tickle of his breath against my ear.

Asshole.

The wolf started to tell Aaron his tale of woe. I barely heard him through the fury clouding my mind, and under that, the weight of the Moon pressing down on the back of my neck. The same weight as I'd felt when Gabel had presented Gardenia to Anders. The weight of the future groaning onto its path.

That terrible set of decisions on Gabel's part had haunted us for a long time.

Aaron turned and asked, "Your opinion, Luna-Oracle?"

"Of what?" I asked.

Aaron gestured to the wolf in front of him.

"He is not here to hear *my* opinion," I said.

"No, but *I* am."

I stood, brain on fire as the storm roared across the sky towards us, and a west wind blew my hair about my face. "This has gone far enough, Aaron. I'm returning to SableFur, immediately."

Aaron got to his feet, scent clotting with blood and bone-deep violence. "Not with the storm coming in. You will remain here."

"I am not afraid of a storm."

He matched me step for step. "Perhaps you should be. I am the one who goes out to meet it, am I not? That is what you've seen in your visions?"

I scrambled back. "I am leaving, Aaron. Don't make me say something your pack doesn't want to hear!"

"It's what *you* don't want my pack to hear. I've been civilized to you, you've been treated like a guest, I've made myself clear." Aaron loomed over me. I held my ground as he growled, "You are *not* leaving. I've explained to you you are the only one. My *only* hope for the future. I killed my family to save this pack. Do you think abducting *you* to keep you out of Gabel's grip is going to shock them?"

I glanced, quickly, at the IceMaw standing around. The two warriors didn't seem shocked, and everyone else was not nearly as horrified as they should have been. Uh-ho, so much for thinking my big reveal would buy me a safe, but hasty exit... maybe I was about to get that downgrade to a dungeon suite.

"They will *thank* me for castrating Gabel's future." Aaron seized my Marked arm. The diaphanous fabric of my shirt tore under his fingernails. "Without you, Gabel's future rots."

I tried to yank free. His grip bore down hard. I snarled, "Then show them what you can never have! Howl all you want about I'm the only female the Moon lets you dream of, but show them your own future is just as dead as Gabel's!"

He clenched down, raking claws through my shirt, and grazing my skin. Blood welled up from the Mark and stained the tattered ribbons of my shirt.

In the darkening sky, the pale blue halo around the Mark seemed to glow, and my marked eye pulsed dangerously under the weight of Aaron's prestige and resolve. I summoned every shred of dignity and prestige and authority I could muster. "I am leaving, Aaron, and going back to SableFur. If you keep me here, you'll have to acknowledge I am not your guest and never have been. I am your prisoner."

"Keep you prisoner? No. But let you leave? Never," Aaron

said, still holding my arm in a grip that felt like being stuck in rocks.

The storm whipped my hair out of its clamp, tore the ribbons of ruined fabric and sent them scattering across the patio.

The grip on my Mark compressed so tight my throat tried to explode. My marked eye went blind from pressure and sharp pain, and I thrashed backwards. He lunged, driving us both into the side of the house, and pinned me with his weight.

"Get off me!" I screamed.

"I told you," he growled in my ear. "I will stop at nothing, and I will pay any price."

"If you kill me your future dies," I rasped. Every inch of his body weighed on mine like a stone, heavier than Gabel, heavier than Hix, heavier than the Tides themselves. I couldn't breathe, but I could taste his salt-and-snow scent on my tongue.

He whispered, "I'm not going to kill you."

His other hand twisted into a snowy white claw.

WHAT HE HAS, WHAT HE WILL LOSE

The first touch of the Mark is ice.

The next is pain.

And then there is nothing but pain.

He pressed deeper, carving trenches into my skin and into my soul.

I screamed, and screamed, or tried to, I couldn't breathe around his weight and the suffocating agony.

No.

My soul twisted like a towel, split down the middle, and—

…*Gianna*…

…*Gianna!*…

It went on forever.

Aaron staggered back. Blood soaked his sleeve. Dripped off his hand.

I collapsed to my knees.

I couldn't breathe, scream, cry. My soul convulsed. Agony wracked me.

More agony than I had ever known.

And it didn't stop.

Blood obscured my vision and bubbled through my fingers. My sleeve hung in ribbons, and my soul in knotted tatters.

This can't be happening.

But Aaron was inside me now too. Cold, sharp-edged, unmoving, like a raw lump of quartz

I rocked back on my heels and cried out, brain spinning.

Aaron pulled off his shirt. Blood welled up out of a carved set of trenches on his arm.

No. It can't be. This can't be happening.

Then he turned attention to me, a bright triumphant gleam in his eyes, and inside us, shining like sunlight on unpolished quartz. He reached down towards me.

"Don't touch me," I choked, struggling to stand. My head throbbed. I couldn't see out of my marked eye. My limbs wouldn't obey. I sobbed and gasped at the same time.

"Let me help you, my love," Aaron said.

"Don't touch me!" I tried to shout. My soul convulsed, and I screamed. "You aren't my mate!"

Make it stop, make it not be true, make it stop.

"Take her to my rooms," Aaron, breathless and triumphant, ordered.

This isn't happening…

I WAS IN HIS BED.

I yelped and flung off the blankets and jumped out of bed. Or tried to. I jerked and fell out of bed and landed hard on my injured arm.

I moaned.

What was the point?

Rain slid down the window panes.

The barren room reeked of Aaron, and the scent repulsed and soothed.

Gabel's hot coal pulled downward. Instinct sent my soul yearning for the closer wolf with a scent that erased my memory of Gabel.

No. Gabel smelled of ash and burning. I struggled to conjure the memory, and Aaron's Bond blotted the memories like water on ink.

My blue Mark was still intact, but it hurt like a cruel bruise. I choked on a sob. Then realized I couldn't see out of my other eye. I touched it. Still had an eyeball, but it was dim.

Aaron didn't have anything under his bed. Not even some dust bunnies,

He'd Marked me. He'd Marked me.

And it had held.

He'd warned me he'd stop at nothing…

The wracking pain inside me was like my soul trying to peel away from the inside of my skin. I tried to crawl back on the bed, but my soul had had enough, and I collapsed, feverish and wretched.

…*Gabel, where are you…*

…*I am lost…*

…*you promised…*

STRONG ARMS LIFTED me back onto the bed. I stirred out of my stupor. Aaron.

I struggled against him. I didn't want to be in this bed, in this room, in this pack, in this relationship. "Let me go," I rasped, fighting to stay above the waves of disorientation and pain inside me. I had to get out of here. I had to leave, get away from him…

He'd Marked me.

"I'm not touching you," he said mildly.

"I don't want to be in this room."

"This is your den," he said.

"I don't want it," I choked out.

"Then when you're feeling better, I'll show you the other options. I'm not attached to this room."

The weight of two Bonds crushed whatever resolve my soul could have provided. There was him, and there was Gabel, and I sensed Gabel's fury and... Gabel knew.

But Gabel wasn't here.

"Gabel is still in the north holding Adrianna at bay," Aaron said, as if he could sense what I was thinking.

Maybe he could.

"He isn't coming," Aaron said evenly. "I told you he will not risk losing his crown for you. He knows there's nothing he can do for you now. He's made his choice on what's most important to him."

Smug bastard. "Can you sense him?"

Aaron's mild expression turned dark.

I managed a smirk. "Unexpected bonus or curse?"

Aaron bent low over me, too low. His scent clouded my nose, and the Bond squirmed, thumped, and my soul twisted, confused and flailing. He ran his thumb over my lips.

"No," I whispered, sensing the pressure of desire building. His or mine? I didn't know, I didn't want to know. I wanted it to stop. I couldn't—I *wouldn't*. No matter how much the Bond demanded that I accept his body within mine, or feed it what it wanted. I *wouldn't*.

You swore that to yourself with Gabel too. You've broken that promise to yourself before.

No. No. *No.* Not this time.

Aaron stood. "I will endure anything for you. Even your hatred and even your contempt. Even Gabel's soul within breathing distance of mine. I'm sure I will turn it to my advantage in the end."

ABANDONED/CLAIMED

Aaron's unrelenting presence rubbed my soul raw. He would not stop. Gabel had shifted and moved, at least, from mocking and laughing, darkly playful, cruel, but it'd always felt like there was some give in him, even if I couldn't be free.

Aaron was unmovable. A stone.

I forced myself to look at my new Mark in the mirror. The blue one on my left arm—Gabel's—thrummed, the blue halo moving softly, strangely reassuring. The Moon hung in my mind, waiting, but with Her Eye wide open.

The vision in my marked eye had started to return, but I could only see shadows and light, and my eye kept trying to focus, like there was a foreign body inside the globe I couldn't get out. Aggravating.

I traced the Mark, trying not to think about how he'd carved it as he'd pinned me and roughly cut the design into my body.

"Instrument," I whispered to myself, tracing the design. Embedded into the design was clearly the rune for *instrument*, and the rune for *balance* bisecting it, and although it was hard to tell, I thought I could make out *courage*. Maybe it was something else. *Pack* was similar to courage.

Maybe it was the design Kiery had seen.

I'd never heard of a she-wolf having two mates and two Marks. I'd heard of ancient Lunas who had refused to take an Alpha and instead kept consorts to produce heirs from, just like King-Alphas who had had concubines for the same purpose, jealously guarding their power from the reaches of other ambitious wolves. I'd never heard of two males sharing the same female. At least not in the formal sense. Not even identical twin pups had shared a mate, even though they were a soul split between two bodies, so it was said.

My mostly sightless marked eye stared back at my reflection. The pupil was blown, nearly devouring the white sliver of moon hanging in the iris.

I dragged myself down the hallway to Aaron's office. I practically fell through the door, sending all the wolves with him startling and jumping and falling over themselves.

"Fuck," I breathed. The endless windows poured with rain, and the sky was so dark, and it was like being *inside* the storm. Tiny pellets of hail pattered the glass during brutal wind gusts.

"Leave," Aaron gestured to the wolves.

They filed out, murmuring *Luna* to me as they did so.

Aaron tried to take my arm to steady me. "Don't touch me."

"You've already fallen several times," he said, his tone neutral, and his presence that unforgiving lump of rock. My soul yearned to lean against him at the same time it was painfully repulsed by him.

Somehow I ended up in one of the chairs. "How dare you. You fucking monster."

"How am I different?" Aaron asked. "How am I *any* different from what Gabel did to you?"

I clutched my arm and tried not to double over in pain.

"Gabel did it because he was a bored, arrogant fool that wanted a plaything. Part of me will never forgive him for what he did. You didn't do it for a plaything or sick amusement or because you're so arrogant you decided pissing at the Moon would amuse you. You did it to own me. Gabel tormented me, he humiliated and degraded me, but he did it for small, stupid, petty reasons. You? You forged this out of hatred!"

Aaron shook his head. "No, I did it out of love. Love of you, love of my pack, love of the future for our species. You had the lure-scent when you shouldn't. I am a wolf willing to act, no matter how cruel or desperate. I did not do this to hurt you. One day I hope you understand that."

"Don't you dare talk down to me," I rasped. "The Gabel that Marked me was a cheap imitation monster. The Comet on the wrong path, not the Moon's true Destroyer."

"Can you honestly tell me you love him for what he is, and not despite of his many flaws? Do you really want to give birth to pups in his image?"

I loved Gabel, and I could...somehow...accept what he was, but Gabel was Gabel. I'd been stripped of my choices. Pups like Gabel? I...

Aaron spared me a cocky smile or laughter, and just told me, deadpan, "You want to think this is different, but it's not. It's only more monstrous to you because you thought me above it. All considered, I'll take it as a compliment."

I sobbed once. "Shut up! Shut up, shut up, shut up!"

"Did I hit a nerve?" He caressed my hair.

My heart broke as it overflowed with the instinctual desire of *yes, touch me* and the utter revulsion of his touch *I am not for you*. "Shut up, Aaron!"

Aaron gently pulled at strands of my dark hair. He said, softly, "Nothing is different, as much as you beg for it to be. Be as angry as you like, my love. Unlike Gabel, my monstrosity will stop here. I will never intentionally humiliate, degrade, or imperil your life for my sick amusement. I'm surprised you're so furious. My reasons for doing this at least have some basis beyond *I was bored*."

Through the hot haze I recognized the element of truth in his words: I'd sworn to Gabel I'd never forgive him, that I'd hate him, but even as I'd done it, I'd known my chances of escape were almost zero.

Aaron's words had the same ring. Like oil sliding over water: the words being the oil, the truth being the water.

"You are looking at what happened with Gabel through the context of distance and time," Aaron said.

"I haven't forgotten what he did to me either," I snarled.

"No, but you still took the vows, and still love him despite it," Aaron said. "Who's to say you won't eventually come to see that what I did was necessary, and while perhaps not forgive me for it, set it on a shelf and out of the way."

I growled.

"Do you want the world to end? Do you want to be queen of a burned kingdom?" Aaron pressed. "Because you know that's what he is, and what he will do. I have vowed I won't let it happen. You had the lure-scent. The Mark held. Now Gabel cannot kill me without imperiling you. Granted, I no longer can kill him, but I have his Luna, and I will not let him near you."

"What are you saying?" My brain was so addled I needed him to spell this out for me, and Aaron clearly liked to hear himself talk. Maybe he'd say something useful.

But what was useful with this Mark on my arm?

"What I've told you before: that without you, Gabel's kingdom turns to ash. Even if he kills Adrianna, even if he prevents SableFur from splintering, even if he *does* crown himself King, it won't matter. The pups you bear will be mine, not his, and his kingdom will die when he dies."

"Fuck off," I spat at him, although inside I quailed. I'd told

Gabel much of the same when we'd first met: that his kingdom would be nothing when he wasn't strong enough to hold it together, and that a Luna was his only hope to see it endure.

"I'm fairly sure if I tried to consummate our love in the near future I would leave without my cock," Aaron said with a smirk.

"Oh, you'd be *lucky* if I stopped at your cock," I snarled.

Aaron chuckled. "Speaking of my cock—"

"Let's not."

"I have already informed my senior wolves that we consummated the Bond," Aaron said, expression sharpening and turning into something hideously feral. "They were... aghast, but I left out details."

"You did *what?* Why did you do *that?*" I exclaimed.

"So there is no doubt in their mind who the Luna is," Aaron said. "We will formalize the vows at Solstice this winter. That should be plenty of time for your SableFur and Iron-Moon concerns to die a natural death."

"So you told them you raped me. Wow, Aaron, you really are ticking off every box. Familicide, rape, what's next? Going to kill one of our pups?"

Aaron shook his head. "Never. And I did not tell them I raped you. I told them we consummated our Bond. You can tell them whatever you like or nothing at all."

"How about I tell them the truth?"

"I suppose if you want to?" Aaron said. "Though I'm not sure what good you think it will do. I have told them you are the Luna of IceMaw, and that that word is to be spread throughout the pack."

"How are you explaining my IronMoon and SableFur connections?"

"Considering you never publicly reclaimed Gabel, and you're about to be overthrown in SableFur, why bother? I abducted you, I Marked you, you're now my Luna." He shrugged. "The word is already going through the pack that we will announce at Beltane, and come Solstice, take the vows, and we have started on pups. The pack is pleased."

"How deranged is your pack that the details of this isn't bothering them?"

"Compared to the alternatives, I'm a veritable saint." Aaron chuckled.

This was insane. This was crazy. But what did I do? He was already telling his pack. I'd sworn to myself with Gabel I'd never stay with him, but that'd lasted six months. I knew what the Bond was about. I knew how it warped and twisted your mind, and I knew how the Bond didn't take root unless the souls were compatible.

Kiery had told me I'd never been *afraid*. But for the first time... I was afraid. I was as afraid as any acolyte shoring up her courage to step out onto the Tides once more. Was this what they felt? This horrible fear that maybe, this time, they'd be lost?

Gabel had left me dancing at the end of the Mark, telling IronMoon we *might* take the vows. That I *might* be their Luna. I had been *Lady* Gianna for lack of anything else to call me. Aaron was doing the opposite: boxing me in, smothering me, jumping ahead so I had no chance of escaping on the way there.

"I am sorry it came to this. I hope one day if you can't forgive me, you can at least make peace with it the way you made peace with Gabel for the same offense," Aaron told me, so sincerely I almost believed he might be sorry.

But he *wasn't* sorry. Whatever genuine apology he had inside him was locked up in that stone heart of his, same as bones locked up in the SableFur tombs. "I know you aren't sorry, Aaron, and you never will be. You might regret you had to do it, but you'll never feel guilty."

"Do you think Gabel is sorry for how you've suffered for

him? Do you think he's sorry now that he's let me keep you, how he's not going to come for you, how he'll leave you here instead of give up Adrianna's head or SableFur's throne? Don't be naïve. I told you I would never have given you up. Do you believe me now?"

I stared at him. "Yes. And that's what makes him better than you."

"How does giving you up and sending you to SableFur make him better than me? He violated his vows," Aaron demanded.

"Because I told him to!" I snapped. "He refused, but I begged him. He did it for me."

Aaron's expression turned horrified. "Dear Moon, he has warped your thinking. I can feel him through you, and it's like being haunted by a nightmare. I don't blame you for it. You had to survive. But it's over now. I won't let him have you."

"I have two Marks, why can't I choose? Why can't I have both of you?" I argued, trying to find some way out of this nightmare.

"Because I will call no wolf King, and this is the way to prevent it," Aaron said.

"Then let me contact SableFur. Lucas. Kiery."

"No," Aaron said.

"They'll think I abandoned them to marry you!"

"I will tell them the truth. And Beltane is in two days. You know what we will be doing."

"Not a chance," I said.

Aaron chuckled. "You're the point on which light and dark turns, and no one is going to turn anything a darker shade when they look at the long-view. Don't you see that *you* do not choose, you just force all the rest of us to decide what bad bargains we're willing to make? You're just one small sacrifice in the grand scheme of things."

Holy Moon, was he *right*? Was that what the Balance-

Keeper was? I was the keystone in various plans and schemes, some bog/river/thicket to be traversed, some grand test to be passed—while I *never* got a choice in any of it? Was I just some shitty cosmic messenger that delivered riddles to the real players?

I whispered, "Gabel *will* come."

Now Aaron looked annoyed. "Every time he takes his eyes off Adrianna she chews through his forces. He is outnumbered five to one, with no where to run, no allies to summon to him, and no respite."

I looked away from him, jaw trembling.

"I won't let you return to SableFur or have contact with them—it'd be pointless—but I will send for the human doctor Ana if you like. I'm sure she'll have a number of choice things to say to me that will improve your mood, and I know you trust her."

"Send word to her to get out," I told Aaron. "Just see that she goes somewhere safe and back to her human life."

Ana didn't want to go back to her human life, and she'd promised to follow me into whatever, but she hadn't signed on for this.

"Easily done. I have work to do. You can either sit with me, or I'll escort you somewhere out of my company to rest. We may not be taking the vows in two days, but you are the IceMaw Luna, and I know the pack will want you at your best for Beltane."

"Then I guess you should have thought of that before you ripped my arm and soul open again!"

Gabel had never insulted me with an apology. If he had it to do over again, he would have done some things differently. Aaron wasn't sorry, and he wouldn't change anything.

And it was impossible to really hate him like I wanted to. The Bond wouldn't let me, and I just couldn't: he'd done what he'd done out of the absolute belief he'd had to do it. His

absolute conviction to prevent the future that Kiery and Anita
had seen.

I didn't want to be Queen, I didn't want Gabel to pursue
this dream of being King, I didn't want Adrianna's pups to be
disgraced orphans. I didn't want my people to pay the price for
Gabel's ambition or SableFur's sins.

Aaron was the one who could make this fire burn itself out.

"I hate you," I whispered. Not anymore than I hated
Gabel. I hated this and what he'd done, and how it was all
wrong and fucked up and unfair.

"I know," he said sadly. "I've hurt you, and I am so sorry
that now you have scars in your spine like I do."

…*Gianna*…

I wasn't going to be trapped here with him.

The storm was here, the sun had set, and the scythe-Moon
had fallen.

I shouldn't go back onto the Tides, but I'd do it because
Aaron didn't think I would, and Gabel would forgive me if
I did.

THE FULCRUM

THE VISION IN THE METEORITE BOWL

I staggered and fell.

"Ow," I said, picking myself up off the stone floor. I got to my feet. I still had no sight in my marked eye.

Gabel's Mark glowed softly against my skin, like the Moon shining behind storm clouds, and the blue-gloss shone like moving water, shifting like an ocean at night. Aaron's Mark was bone-pale and raised, like a Mark that had been on my arm for fifty years.

I traced it. Balance, Pack, Instrument, ragged and raw from the force of the Marking. He didn't know about the instrument rune, so it hadn't been conscious on his part.

I checked the rest of my body. I wasn't cut up like I had been in the storm vision with the she-wolf.

And here I was, back in the temple. The stone altar was here in this little alcove, but the trinkets from before were gone. I crawled out the window and slithered onto the ridge.

It was raining. And not just a nice jungle drizzle, but pouring rain. The sky was completely obscured by cloud, but I sensed the sun had set.

This place had always been balanced between those two times: that moment just before the sun set, and night arrived.

The rocks were slick from the rain. I felt my way up them on my hands and knees, sliding down a few times, and struggled under the driving rain.

I reached the top of the temple and looked down. There was just enough light to see that all the rain from the temple coursed down into the jungle below and flooded it. The water lapped lightly at the bottom of the temple.

At the top of the temple were two lines of lanterns made of fangs laced together with sinew dangling from poles of spinal columns, with the chains suspending the fangs gripped from the skull of wolves. Dancing flames sputtered in the driving rain. On the altar was a large balance scale.

The rain plastered my hair against my skin. Lightening occasionally split the sky, and in the distance thunder rumbled. I approached the scale. It was simple in shape: stand, beam, two plates suspended by chains.

The stand was bone, the plates made of silver, the chains iron. The beam was a luminous sliver of Moon: the scythe-Moon, the chains dangling from the very edge of the delicate tips of the crescent. The fulcrum —the center point on which the beam would tilt, the point of pure balance —was an eyeball.

A human eyeball: hazel, pupil dilated, the shoreline of hazel lashed with a white crescent.

Arranged on the altar were dozens of fangs mixed with shards of blue tourmaline, white quartz, and black obsidian, and a set of balance weights made of silver.

The empty pans danced in the wind, jangled in the driving rain, sending the beam tilting this way and that against the fulcrum.

I realized, as I reached for the eye—

The eye in my own head was gone.

I touched the blind socket. The eyeball was gone. In its place was a hole.

The hole in my soul was the fulcrum. The point on which light and dark turned.

I picked up one of the silver balances. It burned. I judged its weight, set it down. Chose the smallest one. It burned and weighed just as much. I tested each balance on the scales and ignored the pain handling them caused: despite their size, they all weighed exactly the same.

I touched the curve of the beam. The Moon's soft cold balanced against the razor-sharp tips of the crescent. I pressed my fingertip into one edge. Blood trickled down the beam, quickly diluted by the driving rain.

All evidence of the runes I'd always seen, the stones, Gabel, Aaron, even myself were gone. No crowns, no necklaces, nothing.

Just this scale, and the storm, and all these bones. I plucked one of the bone lanterns out of the jaws of a skull and carried it to the main stairs.

The stones were slippery, but the lantern's flickering light was enough to pick my way down the sides of the temple. I'd never gone beyond the tier I entered on, and the bottom of the stairs had always descended into the jungle below.

Five tiers from the top, I met the rising water. It lapped the sides of the temple, surface pummeled by the driving rain, and the trees bowed under the weight of the rain, and everything alive in this place silent.

The water was warm. I crouched down and put my hand into it, then scooped upwards.

Fangs.

I dropped them with a yelp and almost fell backwards. Then I reached in again and scooped up another handful of water. Jungle debris, fangs, and two runestones: a tourmaline courage, and an obsidian love. Another handful yielded more fangs and three runestones: a tourmaline love, and two obsidian balances. I set all it aside, scooped out another handful, then realized I could scoop forever and I wouldn't get all the fangs.

I sat down on the wet stairs in despair as the water rose higher. I waited for I don't know how long, hoping for a break in the clouds, or the rain to let up, or something to change, but nothing did, and in the end, as the rain rose to my knees, the only thing left to do was to go back up the stairs. The scales still jangled in the storm as rain and pellets of hail pummeled the pans, and the beam swung back and forth wildly on the fulcrum under the constant impact.

I returned the lantern to its post, and as I did so, the rain became a deluge that pushed me to my knees, and I could not breathe—

The Tides coughed me up.

I woke up gasping and choking, then pain splintered my soul like the lightening across the sky in the vision—

Aaron grasped my hands. "You're fine. You're here, it's this world."

I woke from one nightmare to another. I was back in his bed, and he'd been sitting in a chair at my side. "You *moved* me?" I wheezed. Because I was full of thoughtful commentary right then.

"What did you do?" He was still holding my hands.

I tried to yank away. He didn't let me go. I ignored him a moment. It was daylight, but, "Is it still raining?"

"Yes. Half the years it rains during Beltane," he said.

"How long was I gone?"

"Overnight," he said, staring at me, troubled. "What did you see?"

I shook my head and wriggled one hand free to touch my eye. My eye was still there. I blinked. The vision still hadn't returned. I just saw shadows. But my fingertip had a pin-prick on it. I rubbed it against my thumb.

"What is this from?" Aaron asked, indicating the bite marks on my blue-gloss arm.

I realized I was *naked*. The asshole had taken my clothes off. Anger made me a bit faint, "what does it look like? A bite."

"From a wolf," he said.

"And this," I shoved my pin-pricked finger at him. "Was from a set of scales, and these bruises from falling in my vision. Stop it, Aaron."

"Silver burns." Aaron clutched my hand and looked at my palms.

Well, hell, he was right. I had minor silver burns on my hands. Went with all the other scars.

Aaron bent close, and said, "Do not do that again, Gianna. I didn't give you those bowls for you to dangle yourself into the abyss where I cannot reach you."

Gabel had sworn he'd find me wherever I went. The memory of that vow crowded out against the intensity of Aaron's concern, forced upon me by the Bond between us. He still held my one scalded hand. His palm was warm, and our hearts beat together.

He kissed me. Gently.

So gently it took about ten seconds for me to realize what was happening, and process the warmth/pain. My skin flushed, the Bond with him sighed, and the one with Gabel slipped—

"No," I gasped, yanking away. "What are you doing!"

"Kissing you. And your being does not object."

I snatched my hand away from him and pawed at my lips, which burned and stung pleasantly from the warmth, and I keened as the Bond with Gabel woke, and the one with Aaron howled for more. "I just came out of a vision! You fucking scavenger!"

"Gianna—"

"I know, the Bond, I've been down this road." I turned away from him. I was trapped here with this wolf, and no one was going to come for me. I had to manage on my own. I was alone in this. The temple had shown that. The storm would not stop. The clouds did not change. The Moon would not help. I was alone with the scales, the silver, and a pile of shattered stones and fangs.

Aaron quietly retreated from the room, leaving me alone with my thoughts, my misery, and now, my guilt.

LIGHT & DARK TURNS

The IceMaw wolves had started to arrive for Beltane the previous day, and now there were many of them camping out on the green lawns and in the forests and along the paths, despite the inclement weather. They all filed in neat and orderly for breakfast that morning, even if they had to take their plates throughout the house and even into the rain.

They crowded around for Aaron's announcement, which involved me.

"Wolves of IceMaw," Aaron said, actually standing up on his chair for this, his voice pitched and carrying easily despite the rain pattering the roof. So, so, *so* many wolves had come to Beltane. "I wish to present to you your new Luna. We will take the vows this winter, at Solstice, as we must unravel her concerns from the north, but yet my pup may be in her belly before then. The future may be here now."

He was such a liar. But a really convincing one and IceMaw ate it up with howls of delight.

He took my wrist and hauled me up onto my chair so I was

forced to look at all of the IceMaw while they howled and applauded.

"You will celebrate with us this evening!" Aaron told them, "IceMaw's future is here, and she will carry it in her belly!"

Even more howls. Fervent howls. Well. No doubt that IceMaw thought was just fabulous. And Aaron's control over them was absolute.

"I am going to kill you," I told Aaron under the din.

He grinned. "Is that what you told Gabel?"

I growled. "I'm going to tell them the truth. That you are lying about fucking me."

"Go ahead." Aaron shrugged. "It really doesn't matter. You're still their Luna because I just made you their Luna."

That sounded like a trap to me, and eviscerating Aaron's credibility in front of his pack would end badly for me if I was now their Luna. Plus I had a few other complications. I was furious and miserable, but I couldn't be stupid. "I'm still Luna of IronMoon and SableFur. Guess that makes me a Queen, doesn't it? So much for your bullshit to not be King."

We stepped down off the chairs as the din quieted. Aaron said, undisturbed, "We've had this conversation, and I did just acknowledge your concerns to the north. Everyone here knows those are going to die a natural death."

"What about my *other* Mark? *That* might be a problem, wouldn't it?"

"You mean the Mark that looks like a blue-gloss tattoo? I've told them that the Moon gave you Gabel's soul in penance for his wrongs against you, and you're the Balance-Keeper, and that his obsession with you a sacred matter we must be patient and permit to play out as the Moon intends. I can be really quite devout when I want to be." He rolled his eyes and smiled. "You keep acting like I haven't thought this through. Gabel was thoughtless in his actions towards you. An animal of the moment. My Marking of you was rash, but it was not impulsive. I had already decided it would be my fallback plan. I don't believe Gabel's death—now that you are bound to me —will result in your demise. I'm quite confident in that, actually."

Her Instrument. I shuddered. "You're wrong. You and Gabel were fighting over me. I died from it. The world rained glass and stars and the Tides boiled."

"Then I will have to be very, very careful, won't I?" he said, unrepentant and, more terrifyingly, unconcerned.

THE RAIN WAS STILL A DRIVING, unrelenting rain. This didn't seem to have any of the IceMaw concerned about Beltane. As Aaron had said, it rained regularly in the spring down here, so a soggy Beltane was still Beltane. Probably with more mud-wrestling.

I had moved from the bedroom to a small alcove on a glass-paneled hallway on the second floor, that afforded an unusual and beautiful view of the rear of the house. There were two chairs on a plush rug, and a little table. One of the wolves had set out a cup of tea for me, beaming as he'd done so, and whispering my title of *Luna* with obvious delight and a murmur that the IceMaw midwife had made the tea especially for me.

Damn. Breaking this pack's heart... they just seemed so damn *happy*. Aaron had draped a very pretty translucent veil over the truth.

Aaron captured one of my scalded hands and tried to bring it to his lips. "Surveying your domain, my lady?"

I yanked out of his grip. He didn't say things like that to needle me—not like Gabel. He did it because it was *true*, and he wanted me to accept it was true.

"What do you see out that way?" Aaron asked.

"Rain," I said. "Nothing but rain. And bonfires-to-be. And the storm."

"If I could make the rain stop for you, beautiful one, I would do so."

"Who said I wanted it to stop?" I looked at him sideways, seeing the burning row of bone lanterns and the scales. Aaron was a rock in my gut, a door I couldn't open. Gabel seethed within me like lava. "It suits my mood. Go away."

"I think I will sit here with you," Aaron said. "I savor your presence, even if you loathe mine."

We sat in the miserable quiet for a while longer. I didn't know what purpose Aaron served any longer in the Moon's design, but perhaps he was right: that I was just a fulcrum. Other people put things on the scales and weighed the cost and reward of their choices.

A shape moved in the distance along the edge of the pond.

A dark, rangy wolf loped down the long side of the pond, carrying a burning branch in his mouth, setting fire to each oil-saturated pyre as he passed it.

My heart surged.

Gabel.

Gabel was here.

He'd come.

"No," Aaron snarled. "*No!*"

"Gabel," I whispered.

"Jarjis!" Aaron roared, sprinting down the hallway.

I stumbled down the stairs to the main level and back patio, where Gabel had loped back along the side of the pond, igniting those pyres as well.

I spun around to face the furious Aaron. "He's *here*, Aaron. He *comes!*"

Aaron ripped off his shirt and stepped out of his pants, his handsome features twisting into a mask of feral fury.

"All your plans, asunder," I hissed.

"Then I will deal with him," Aaron snarled back. "And we will settle this between us, and then you and I can have the life your scent promises. IronMoon is doomed without him. Adrianna will have SableFur back under her control before his corpse cools. He *is* the fool who has no idea how to keep what he has—and I am going to bring you his head!"

Gabel loped around the pond once more, then tossed the torch aside and approached the house through the driving rain. He transformed into his human form. "I am here to reclaim what is mine, IceMaw!"

Aaron strode out to meet him. "Gianna is my mate, and this is her den."

"Not if she says it isn't!" Gabel roared.

"You already broke your vows to her. Go home, IronMoon. You have a war to fight." Aaron paced back and forth. "You and I will not fight. You cannot kill me anymore than I will risk killing you."

"I am not leaving her here with you. I don't have to kill you to break you and free her from you!" Gabel twisted into his nightmarish war-form.

"The Comet indeed," Aaron growled, grinning, and he transformed to meet the challenge.

Gabel howled a challenge that struck the sky like a hammer, and the stars cried in response.

The IceMaw Alpha gestured with one clawed hand to Carlos. "*Protteecct herrr. Thheee Commett and I musstt dancce.*"

"Yes, Alpha." Carlos placed both of his hands on my shoulders.

I shook them off.

Gabel barred his yellowed fangs at Aaron.

Aaron vaulted over the terrace wall. I saw the hairless scars over his spine and my heart, strangely crunched.

Aaron, in truth, was a cripple, and couldn't possibly beat Gabel.

The two crashed together.

Aaron's claws stabbed into Gabel's thigh, sinking deep and

drawing first blood. Aaron snarled, the IceMaw cheered, but Gabel grinned, and twisted his head to bite down on Aaron's shoulder. Yellowed fangs sang deep.

Aaron dug down and tore his claw back, ripping out a maw full of gore. Blood erupted out of the gaping wound and splattered the shining white IceMaw Alpha.

Gabel drove forward, gnawing on Aaron's shoulder and sending the IceMaw reeling backwards, and both war-forms fell to the ground. Aaron's clawed feet found Gabel's belly first, shoved my mate off him, sent Gabel tumbling back.

Ashes and sparks from the pyres started to singe the grass and my eyes.

Gabel snarled and chomped down on Aaron's left arm, biting deep. Blood erupted around his maw. Aaron roared, and with his still-free arm, shoved claws into Gabel's side. Gabel bit down harder. Aaron twisted his claws deeper.

Gabel shoved against his grip and lunged for Aaron's throat. Aaron evaded, sending Gabel tumbling, and the two clashed together again. Gabel shoved Aaron to the ground with a knee. Aaron's good hand moved as if to stab Gabel in the other thigh, but I saw what Aaron was actually going to do: castrate my mate.

Gabel snarled, claws closing around Aaron's mandible, his own claws bloody from Aaron's fangs. I practically felt the creaking of Aaron's jaw. Gabel's grip suddenly loosened, and for the first time, I saw him hesitate in battle.

I stumbled out into the rain, their fury and violence and the churn tearing through me. I dropped to my knees.

The scales jangled wildly in my mind, pounded by rain and hail.

I was going to die. This was how I died.

"Kill him," I tried to shout over the rain and wind. "Do it!"

"*You mayyy dieee,*" Gabel said, struggling to hold Aaron down and defend himself at the same time.

Lucas, have you ever wondered if wolves entering one of our dark ages recognized the dark age as it arrived?

Aaron thought he could stop it, and maybe he could, but it'd only be temporary. I was done being powerless. I was done watching while the stars danced around me. I was done fighting the wrong battles.

It always ended in death and fire.

It only works when there is a fulcrum to break the Bond over. You want that conviction. You don't have it. You wish you did. That is what hurts. You just don't want to look into the abyss. Perhaps Gabel did you a favor Marking you as he did. It spared you the pain of being wooed by him.

This time I had the conviction.

This time I'd swing the scythe.

"Do it!" I howled.

Gabel whipped his attention back to Aaron, and without hesitation, his shoulders twisted.

CRACK.

Aaron's death tore my soul into pieces, ripped it away, and he spiraled down, into a void, out of my reach, out of my grasp, gone, and my soul tried to flee after him.

I collapsed, shuddering, into a pile, clinging to a rocky outcropping in my own mind. The rain drenched and puddled and I couldn't breathe, couldn't think.

"Gianna," Gabel said, his voice far away. His human voice. More howls, wails, where those mine or IceMaw's? I couldn't respond. My body was still there, but the remains of my soul were too small to animate it.

I couldn't think. Couldn't do anything. Couldn't move.

"Gianna," Gabel said again, turning me over in the rain. His soul clung to mine.

I dangled in the abyss, blind, unseeing, wracked with pain beyond comprehending, my spine cracked over the fulcrum.

IN BLOOD & BONE, ALWAYS

Gabel whispered to her, but she didn't respond. She laid there twitching and moaning softly.

He rolled her, gently, onto her back. One arm with their Mark, and the one carrying Aaron's Mark. It was hot to the touch. No human words came. Growls and snarls in his mind, and a high keening for the mind that felt so far away. Her soul howled—for him, or for Aaron, or for both?

"*Giannnaaa*," he spoke her name again, trying to summon her back. She twitched and moaned, saturated with misery. The IceMaw had broken into howls and a few of them had run forward to Aaron's shattered body. He paid them no mind.

She managed to open one eye. The one marked with the white crescent. "Gabel."

"*Wwwolff-ffform, Giannnna. Thennn you caaan ressst,*" he said.

She closed her eye again, and he thought for a moment she was too weak and deranged to obey, but his Luna was an Oracle, the Balance-Keeper, and she summoned the last of her mind and strength to shift into her silvery-blue wolf form.

He slid his bleeding claws under her. He staggered and

limped on his injuries. His body did not want to obey, and her soul howling its agony pulled at his own mind.

So many flavors of grief. He worked his tongue. He could taste them all.

He took one step, then another.

The IceMaw First Beta stood over his Alpha's broken, ruined body.

He did not know. He did not like what his Alpha did. I know that look. Hix gave me that look. I remember it.

Gianna's loss of Aaron was somehow his loss.

We both gambled with her life.

He wanted to give orders that every bone in Aaron's body be broken, and his corpse draped across poles like a tent. Rip off his Marked arm and shove it through his chest.

But he had to leave. This place was not safe.

"*Dooo notttt dessstroyyy hisss fangsss,*" he ordered. "*Herrrr ssssoul bearrsss the burden of hisss wrongs, as it bearrrsss mine.*"

Gabel turned as the driving rain intensified. The Beltane fires fizzled and spit.

"Where are you taking our Luna, Comet?" the First Beta demanded.

"*Sssommewhere ssaaffee,*" Gabel replied, the destination already forming in his mind.

The First Beta looked at Gabel's Marked arm, and very slowly, nodded.

Gabel carried her away into the rain.

BOOK 4: OBSIDIAN ORACLE

THE SCYTHE-MOON HAS FALLEN, AND THE SUN HAS SET

With one swoop of his claw, Aaron changed everything.

At the center of a war that will forever alter the course of her species, Gianna is caught in a nightmare beyond imagining.

The Balance-Keeper, the Obsidian Oracle, the point on which light and dark turns, crowned in bones and blood, has only one choice left:

…which way to swing the Scythe.

Available 2020

UNKNOWN AFFILIATIONS & STATUS

Gianna, Oracle. Former(?) Luna of IronMoon, SableFur, and IceMaw. Mate of Gabel and Aaron.

Adrianna, Former (?) Luna of SableFur

Ana, veterinarian (human)

IRONMOON

Gabel, Lord-Alpha

Flint, Master-of-Arms, Moon's Servant

Hix, First Beta (deceased)

Eroth, Second Beta

Romero, Second Beta (deceased)

Donovan, Hunter

Gardenia, unranked (deceased)

Violet, unranked

Brian, cook

SABLEFUR

Magnes, Alpha, Gabel's father (destroyed)

Kiery, Elder Oracle (primary)

Anita, Elder Oracle (deceased)
Thessa, Oracle (deceased)
Lucas, First Beta
Bernhard, Second Beta
Francis, regional leader
Thomas, regional leader
Evan, warrior
Lulu, Hunter
Walter, Cook

ICEMAW

Aaron, Lord-Alpha (deceased)
Carlos, First Beta
Nandia, Carlos' mate
Jarjis, advisor

SHADOWLESS

Jermain, Alpha (deceased)
Rogan, First Beta, Gianna's father (deceased)
Amber, warrior (deceased?)

MARCHMOON (destroyed)

Holden, Alpha (deceased)

REDWATER

Marcus, Alpha

GLEAMINGFANG (destroyed)

Anders, Alpha (deceased)

Other Oracles & Acolytes

Beatrice, Elder Oracle, AspenBark (deceased)
4 acolytes, deceased
2 Oracles, fate and location unknown, presumed deceased

Other Minor Packs

    EmeraldPelt

    NightScent

    AspenBark

    SpringHide (destroyed)

    SaltPaw (destroyed)

    RockTail (destroyed)

ABOUT THE AUTHOR

Merry is an independent author living in the Napa Valley of California with her husband and two cats. She enjoys coffee, combat sports, casual games, and low budget disaster flicks.

---

www.merryravenell.com
(freebies, festivities, oh my!)

Follow Merry on BookBub

ALSO BY MERRY RAVENELL

The Breath of Chaos Series
Breath of Chaos
Bound By Chaos
Chaos Covenant - *2020*

The IronMoon Series
The Alpha's Oracle
Iron Oracle
Ice & Iron
Obsidian Oracle - *2020*

The SnowFang Series
The SnowFang Bride
The SnowFang Storm - *2019*

The NightPiercer Saga
NightPiercer - *2019*
Separated Starlight - *2020*

Other Titles
The Nocturne Bride
On The Bit
Mirsaid : The Iron Marked

Printed in Great Britain
by Amazon